Becca's
Dance
by
Jordyn Meryl

jm dragonfly

Becca's Dance
by Jordyn Meryl

Originally released by Idyllic Ink Publishing 2014
Author's Revised Edition released by jmdragonfly 2015

Published by jm dragonfly, L.L.C.
Des Moines, IA

ISBN-13:978-1507677940
ISBN-10:1507677944

CHAPTER ONE

"Damn. Damn. Double Damn!"

On her one last good nerve, Becca Young-Hamilton resisted the urge to blast her horn at the car next to her. Instead, she hit her fist against the cream-colored steering wheel of the Lexus SUV.

Cussing inside the safety of her sound proof car. "Damn it ole' man!"

Glancing at her reflection in the rearview mirror, she tossed her burnt almond, naturally curly hair from her cornflower blue eyes, shaking it out of her face.

If the idiot beside me would have either went slower or sped up, I could have gotten over and not missed my turn-off. Now I have to go to the next exit.

Glaring at the older man driving the late model luxury car, she resisted the urge to flip him off.

Calm down, it's still only late afternoon. The early spring hours will keep daylight on longer. I can still get to Aunt Tilley's before dark.

Traveling from the upper Great Lakes area to the northern part of the southeastern states had taken her two days. Last night she stopped at a hotel when she hit the half-way mark. She could have flown, but she wanted the time to be by herself. And the bustle of flying did not appeal to her. The real plus was seeing the landscape change from dull to alive.

Plus your anger is not at him, or the missed exit. It's at the life you so carefully planned that just went to hell!

The stupid car next to her passed, leaving an open space to get into the right lane. Soon she saw the next exit.

So I take the scenic route.

Becca knew the back roads of this countryside like the massive interstates she normally traveled. Aunt Tilley's house on the lake had been Becca's playground as a teenager, then only a few summer weekends as a young wife and mother.

However, today she was going to the lake house alone. Aunt Tilley died almost a year ago, leaving the house to Becca because of the love she possessed for the old place. It shocked Becca at the time, but now, she decided, was the right time to open the gift.

4

Becca hadn't been here for several years. She always longed to come back to the lake. To a peaceful time of lazy days and sunshine.

Was it that perfect?

Kids grow up making their own plans for the summers. Jon, her husband, didn't like the

quiet lake. He went for more exotic vacations, so Becca wrote Aunt Tilley long letters, never getting back to the place of her dreams. Now the kids were at college, in two different directions, leaving her alone in a world she barely drifted along.

The shock of her life came last week when her husband asked her for a divorce. No specific reason-just tired of being married "for-fucking-ever". Keeping the secret tore at her soul, the one she buried deep refusing to allow to rule her life. There were no close friends. No family. She didn't want to tell her children.

Jon can have the pleasure.

Three days ago, standing at the window of another day filled with nothing significant to do, she remembered the letter she received from Aunt Tilley's lawyer.

Take care of business.

Making arrangements to open the house, she prepared a list of things to do. Telling Jon wasn't one of them. He'd lost the right to know what she decided to do, a task she allowed him to control for all their married life.

This morning she threw some clothes in a bag, pictures, 'her things' loaded her SUV.

Turning off the interstate, a thought lifted her spirits.

This feels like home.

Whatever happens, at least this time, I am on my turf.

The car skimmed up and down the small rises on the two-lane road. No reason to hurry.

I have all the time in the world. And nobody else I have to share it with.

A small country graveyard loomed ahead of her at the T crossing, her last turn. Slowing her speed, she laughed silently at the memories of her in the cemetery with the group of local kids she gathered with each summer. Beer, making out, exploring the opposite sex. It wasn't her teen year's memories that kept coming back to haunt her. The summer she turned twenty-two, she'd fallen in love with a local boy. The real thing. She never forgot him, or the desires he awakened.

Why am I going back to that time? I was young and stupid. I've out-grown that...I hope.

Pausing as she made the turn, and saw ghosts of the past in her head. Almost could swear she heard the laughter of the youths of twenty years back.

Shit. They are probably all dead by now.

Sighing at the futilely of the thought. She wasn't that old. Steady foot on the gas pedal, she relaxed taking the curves with ease. The radio played an upbeat song about love in the summertime in northern Michigan. She sang along.

***

"Aunt Tilley." Becca bounded out of her smart little red convertible, raced up the stairs to the large wraparound porch to give her favorite aunt a giant bear hug.

If ever there were a character, it would be free-spirited Aunt Tilley. Dressed in a long denim patchwork skirt, a paint-splashed white oversized shirt, accessorized with chain necklaces, she moved with the grace of a woman half her age. Her dark-brown hair matched

Becca's, long and curly, looking as if it had a mind of its own. Usually barefooted, shoes to Aunt Tilley were only worn when necessary.

Aunt Tilley pulled back, holding her niece at arm's length. "Becca, you are beautiful."

Becca could feel the warmth of love radiating off her aunt. Putting her hands in the back pockets of her jean shorts, she surveyed the lake a stone's throw from the house. A large lake as far as lakes go, full of cat tails, lily pads and ducks. Lots of ducks, always traveling in a row.

"How long are you here for?" Aunt Tilley's voice broke through Becca's daydreams.

Smiling back. "The summer." She let go of a big sigh. "My last summer before graduation."

Heavy footsteps on the wooden porch made Tilley and Becca turn. Becca caught her breath. Walking toward her, a tan young man, shirtless in tight jeans, sweat dripping off a rippled chest. A tool belt hung low around his slim waist.

Damn!

His electric blue eyes captured hers and Becca couldn't look away. "Aunt Tilley, who is that?" She asked in a low voice.

Tilley laid her arm across Becca's shoulders. "That, my dear, is Clay Lester. Ain't he nice to look at?"

Becca pretended shock. "Aunt Tilley!" But a smile crossed Becca's lips. "He most certainly is."

Putting their heads together, the two women giggled.

A raspy, deep voice sent waves of sexual want echoing in the air. "What are you two women giggling about?"

Aunt Tilley said in a tone Becca never heard before. "Just girl stuff. What do you need darlin'?"

Clay removed his work gloves, wiped his forehead with his arm. Sweat dripped from his sun-bleached hair. "Dad said the fence is done. We'll be back tomorrow to finish the dock." His eyes traveled down Becca's body.

Aunt Tilley quickly pushed Becca in front of her. "Clay, this is my niece, Becca. Becca, Clay Lester. His dad owns the lumber yard."

8

Becca stood like a stone. The overpowering attraction to this hunk caught her off guard.

Clay stretched out his hand. "Becca. Short for...?"

"Becca." She finally found her voice. "Just Becca."

Clay's hand felt firm, lingered as he held hers. "Glad to meet you. Be here long?"

"The... summer. The summer."

Since when do I have trouble talking?

He nodded his head, cocked it to one side. "Good. I'll see ya' around."

Withdrawing his hand, Becca didn't want to let it go. "Sure. See ya' around."

Stunned, Becca watched his face as he talked to Aunt Tilley. Sizing him up, Becca took in he was taller than her, maybe a few years older. But undeniably hot.

Becca barely heard his parting words. As he walked away from them, her gaze lingered on the nice ass in tight jeans. "See you tomorrow, Tilley..." He stopped, turned around, locked eyes with Becca.

"You too Just Becca." Winking, he jumped off the porch, disappeared.

***

The gravel on the road hit the car with tiny pops. Slowing her speed, Becca cruised up to the large, blue, Cape Cod style house.

The loss of Aunt Tilley suddenly felt real. There would be no high-spirited woman, who made her own way in life to greet her. Tears popped out of Becca's eyes. The real sorrow of losing Aunt Tilley washed over her. The house beckoned her like an old friend. She could almost hear a voice saying, "Come in. I will wrap your pain in love."

Leaning her head against the cool surface of the door glass, she summoned her courage to push open the door. Stepping out, she turned to open the back door, snickering quietly.

One suitcase, packing light for my journey into the past.

Jerking the bag from her back seat, she snapped it upright as the wheels hit the ground. The small rocks of the driveway crunched under her feet as she dragged her life in one bag behind. Still only early evening, the house looked dark. Climbing the wide stairs to the porch, she crossed over, opened the wooden screen door. Letting it lean on her back, she used the key the lawyer sent her to unlock the new dead bolt.

Becca walked through the large stained glass front door, the glass panels handmade by Aunt Tilley. An artist at heart, Aunt Tilley saw the world from a different angle. Shapes put together created designs. By adding color to designs, a mirage of depth and perception formed. Everything in her aunt's world became colorful, carrying a mystical meaning. That was why Becca loved her so. Many a summer evening they spent dissecting the colors and cross shapes of the sky at dusk. Trees, grass, even the lake never looked the same on any two given nights.

Becca had called a local cleaning service first thing, pleased when they said they could go over right away to get the house ready. Everything looked spotless. All of Aunt Tilley's things were in place as Becca remembered. But there were new objects from her latest travels. Aunt Tilley never stayed put too long. Her lake house would always be home, but the world was her playground.

Rolling the suitcase behind her, Becca walked down the hall to the bedrooms. There were three. Aunt Tilley's and two guestrooms. Becca paused at her Aunt's room. Memories rushed back. The room carried three walls of large windows broken only by a set of french doors looking over the lake. Decorated in taupe and jade, Becca chuckled as she remembered the conversation Aunt Tilley carried on with Clay about the paint.

***

"What in the hell color is taupe?" Clay stood in the bedroom prepared to paint. All the furniture had been pushed to the center, covered with plastic. The walls were bare, all window dressings taken down. It stood proudly waiting for its new coat of paint.

Aunt Tilley, always patient when explaining colors to 'lay people' saying. "Taupe is not grey, not brown, it's taupe."

"That's what they call it?"

Holding up a hand full of paint strips, Aunt Tilley looked at them. "Well, yeah. The one I want is called Traven Taupe."

Clay jerked the card Tilley held up. Turning the card strip over, he read the back. "You're right. That's what it says, 'tavern taupe'. What color is the trim? Bud light?"

"That's Traven not tavern." Tilley smacked him good-naturally on the shoulder. "No foolish man. The trim is Canvas Tan."

"But of course. How silly of me not to know."

Becca stood in the doorway watching the two bicker. So funny together. This was only the second time she met Clay. But her mind did not allow him too far from her thoughts. Becca loved the way Clay stood up to the challenge of Aunt Tilley. But one could tell he would do whatever she wanted.

The bedroom stood divided into two separate rooms. A sitting area in front of the windows with access to the deck by the French doors, with a large arch separating the two areas.

Clay's blue eyes set in his tan face made her knees weak every time he turned them on her. "Is she always this contrary?"

Becca glanced at Aunt Tilley, nodded her head. "Yes, she knows what she wants. Gets what she wants. Simple as that."

Clay's look roamed down Becca's body. She felt like he touched her just with his look. Her skin burned from the inside out.

12

"How about you Becca?" He asked, his voice smooth. "Do you always get what you want?" His gaze moved up to her face. A wry smile licked at his lips.

She looked him straight in the eyes. "Yes, I do. I am my Aunt's niece."

And I want you!

Becca smiled back at him. His grin said he got her message. "Then Traven Taupe it is."

***

Lost in her memories, she still stood in the hallway.

Wait a minute. This is my house. Aunt Tilley is gone. I always loved this room. I claim it.

Marching proudly, she dragged her suitcase behind her, stopping in the middle of the room. Hugging herself, she could almost feel Aunt Tilley's welcoming love.

When the kids come they can have the guest rooms. This is mine.

With her arms still across her chest, she walked over and looked out at the silver lake glistening in the pre-twilight sun.

Welcome home, it seemed to say. Your heart is where it belongs.

My heart. I left it here twenty years ago. I should have stayed. I wanted to stay. But never have I regretted it more than today.

Leaving her room, she checked on the other rooms. When she came to Aunt Tilley's studio, she hesitated before pushing open the glass door. The room, still flooded with light even with the edge of night coming, greeted her like an old friend. The room, an addition to the original house, had been designed by Aunt Tilley. Light and shadows, she always said, the stories of pictures. Windows surrounded the whole area. No shades, nothing to block the light. The whole panorama of the lake lay out like a giant mural.

***

An early supper for Becca consisted of soup and a salad. She'd picked up the fixings just before she left the interstate coming here. Washing the few dishes by hand, she watched the activity on the lake. She saw ducks swimming in a row and an older man fishing from a simple boat, with a small motor and plank seats. The kitchen faced south and, with the beginning of spring, the sun set to her left allowing the soft colors of rose and sapphire to filter down to meet the dark navy blue of the water. Drying her hand on the flour sack kitchen towel, she tossed it over her shoulder and pushed open the back door. It creaked as she walked, then slammed shut. At first it startled her, but then she chuckled to herself. The summers she spent here this door banged constantly during the day and even the night. Except when Becca sneaked in past midnight from a date with Clay.

***

As the two lovers move cautiously over the gravel rock driveway, Becca would 'accidentally on purpose' fall toward Clay. His strong arms would catch her, hold her for a moment. Relaxing his grip, he would take her hand to steady her as they walked silently to the back of the house.

All the windows would be dark, meaning the household had retired for the night. The full, bright moon lit their path. At the porch, as Becca stepped up on the first step, Clay would gather her to him. His firm youthful body pressing against her warm flesh sent desires through both. Becca accepted his lips fully, loving his tongue searching, probing her mouth. Her body formed to his, she wanted to stay in his arms.

When he released her she felt a vacancy. He stepped back, his indigo blue eyes boring into her soul. Stepping across the wood porch, she opened the creaky screen door with care, easing it closed so it stayed silent. Clay always waited for her at the bottom of the porch until she reached her room. Flipping on her light, she leaned out her window to wave at him. Waving back, he would put his hands in his pockets, saunter down the dirt driveway.

Her heart would swell with love as her body flushed with the memories of his passion. He lifted her to the edge, then over. Leaving the window open to hear the night sounds, she shed her clothes, slipped into boxers and a tank. Wriggling between the crisp sheets she fell asleep with the taste of him on her lips, the feel of his hands on her skin.

***

Becca curled up in the old porch swing, leaning her head on the cool chain. She thought back to why she didn't stay with Clay. He wasn't the first boy she kissed or slept with, but he

was her first love.

Lost in her thoughts, a male voice made her jump.

"Ma'am?"

A man about her age leaned on the railing. A large, burly guy with kind dark-brown eyes, short tailored hair. Clean shaven, he looked like a sports jock.

Ma'am. So it's come to this.

"Yes?"

"I saw your car in the driveway and I kind of keep an eye on Tilley's place." He pointed with his thumb back over his shoulder. "I live over there..."

Becca squinted her eyes. Stopped the movement of the swing with her feet.

Couldn't be.

"Robert King." He put out his hand.

"Robby? Robby King? No way." Becca jumped out of the swing, ran down the stairs to him.

"Becca?" His large bear like arms grabbed her, swung her around. "Becca. You look great."

16

She knew she blushed. From feeling like a wash-up, tossed-aside wife, to looking great after several years, she smiled. "Robby. Oh my, you are a sight for sore eyes." She stood back at arm's length looking at a friend from a better time. "You live in your folks' house?"

"Yeah, they passed just before Tilley. My wife and kids love it here as much as me, so we moved back. Left the big city and all. But you? Are you and your family here for the summer?"

The dark cloud covered her happy thoughts. "No. My husband is still in the big city, my kids are in college. This is my trek back to the past. When life was simpler."

The football player bear of a man took her hand, dragging her across the open space separating the two houses. He started yelling about half way to the other house. "Susie! Guess who I found? Oh, I forgot you wouldn't know. Becca. Tilley's Becca."

Becca stopped walking, jerked him back. "Why did you say that?"

Robby looked at her with sorrow in his eyes. "Sorry, Becca. Tilley talked about you all the time. She missed you so. After she died, Susie and I waited for you to come. We were just about ready to give up. It's been a year."

The truth of his words hurt her heart. She dropped his hand, hugged her waist.

Aunt Tilley.

Tears formed in her eyes. All of sudden everything busted through her wall of protection and she started to sob. Dropping to her knees on the cool sand, she let the tears flow. A woman about her age came to them, but Becca couldn't see her through the tears.

"Robby King, what have you done?"

The voice and the woman's touch were calming as she kneeled down by Becca. "I'm Susie. Becca? Are you okay?"

Becca nodded, then shook her head. Blubbering. "I should have come sooner. Aunt Tilley...I loved her...but Jon said no...the kids left...he didn't want me...Robby said she missed me...and I missed her."

Becca saw Robby shuffling his feet. Then she heard Susie's command. "Robby! Go get some cold beers."

Putting her arms around Becca, Susie held her as she sobbed. Every once in a while she patted Becca's back, whispered. "It's okay."

By the time Robby returned, Becca gained some control. Wiping her eyes on her shirt sleeve, she took a good look at Susie. One of those natural beauties with long copper hair pulled back in a ponytail, flawless cream colored skin. A mixture of interest and compassion filled her holly green eyes. Robby spread out a blanket. The two of them moved Becca over to it. Handing Becca a cold beer, Susie listened as Becca babbled on. Robby built a campfire in a ring of stones, returned from the house with a cooler of beer.

The night settled around them. In the light of the fire, Becca watched Susie and Robby. Her hysterics over, she observed the compelling couple across from her. Robby had been quite the skirt chaser when they were young. To see him settled down with a sweet woman like Susie, talking kids amused her.

"So Susie, where did you two meet?" Becca took a drink from her bottle.

Susie glanced over at Robby. "At college."

Becca looked over sharply at him. "Where did you go?"

"State. Don't look so surprised." He chuckled, held his bottle high.

Becca shook her head. "I didn't mean...you just never talked about college that summer. What changed your mind?"

"My dad. He wanted me to go. Made me an offer I couldn't refuse." Robby said in his best godfather voice.

Becca smiled. "And that was?"

"Do it for the old man. I didn't know, but he saved since the day I was born. So I let him pay the first year, then I got a football scholarship for the other three." He took a generous swig.

Becca tiled her head. "What did you study?"

Robby finished his swallow. "Architecture. I worked for a fairly large firm, I was the CEO."

Impressed, Becca smiled. "Good for you. So you went to the city to work?"

"Yeah, Dad wanted me to get out of here, so Susie and I settled in to work the corporate lot." He looked back over at Susie.

Becca turned to Susie. "What do you do?"

"I worked my way through education to become the Superintendent of the largest district in the state."

Becca looked back and forth between them. "You gave it up to move here?"

Robby took a sip of his beer. "Yes. We never saw each other. Someone else raised our kids."

"So now what do you do?"

"I run an online designing firm. Work right at home." Robby waved towards the house.

Susie leaned back. "I teach Literature at the local high school. By the way, about 'that summer'. You were part of it?"

Robby and Becca exchanged looks as their minds flashed back.

***

"Just grab the knot on the rope, push off with your feet. When the rope stops to swing back, let go." Robby patiently explained to Becca.

Becca stood on the edge of a rock cliff at what seemed like miles above the mocking lake.

"Are you fucking kidding me?" She glared at Robby.

Strong, young muscular arms reached around her, taking her hands in his, placing both sets on the rope knot, his on top.

Clay.

His voice vibrated in her ear. "Just hold on."

With those words, she soared across the lake with Clay's firm body plastered against hers. At the point the rope hesitated to swing back, Clay pried her hands from the knot, plunging her down. She closed her eyes, took a deep breath, holding it. His fingers intertwined in hers as they hit the water together. Like a bullet, she shot downward, the water covering her head. His hands released her as her body spun like a swirling top. Her eyes still closed, she felt hands around her waist stopping her motion. Upward the two bodies floated to break the water at the same time.

Becca took a deep gulp of air. Opening her eyes, face to face with a smiling Clay, her hands rested on his broad shoulders, his hands on her waist. Treading water together, she couldn't help but let a large gush of laughter escape. Clay joined her, pulling her into him. Hugging his neck, fully aware of their bodies intimately melting together, she let the water pull them apart and looked into his eyes. But his eyes were looking down.

"I think your suit got twisted." A wicked smile played around his mouth.

Jerking her head down she saw while not exposed, her swimsuit top revealed most of her right boob. Releasing Clay's neck, she adjusted her top as he held her, watching with a spark of amusement flashing in his smile. When she felt everything back in the proper place, she looked up at him, narrowed her eyes.

"Enjoying the view?" She admonished him.

His sexy smile always knocked her in the stomach. "Yes, I certainly am."

With no warning, he licked the water from her neck. Smacking his lips, she felt delightful sensations rising. Wiggling out of his embrace, she started swimming for the beach. She could hear the water splashing behind her. He never overtook her, although she knew, as a strong

swimmer, he could at any moment.

When she figured her feet could touch the bottom, she stood, marched up the beach to her blanket. Grabbing her beach towel she plopped down, glared at Clay finishing his walk toward her. Reaching her, he stood dripping wet, water glistening off his golden tan torso. With the sun behind him, she could barely see his face, but his electric blue eyes flashed wickedness.

"Want to go again?" The challenge spiked his tone.

While his offer was tempting, her awareness of her body, still trembling from the strong feelings his touch produced in her, prevented her from accepting.

22

"Later. I want to get some sun." She laid back, closed her eyes, gripping the blanket at her sides to ease her shaking.

"Okay, later then." He stepped over her head, leaving drops of water in his wake. She forced herself not to turn her head to watch his beautiful tight ass walk away.

"Now that's a hunk of a lot of male." Gwen, Becca's best friend when she stayed at Aunt Tilley's, said as she plopped down next to Becca. Fluffing her long auburn hair back, the red in it sparkling in the midday sun, it looked like a lion's mane. Her ginger skin tanned from the endless days down on the lake, Gwen laughed with her frosted purple eyes.

Becca released her grip, letting go of the laughter she kept down while around Clay. *"Oh my God. He can get my juices going."*

"Good or bad juices?"

Becca raised up on her elbows just as Clay swung his gorgeous body out across the sparkling blue water. Doing a spin when he let go, he looked like a dancer in motion. In a graceful form, he split the water. The crowd on the beach cheered and clapped. The girls especially made a big to do when he surfaced.

Shaking her head. *"Both. And he has way too many groupies for me to even think I had a chance."*

Gwen gave her a staunch look. *"So you give up?"*

"Not give up, being practical. I have a year of college left. Then maybe grad school. Not working on my MRS degree."

Gwen lay down next to Becca. "You may regret being so practical someday. If I could have him every night, I could begin a whole new line of education."

Together the girls giggled...

***

"Hey, that was a summer. Right, Becca?" Robby's words snapped her right out of her trance.

"Yeah it was." She almost regretted leaving the cocoon of the past.

Robby got up to get another beer. He motioned to Susie and Becca. Both nodded their heads yes. Handing them bottles, he paused at Becca. "Every boy had a crush on Becca that summer, me included."

Becca laughed as she took the bottle. "Really?" Her disbelief sounded in her voice.

Robby sat back down. "Everyone except Clay."

Becca caught Susie's sharp look first at her husband, then over at Becca.

Heaving a sigh, Becca looked out over the lake. "Yeah. He just played me."

Robby chuckled. "No, Clay wasn't playing. He was in love. You broke his heart when you left."

***

When a tempest forms over a lake it takes on a life of its own. Becca stood at the backdoor with her arms folded, waiting for the thunderstorm to hit. The floor vibrated from the rolls of thunder. Large powerful flashes of lightening turned off the outside night lights, giving the impression of daylight. Never to be one to fear bad weather, she remembered Aunt Tilley taught her to take them head on.

A box on the nightstand in the bedroom carried the message. "Life isn't about waiting for the storm to pass, it's about learning how to dance in the rain".

As the downpour washed sand back into the water, Becca knew now why she did not come to see Aunt Tilley.

Guilt.

A storm of life changed Becca. Even though a long time ago, it shaped her life in a way she did not want. But she did not fight it. Her belief centered on the fact that things happen, so make it as easy for yourself as you can. Her path of least resistance produced regrets with unchallenged fears.

Resigning herself to the beginning of a spiritual journey, she did the natural thing and checked the windows in the house. The studio windows leaked like a sieve.

I need to get some caulking to seal these better.

Good. A physical duty to put on her 'to do' list.

Becca's Dance

CHAPTER TWO

The morning started well. Becca slept late. No alarm clock. No husband giving her directions for the day. No first thoughts of her calendar reminding her what to do.

"You broke his heart when you left."

The words echoed through her head.

Did I really? I never wanted to break his heart. I wanted to come back.

But life and expectations lead her down a different path. Jon Hamilton, the up-and-coming executive, offered money, prestige, a safe place to hide. So when he chose her, she didn't have the courage to say no.

The fresh spring breeze moved the lace curtains. Jon would never allow an open window. Their house was always at the same temperature, winter or summer. A perfect seventy-two degrees. Just like their life. The same, day after day, the perfect life.

So why the hell did he grow tired of it? He created it. Rat bastard!

Her anger made her jerk the covers off, leap from the bed. At home, her first act would be to take a shower.

Not today. First, a cup of flavored coffee in her jammies.

Padding to the kitchen, she fixed her flavored coffee in her new coffee maker, purchased at the shopping mall on the way to the lake. The caramel colored liquid poured into the single cup, releasing a fantastic aroma. Picking up the large mug, she wrapped her hands around the warmth. Holding it up, she savored the smell as she walked out to the porch. Taking her favorite seat in the swing, she watched the ducks on the lake. A thought struck her.

What time is it anyway?

Who the hell cares?

Leaning back she relished her new-found freedom. The ringing of the phone disturbed her new world.

Damn.

Sitting her mug on the side table she went into the house, picked up her cell phone. The caller ID showed Carter, Aunt Tilley's lawyer.

"Hello?"

"Mrs. Hamilton?" A strong male voice.

28

Becca cringed at the Mrs. Hamilton. "Yes."

"Hi, this is Lloyd Carter."

A pause.

"Mrs. Hamilton? I'm Tilley Young's lawyer. Are you getting settled in okay?" Not sounding like most of the lawyers she knew, he sounded personal.

Becca leaned against the wall. "Yes, everything is great. Thanks for sending me the key."

"Not a problem. Now that you have taken possession of the property...You are taking possession?"

Becca chuckled. "Yes."

"I have some papers for you to sign. Can I stop by?"

Shrugging. "Sure what time?"

"In about an hour?"

So much for a leisurely coffee in her jammies. "That would be fine, Mr. Carter."

"See you then. Bye."

"Good bye."

Pressing the button to disconnect, she laid the phone on the table. Pushing off from the wall she went out to retrieve her cup.

Guess I'm taking a shower now after all.

Bounding down the hallway, she danced into the bathroom to an imaginary song in her head.

***

Becca did make a 'to do' list in her head while showering. After the lawyer man left, she wanted to explore Aunt Tilley's art studio, the one room she avoided yesterday. The memories so good, she wanted to savor them all by herself. And have all the time in the world to do it.

She dressed in some jeans and a denim shirt, new items from the mall. Since Jon never allowed her to wear everyday jeans, she relished the feel of the soft material against her skin. Pulling her hair into a pony tail, not all of it wanting to go in, small locks stayed free, giving her a messy feeling of freedom.

I like unkempt. Kind of like ruffled.

A knock at the door sounded just as Becca reached the front room. Heaving open the solid wood door, she held out her hand to the nice-looking man in an off-the-rack suit.

How do I know that?

Jon taught her with all his custom-made suits. Still, she liked this guy. He looked real, trustworthy. Besides Aunt Tilley picked him, so he must possess a good spirit.

"Mr. Carter, glad to meet you. Come in." Becca pushed her hair out of her eyes.

He extended his hand. "Mrs. Hamilton…"

"Becca. Call me Becca. I'm not real fond of Mrs. Hamilton right now. Do you do divorces?" Seeing his confused look. "Never mind."

Standing in the foyer, Becca looked around. "Where do you want to go?"

"A table would be nice." He held up his briefcase. "I have some papers for you to sign."

"Sure." She looked in at the bright dining room and motioned with her arm. "In here. It's nice."

Mr. Carter put his case on the table. "You don't remember me."

Becca sat on the chair across from him, cocked her head. He looked familiar, but... "I don't remember a Lloyd...wait Sparky?"

The man chuckled. "Yes, Sparky. How are you Becca?"

She slapped the table. Sparky was part of that summer. A fun loving, tall, lean kid, possessing sex appeal in a quiet way.

"Sparky, so you're Aunt Tilley's lawyer?" Folding her arms over her chest, bobbing her head. "A lawyer."

"Yeah a lawyer. Go figure." His chuckle warmed her heart. Pulling papers out, he started explaining something or other to Becca, but her mind went back to 'that summer'.

***

"Sparky, hit the fucking ball." Clay and Robby's voice chimed together. The fun game of beach volley turned serious. Becca stood on the other side of the net from Clay. The veins on the side of his neck were pulsing.

How can men get so intense over a stupid game?

Looking back at her teammate, Sparky served the ball just out of Clay's reach. Robby went for it, so did Clay. Clay stopped. But so did Robby. The ball hit the sand in the space between them with a thud. For a moment, they just looked at it. Then they raised their eyes to each other and started arguing over who should have hit the ball.

Sparky came up behind Becca and laid his arm across her shoulders. "It's sad to see children fight."

The two laughing stopped the fight as Clay and Robby turned to glare. Clay picked up the ball, slammed it on Sparky's legs. "Just hit the fucking ball."

***

Sparky slid some papers over to Becca. Embarrassed she hadn't been paying attention, she tried to focus and remembered some of his words.

Aunt Tilley's house. Did she want to take up legal resident of the property? The first paper.

Becca reached for it. Glancing at it, she got the point of it. It gave her the right to live in the house. That she wanted. Her signature flowed over the blank line with the highlighted "X" on it.

Next.

"Now this is Tilley's bank account. She added you several years ago, so all we have to do is verify you are Becca Young-Hamilton, and it's good to go. Sign there."

Again the highlighted "X". Becca glanced at the figures. Did a double take.

"Are you sure the decimal point is in the right spot? There are a lot of numbers here."

Sparky smiled. "You had no idea? Tilley was quite wealthy. Her artwork sold all over the world."

The stoneware vase on the buffet behind Sparky scoffed at her. From some far-off country. As is most of Aunt Tilley's stuff.

Her trips.

She always asked Becca if she wanted to go, but Jon made other plans. God forbid she

screw up his precious plans.

Becca shook her head. "No, I didn't."

Sparky lowered his voice. "She loved you very much. Missed you."

Tears formed in Becca's eyes again. "So I've been reminded." Through the blur, she scribbled her signature.

"I'm sorry, Becca. Tilley was just such a kind spirit. We all miss her."

Becca wiped her eyes. "I know. I am angry with myself for not coming back sooner." She shook the bad thoughts from her head. Smiling, she angled her head. "Thanks for everything. I'm glad she had you."

"We're the lucky ones. We had her."

She leaned back in her chair. "So, Lloyd Carter. What have you been doing for the last twenty years?"

"Normal stuff. College, marriage, kids..." He gathered up the papers, separated them into two piles.

Becca smiled to herself.

Most lives are the same aren't they.

He handed her one set of papers with a navy blue checkbook. "I married Jillian Owens. You remember?"

Becca perked up. "Yes, Jilley. Oh my god. How sweet."

"Yes, we live on the other side of the lake. She's in Chicago now, but when I told her you returned, she was so excited. She'll be back by the weekend. Come to our house Saturday night for a cook-out?"

Nodding, she accepted. "Yes, I would love to."

Sparky rose from his chair, put his papers back into his case. "We'll see you then. Robby and Susie are coming. You know they are your neighbors."

"Yeah, I met them last night. Great. I'll hitch a ride with them."

Pausing, Sparky looked at her. "Are you alright? You said something about a divorce when I first got here."

Standing up, she stuck her hands in her back pockets. "Yeah, well. My marriage is dead." She tried to make light of it.

34

Sparky took her seriously. He walked around the table to hug her. Against her hair, his words sounded. "You're back home now, Becca. With people who will take care of you."

Wrapping her arms around his back, burying her face against his chest, she felt the comfort and strength she could draw from these people.

Thank you Aunt Tilley.

***

"Hey Robby." Becca leaned over her porch railing, waving to get her neighbor's attention. He acknowledged her, sauntered over.

"Yes, girl." The ever-present smile.

Leaning her folded arms on the top rail, she smiled at having an old friend as a neighbor. "Rummaging through Aunt Tilley's studio after the storm last night, I found several widows leaking. I think I want to replace them all. Got any ideas who I can call?"

Robby patted the rail. "I know just the guy. I'll call him and set up an appointment. Any special time?"

Becca stood up. "That would be great. Thanks. Anytime. I am just hanging."

Robby looked up at her. "Are you thinking of doing some painting?"

"I am. Being back here, looking at all of Aunt Tilley's works, I have the desire to dive in and do it."

"Good for you. If I remember you were fairly decent." Robby winked.

Becca crossed her arms across her chest. "I don't know about that, but I did have a passion for it. I think it is time to rekindle."

Robby chuckled. "Yes, rekindling passion is good. Very good." He turned to walk off. "I'll take care of getting the windows replaced."

Becca yelled at his back. "I can pay. I have money."

Robby yelled over his shoulder. "Was planning on it."

Becca snickered at his remark as she went back into the house, to continue her studio clean-up mission. All artist studios looked messy and cluttered. To keep a good flow of work going for hours the truth is, they know where everything goes.

Becca didn't realize how much she missed the rainy days she and Aunt Tilley would spend hours in this room, losing track of time.

Sorting through the boxes, she found a crate with her name on it. Pulling a canvas out, a sheet of paper fell to the floor. Leaning the crate back against the wall she abandoned, for the moment, her efforts to unpack and picked up the piece of handwritten stationery.

The handwriting looked so familiar.

Dearest Becca,

Over the years, I saved the paintings you did when you spent the summers with me. I always hoped you would let the dream of your soul control your whole being, releasing the artist deep inside. Your visits became farther and farther apart. So I crated them up, knowing when you did come, after my death, you would remember what you once so dearly loved. In my heart of hearts, I know life did not turn out the way you expected. You have two beautiful children and a fine husband. But little by little I watched the joy of life fade from your eyes to be replaced with the duties. Look at your drawings. Let your memory go back to the feelings used to create them.

All my love forever,

Aunt Tilley

Becca went crossed-legged down to the floor. Tears dropped from her eyes landing on her legs. She wiped at them with her dusty shirt sleeve.

Oh, Aunt Tilley. You knew me so well. I am so sorry I didn't come more. But I figured I

had all the time in the world. But we don't, do we?

Hoisting herself up, she went back to unpacking the box. The first image of the lake looked rough, amateurish. She still remembered how the paint flowed as she experimented with all the colors. It ended with more paint on her than the canvas. Aunt Tilley suggested framing her shirt instead. But Becca loved the shirt, wore it every time she came in to paint.

Where is it?

Becca looked over at the hooks that always held the smocks and aprons.

Nothing there.

Where would they be?

She glanced around.

Surely, no one would toss them out?

Later. I will look for them.

Canvas after canvas she pulled out. Each a little more structured, sharper. Turning one around, she saw where Aunt Tilley numbered and dated them.

Becca's Fifth. Kind of like Beethoven's fifth.

Even made her chuckle to herself. The last one, the biggest, hit her with the most impact. It was of a stunning young man, standing on the dock, leaning on the pilasters. His sun streaked hair blowing wisps in his light-blue eyes. His award-winning smile almost real, showing white teeth, crested a deep humor that always made her laugh.

Clay.

Becca stared at it for several minutes as sweet memories washed over her. The summer love you never forget.

Turning it around, this one Aunt Tilley had titled-Becca's First Love.

How many times over the last twenty years did she think of him? A million? What if she stayed the day he begged her? Would she be seeing her marriage end? Or would they have been like Robby and Susie, renewing their love in the solitude before kids, jobs, life.

Becca sat the picture on the floor, stepped back to look at it.

Where is he? Did I actually break his heart like Robby said?

A loud pounding on the door sharply interrupted her thoughts.

Wiping the dust from her hands on her jeans, she pushed loose wisps of hair from her face. Still thinking about Clay and that summer, she absent-mindedly opened the front door to the person waiting for her.

She gasped, gripped the door for support.

"Clay. Clay Lester." Older, but even more handsome than before if possible, the face from her canvas came alive.

In tight jeans, with a plaid flannel shirt open just enough to show the beginnings of his chest hair, his electric blue eyes still as bright and knee-weakening as ever.

Smiling, his eyes traveled down her body. "Becca. You look fantastic."

She felt it was a lie, but hearing the familiar voice still brought back sparks of his charm.

Catching the loose hairs, she tucked them behind her ears.

"Clay...what are you doing here? I mean I'm glad to see you and all...why are you here?" She knew he still held the ability to fluster her, making her jabber, but...

"Robby said you need some remodeling done. Windows? Tilley's studio? Ring a bell?"

I always hated it when he showed cool, calm and collected, and I was not.

"Yes...okay..." Becca looked behind her for... what? Support? "Come in...It's..." She waved her arm in the direction.

Clay pushed passed her. "I remember where it is."

The flashback crossed Becca's mind.

Yeah, they made love for the first time on the table. And later the floor...and against the wall...

Even her thoughts were jabbering.

Passing a mirror, Becca saw the reflection of a disarrayed woman. Fly away hair.

Is that dirt on my cheek? Shit. Robby could have warned me he was coming.

She continued following Clay and she entered the studio just after him. His attention focused on the windows as he strolled over to them.

Did he just pat the table?

Shoving her hands in her back pockets, she watched him move about the room. With nothing to do, she glanced around until her gaze landed on the portrait of Clay she had sat down to answer the door.

Jerking her head to see if he was looking in her direction, he was still busy with his tape measure. She started meandering

40

toward the picture. With his back to her, he measured, wrote on a pad. Reaching the crate, she slipped the canvas inside.

He said something.

"Sorry, what?" She moved away from the spot, wandered toward him.

He turned around, looked at her, glancing around suspiciously. "I would suggest sun shield glass. Allows in the light, but not the harmful rays."

Becca shrugged. "Sure sounds good."

Clay narrowed his eyes. "They're pricey."

"Fine, just give me a bid, I'll get you a check." She placed her hands on her hips, leaning on one leg, then the other, finally standing with both legs straight.

Clay ripped a sheet from his pad. "Yeah, I forgot. You married well. Money's no problem?"

"No, it's not like that…I just…" He eliminated the distance between them. Standing so close she could smell his scent of musk and…

Sawdust?

Her insides went to jelly.

His look bore into her. Taking her hand, he slapped the paper into her palm. "When do you want us to start?"

Her voice barely above a whisper. "Anytime."

His voice sure, commanding. "I'll call. Let you know when we can start."

Becca angled her head. "We?"

Clay's look hard, cold like a freezing rain. "My sons and I."

It took a lot of will power to keep her jaw from dropping. "You have sons?"

He chuckled. "Six of them. Three work with me."

"Six sons?" Now her jaw did drop.

"Yeah. Did you think I just waited around for you?" A smirk lingered on his lips.

His words took her back. At a loss as what to say, they stared at each other. Then he frowned, turned away. Becca froze in her spot. She heard the front door slam.

Looking down at the crinkled paper in her hand, she saw the large lettering, 'Lester and Sons.'

***

"What are you gawking at, Robby?" Susie said as she walked into the kitchen, surprised to see her husband almost falling out of the window.

"Clay Lester. He's over at Becca's giving her a bid on her windows."

Susie stood stunned at her husband's antics. "And you didn't tell her he was coming?"

"No, that would have spoiled the surprise."

42

"Robert King, when are you going to learn women don't like those kinds of surprises?" She slapped him with her dish cloth. "Get out of the damn window."

Robby scampered down from his perch. "She's coming over. Act natural."

Becca knocked hard on the back door but didn't wait for an invite. "Robby, I know you're in there. I saw you in the window."

"He's here." Susie stood against the counter, her arms crossed, glaring at her husband.

Robby took a quick seat at the table and looked up at her as he shrugged.

"You set me up." Becca's words entered the room before her.

Robby gave his best innocent act. "What? You wanted someone to put in new windows. Clay is the best."

Becca stood in the middle of the room, hands on hips. "You didn't say anything last night about him still living here."

Robby shrugged. "You didn't ask. Anyway, where else would a Lester live?"

Becca stood over him glaring. "What's your point, Robby? He's married. Six sons. A wife. It's like dangling a carrot in front of a donkey." She turned to leave, but his words stopped her at the doorway.

"He's not married."

Becca turned back, looked first at Susie, who raised an eye brow and nodded. Then over at Robby, who sat there with a Cheshire cat smile stretched wide across his face.

"What?"

"He's divorced. Has been for several years." Robby leaned on the table with one elbow,

darn cocky and full of himself.

Becca shook her head. "Doesn't matter."

Susie looked over at Robby. "Does it matter?"

Robby leaned back, chuckled. "Oh, yeah. It does. To both of them."

***

Becca

Clay sat on the deck of *Brick's Bar* ready to drink the pitcher of beer in front of him.

The sun settled down on the infinity line of the lake, shooting soft colors of pinks and purples. Clay propped his feet up on the chair across from him, letting his memories cascade over him.

Becca

Seeing her again hit Clay harder than he wanted. Convinced he got over her, that the wall he had built would hold strong, he was dismayed that it cracked at seeing her. Twenty-some years, still smitten as bad as when she walked into his life.

***

A spring day warmer than usual welcomed May. Just returning from college, Clay now wanted to settle down to work with his dad. The only son in a family of five girls, his sisters had married and moved away. He stayed. This is home. Clay, his father Paul Lester, his grandfather Oscar Lester. Greats and greats before him. Clay's roots run deep; he liked that. His sons, their children, would be born and raised on the land he loved. He never wanted to live anywhere else. College had been an experience, now out of his system.

Working on the dock for Tilley Young gave him a feeling of fulfillment. He hadn't worked with his hands for months. A brain full of 'book learnin', he wanted to feel wood. His father owned the local lumber yard, Lester Bros. His uncles worked in the wood trade in some respect. Uncle Hoarse made the most beautiful furniture in the state. Uncle Ted did remodeling and custom work. Uncle Carl did the books. A math whiz, he made sure the company made money.

His young, strong hands gracefully ran down the pilaster he just finished. Almost done. One more day, then Tilley could dock her boat. Jumping down off the dock, he stood knee-deep in the crystal blue water.

"Uncle Ted. This is about done. I'm going to go up, tell Tilley to take her boat out of dry dock. I know she is just itching to go fishing."

"I'm sure she is." Uncle Ted went to school with Tilley. Old dear friends, if anything ever happened between them, Clay didn't know. Uncle Ted never said.

Putting his gloves back on, Clay placed his hand on the dock, jumped out of the water. Picking up his tool belt, he buckled it around his waist as he walked to the front of the house. His shirt had come off hours before, welcoming the warm rays of the sun after a long, cold winter.

Grabbing the porch brace, he swung up onto the landing. Stopped dead in his tracks by the beautiful young girl standing next to Tilley, he leisurely walked toward the two women in a slow saunter as he took off his gloves. He wanted time to size up the girl.

His eyes first saw the ample breasts pushing against her thin shirt. Her legs, long, toned and tanned. He smiled to himself, thinking of that body pressed up against his. Cornflower blue eyes flashed mischief and fire. Ready for some fire in his life, he stretched out his hand. She put her small hand in his. He rubbed his thumb over her silky skin.

Watching her face, he could tell he disturbed her senses. Clay knew how to decipher women. In college, a long affair with a female professor taught him how to read a woman's body, then meet her needs. It proved to be a good lesson to learn.

When he released her hand, the movement measured and purposeful, he turned his attention to Tilley. Watching Becca with

46

his side vision, he could smell the sex on her. Like a blood hound, he knew when he aroused.

Leaving her with the promise of tomorrow, he jumped off the porch. He felt her eyes on him, and he smiled. Summer looked a whole lot better.

***

"Clay." Sparky's voice ended his thoughts. "Mind if I join you?"

Clay slid the pitcher over to Sparky's side of the table as he sat down. "Knock yourself out."

Sparky poured the rich, yellow, bubbly liquid into his glass. "So I got a call about a week ago from Becca about coming back to claim Tilley's house."

Clay gave him a smug smile. "I saw her today, sport."

Disappointment showed all over Sparky's face. "Damn! I wanted to tell you. So why did you see her? Rekindling old flames?"

"Not a chance. Burnt once is enough. Anyway she's married."

"Not so sure that is going to be her status for long. She hinted at a divorce."

Now Sparky got his attention. "How so?"

"Asked if I did them. So why did you see her?"

"She wanted some new windows. I got the impression hubby is buying them since money's not an issue."

"Wrong again, sport."

Clay cocked his head, studied Sparky. "Spill."

"Nothing big. Tilley left her a shit load of dough."

"Really?" Clay leaned back in his chair, ran his tongue around the inside of his mouth.

Sparky dropped a bomb shell. Clay's look probably said it all.

Clay chuckled, picked up the pitcher, poured more beer into Sparky's glass, then his. "Tell me more."

"Nothing else to tell. She's here, alone. Lookin' good. Don't you think?"

Clay nodded in agreement.

"So, we are having a cookout this Saturday. Coming?"

"Sure." Clay liked Sparky and Jilley's parties. They were relaxing, casual and fun. Many

life-long friends. He could go alone, not feel like he needed to explain.

Sparky hit him with the final bomb. "Becca will be there."

Jordyn Meryl

CHAPTER THREE

Not a good night for sleeping. Becca's mind went back to Clay every time she closed her eyes. Her body ached from the sweet memory of how he made her feel. Like a woman desirable, alive. He still had the same effect on her.

When did I become unattractive? Capable of being discarded?

Even today with his eyes flashing with anger, she felt the stirrings of her youthful desires.

Why is it so hot in here?

Throwing back the covers, Becca went to the French doors, yanked them open. The night's cool lake breeze reminded her of the feelings and sounds of that summer.

***

The sound of a truck rattling down a bumpy dirt road, kicking up the gravel, told Becca Clay was close. By the time she got to the window, the clouds of dirt billowed behind him as he barreled

50

passed Aunt Tilley's house. Even the flash of him sent hot licking flames up her body. Pushing open the screen door, she stood on the porch, watched his dust. Collapsing back against the house, closing her eyes, she waited as the shakiness of her body subsided. Her hands on her thighs felt hot. Rubbing them up and down, she closed her eyes, saw Clay's face. Saw that wicked smile playing around his lips.

"Becca?" Aunt Tilley's concerned voice interrupted the enjoyable fantasy.

Becca sighed. Opening her eyes she looked at her aunt. "I'm fine, Aunt Tilley."

Aunt Tilley walked to the banister, turned her head in the direction of Clay's retreat. "Was that Clay Lester's truck just went by? Seems he goes by here a lot lately." Aunt Tilley turned, winked at Becca. "He must have a job going on down the road. Otherwise, I cannot see any reason he would be traveling down this old dirt road so much." Pushing away from the railing, Aunt Tilley sauntered into the house. "No reason at all."

Becca's eyes followed Aunt Tilley's departure into the house. The screen door slammed behind her.

"Becca?" Robby King's voice cracked as he walked up the steps.

Refocusing on him, she watched the boy who lived next door come to stand in front of her. "Yeah?"

"Beach party tonight. Down by the dunes. Start gathering around noon. Going?"

"Sure. Sounds good." Becca's heart jumped. She could watch Clay, still be protected by the group.

"I'll give you a ride?"

Becca nodded. "Sure."

Robby smiled. "Noon?"

She started for the door, a truck horn behind her stopped her in her tracks. As she

twisted around, Clay's black truck skidded into her driveway. Bringing it to a sharp stop, his head half way out the open window, he leaned his elbow on the door frame.

"Hey guys." Even his deep, rough voice gave her chills. "Goin' tonight?"

Robby shuffled over to the side of the porch. "Becca and I were just talking about that…"

Clay's eyes switched from Robby to Becca. "…and what did the lovely Becca say?"

Robby looked over at her. She felt his stare, but her eyes were on Clay. She straightened up walked to stand beside Robby. "Becca said for Robby to pick her up at noon." She narrowed her eyes at Clay. Her looked dared him.

His words sent sharp flames of heat to her breasts. "Then I will be here at noon to take the lovely Becca to the party."

She concluded for him. "And Robby."

52

Clay licked his lips, let his eyes followed her body down. Bringing them up, he smiled. "But of course, Robby too."

For a few seconds, they just stared at each other waiting for the other to blink.

Robby cleared his throat. "So…noon?"

This broke the spell between them. Clay snickered. "Noon."

Shifting the truck in reverse, he nodded at the couple, winked at Becca. With the skill of a stunt driver he backed up, out to the road.

Becca gripped the rail of the porch. She now felt all too eager about this afternoon when Clay would pull into her driveway.

She almost forgot about Robby. Her mind was already on what to wear, coupled with the thrill of sitting next to Clay in his truck.

"Robby! Guess we'll be going with Clay today." She patted his shoulder, bolted into the house, leaving him standing outside.

***

A few minutes before noon, Becca saw Robby coming across the lawn separating the houses. She had changed her outfit five times, wanting to look sexy, but modest. She settled on jean shorts, a light-blue V-neck sleeveless tee, and, after raiding Tilley's closest, she found a long denim vest. In her jewelry she found a dragonfly pendent with matching dangling earrings. White canvas Keds completed the outfit. Wearing her swimsuit under her clothes, she stuffed a towel into a beach bag, threw it over her shoulder, and went out to greet Robby as he climbed the stairs.

"Wow! Becca you look great!" Robby's approval became visible in his eyes. Becca smiled to herself. They both jerked toward the driveway as they heard tires on gravel. Clay smiled as he brought the truck to a stop in a cloud of dust. His long, tan arm snaked out to open his door from the outside. As his jean short clad legs uncoiled from the cab, Becca couldn't help but watch, forgetting to breathe, with her mouth slightly open.

Stepping back, Clay bowed. "Your carriage awaits m'lady."

Becca walked sure and quick to him. He straightened up, let his glaze sweep over her.

"Nice." He raised an eyebrow.

She brushed by him, but not before the touch made her feel chills. He laughed as he stepped back. She looked at the cab, realized it stood a little farther off the ground than she expected. Looking down she saw the running board. Lifting her foot to the ledge, she looked for something to grab. Then she felt strong hands on her waist, lifting her up, into the seat.

Clay spoke in her ear. "Here let me help you."

Her first instinct to do the 'I can do it on my own thank you', but the feel of his hands, the warmth of his breath became a spell she did not want to break right now. Allowing him to lift her, she turned, plopped her butt on the seat. With her firmly in the seat, Clay pulled himself up to stand on the running boards. Becca froze.

54

She knew she should scoot over, but her senses were screwing with her, her bearings crossed. Clay stood for a moment looking down at her. She ran her hand around the steering wheel, a smooth, shiny, black onyx finish.

"Are you going to drive?" His question snapped her back.

"What? No. No."

He leaned down, whispered against her neck. "Then you need to slide over sweetheart. You're in my spot."

Her body obeyed. Still when he sat, his leg touched hers. Hot bare skin against hotter bare skin. He put his arm on the back of her seat. Looking out the window, he backed the truck around. When he stopped to change gears, he paused, looked at her. Her eyes locked with. He winked, moving his arm to her shoulder. Made her wish they were alone. His lips were only a micro speck away from hers. Lowering his arm, it brushed her shoulder. He smiled, turned the truck toward the road...

***

"What the fuck!"

Becca came straight up from her bed. It sounded like a bull dozer drove into the room next to her.

No, but almost.

A large machine roared pass her French door, which she left open last night. Untangling from the covers, she touched the rug with her bare feet. With one quick step, she jumped at the doors trying to figure out what interrupted her sleep. Stepping onto the deck, she saw a handsome young man driving a fork lift full of windows. Another equally as handsome kid came into her sights on her right side.

"Ma'am?"

There's that ma'am thing again.

"Yes?" She noticed his eyes lingered on her body. Then it dawned on her. She was scantily dressed in a short, thin strapped, silk gown.

Just then Clay walked around the corner. His mocking smile took over his whole face. "Becca? Did we wake you?" His glaze slipped down her body.

Suddenly she felt naked. Crossing her arms over her braless bursting breasts, she

shifted from one foot to the other. "Well...sort of. Didn't expect you."

Clay leaned on one leg as he stood on the steps. "Sparky verified your check would clear, so I had an opening, decided to get those windows in." His eyes roamed over her body, slow and sensual like he did when they were young.

Becca felt the same heated sensations.

Stop it! I am an adult woman. Not a starry-eyed girl.

She still felt uncomfortable. Like the first time with him.

Clay straightened up. "Where are my manners?"

Where indeed! A phone call would have been nice!

56

"This is my son, Andrew. Kevin on the fork lift. And…" A boy younger than the other two came to Clay's side. "This is Stephen, my youngest." Becca's heart caught in her throat. While true Clay, still as handsome as ever, but this one…this one is the spitting image of his dad when she knew him.

Becca stood shelled-shocked.

His sons. They could have been hers.

Tearing her look from Stephen, she locked looks with Clay. His eyes told her he knew where her mind went.

Finding her voice weak, she tried to sound confident. "Nice to meet all of you. Now if you will excuse me. I need coffee."

Turning on her heels, she exited with as must grace as she could muster. Feeling his eyes on her, she knew how short her gown was and what it showed. Her butt, but with panties.

Thank god.

No time for a shower, she went to Tilley's large walk-in closet, grabbed the first pair of jean shorts she found, a bra and a V-neck tee shirt. Dressed, she padded barefooted down the hall to the kitchen. As she waited for the coffee to brew, she watched out the window. Clay and his sons had a special rapport. He gave directions, they followed them. Hearing the beep signaling the coffee's done, she poured a cup. Having removed his top shirt, Clay's muscles pushed against the thin fabric of his tee shirt.

Becca remembered the feel of his chest when he would kiss her good-night.

Okay. I am a grown woman. A warm, gracious woman who would offer an old friend a cup of coffee. I can do that.

Holding her cup close to her chest, she pushed the squeaky back screen open.

All four of the Lester boys looked up. Three waited in expectation. Clay smiled.

Addressing him in what she hoped sounded like a civil voice, she offered. "Clay would you like a cup of coffee?"

"Sure. Give me a minute. I'll be in."

Becca stood still speechless.

In? I figured I could bring it out to him.

"Okay. Whenever." She bolted into the house. As the door slammed shut, she leaned

on the counter.

In. He's coming in.

She glanced around the kitchen like a trapped animal.

I didn't expect to be in such close quarters with him. Where can we sit so we are not close?

Too late. The squeak of the door told of his entrance. She moved to the coffee machine. Grabbed a cup from the hooks, pushed the button.

Turning, her next words surprised her. "Still black?" She lifted her face to look in his eyes.

58

His eyebrow arched. "You remember?"

Becca waved it off. "I guess some things just stay with you."

He took the cup from her and his fingers brushed hers. She picked up her cup, walked to the small kitchen table. Motioning him to sit across from her, she admired his easy stride as he took a chair, sat down.

Taking the first sip, his eyes looked at her over the cup. Sitting down, she played with her cup waiting out the silence.

"So Becca, what have you been doing during for the last two decades? I know you're married…"

She stopped him. "How do you know?"

"Tilley told me. Children." More a statement than a question.

Not willing to volunteer any information. "My daughter and son are at college."

He took another sip. "Husband coming soon."

"No." Her defense shot up.

None of your damn business.

One eyebrow shot up. "So you're just on a… sabbatical?"

Drawing a deep breath, she raised her head. "Just taking some time for myself."

"I see." There it is. His 'I am way ahead of you' look.

His simple response raised her radar. Becca jumped up. "No, you don't. It's my business. I came here to get away from other people running my life."

Clay stood, took his cup to the sink. Turning around he leaned on the counter. "Okay Becca. Whatever you say."

"I say I am fine on my own."

He shrugged. "No problem here. You always did what you wanted. I guess I just have a hard time believing there's someone else running your life."

The statement took the wind out of her sail.

I was once independent. Stood up to anyone. When did I become a wimp? When I accepted I had no control over what happens in my life.

Looking down at the floor she realized she was not the same girl who fell in love with Clay. That girl had left the building.

Clay's words cut through her thoughts. "What happened to that girl?"

Becca gritted her teeth. "She grew up. Became an adult."

Their eyes locked. He spoke first. "Did she now?"

Without waiting for an answer, he went to the door. Turning his head, he spoke to her over his shoulder. "It will take only a couple of days to finish your windows. Tomorrow we will be back around the same time...you might want to be dressed. While I enjoyed the view, I would prefer my boys not ogle you. It slows down their work."

"Ughhhh." She threw her cup at him. But he moved quickly out the door like he expected her reaction. The cup hit the wall, shattering as it fell to the floor.

***

The cold beer went down Clay's throat smooth, his mind a jumble of conflicting thoughts. Sitting in his truck, he leaned his head back against the cool leather.

Becca

She walked out of his life twenty-some years ago. He thought the pain would never stop. After six months of drinking and whoring around, he accepted she was not coming back.

"Hey bud." Robby slapped the passenger's side of the truck. Jerking open the door he jumped in. "A beer for your thoughts."

Clay opened the cooler, tossed a bottle to Robby. Robby popped the top, took a drink, sighed. "So now your thoughts?"

Clay took a big swig. "Not important."

Robby snickered. "Oh, I think they are. Becca."

Clay narrowed his eyes at his friend. "So?"

"I saw you over there putting in her windows. She's lookin' good isn't she?"

Clay looked over at her house. "Yeah. Becca always did look good. But I am pretty sure she is not here to rekindle an old, long forgotten love affair."

"She might." Robby displayed 'a-know-it-all' tone.

Not in the mood for games, Clay gave Robby a stern look. "What are you talking about?" His tone as flat as his interest.

"Her husband left her." Robby answered in a solemn tone.

The words felt like a punch in the stomach. "She never said anything."

"That's what she told Susie and me." Robby leaned back with a smug look on his face.

Sitting up straighter, Clay thought back to the scene in her kitchen.

People running my life.

That didn't sound like his Becca.

My Becca? She stopped being my Becca a long time ago.

Robby stared at him.

Clay did not for a moment buy this. "You're crazy. She picked her life. She got what she wanted."

Robby looked over his bottle at Clay. "Did she?"

"Oh, stop this shit. Becca made her choice. So did I. We are ancient history."

Smug Robby. "So maybe history needs to be revisited. It seems neither one of you made a choice you could live with...forever."

"Stop it, Robby. I have six great sons, a successful business. My life is good." Clay, on the edge of impatience, spoke with a sharpness. This conversation dug at him.

"And you forget I sat here with you for six months while you grieved for Becca. Was the best man at your wedding to the bitch of Lester County and your shoulder to cry on when you realized you no longer loved her, if you ever did."

62

Clay fought his rising anger. "Your point being?"

Decreasing the bluntness in his voice, Robby gave it the old college try. "She's back in your life. Do something about it."

"Like what, Einstein?" Clay gritted his teeth.

Leaning forward, Robby spoke directly to Clay with a low, in-your-face honesty. "Woo her. Turn on the Clay Lester charm, sweep her off her feet."

Clay just shook his head. He couldn't change the raw fury knotting in his gut every time he thought about her.

Robby got serious, his words pointed. "You two should have been together. It was so obvious."

A muscle jumped in his jaw. "To everyone but her."

"No. It was obvious to her. She just ran away. Don't give up. She is the love of your life and worth it. What have you got to lose?"

"Another heartbreak." Clay watched the bubbles in his beer float around.

"So be honest. Does it hurt any less when you see her?" Leaning back, Robby cocked his head.

Strong, coarse, edged with an absolute calm, Clay answered. "I try to stay angry enough not to think about it."

Robby chuckled, wrinkled his forehead. "And how's that working for you?"

Clay laughed quietly. "I made her mad enough to throw a cup at me today."

Robby threw back his head, hooted. "She still has the fire. So make it work for you. Angry sex is great."

Clay laughed, really laughed. The memory of their angry love making washed over him.

Gawd! What he would give to have that back again.

Resuming his comfortable anger, he threw his empty bottle back in the cooler. "No! We picked our paths. We live with our choices. Done deal"

"Really old wise one..." Robby's smirk rekindled Clay's crimson haze fury.

Clay faced Robby. "Look. I am tired of people lecturing me on what I need or who I need."

Robby's words echoed inside the cab as he took a swallow. "Touchy."

***

Cold beer filtered down Clay's dry throat satisfying his thirst. Sitting in his truck, under the shade of Tilley's mighty oak, he watched Becca and Tilley through the windows of their house. Never did a girl make his knees weak like her.

He remembered seeing her years ago, a teeny bopper with a pony tail and braces. Everyone knew Tilley's niece from the city. She always seemed terribly young. Never paid much attention to her, since he only showed up during breaks from college.

64

But today. Today she stood all grown up and striking.

She and Tilley were working around the kitchen. Joking and dancing, they made him smile.

The pound of a hand on the passenger side of the truck jerked Clay from his thoughts.

Robby leaned in the open window. "Got another one of those?"

Clay nodded, motioning toward a cooler on the floor. Robby crawled in, grabbed one from the ice. Closing the lid, he twisted off the top, took a large gulp.

"So whatcha doin'?" Robby leaned back, looked across the way.

"Nothing. Just chillin' down after a workday. You?"

"Just finished helping Dad with the garden. It's going to be a bumper crop." Robby chuckled.

Leaning back against the leather seats, Clay smiled. "Always is." He sighed. "Summertime. Greatest time of the year."

"So I see Tilley's niece is here again this summer. Becca isn't it?"

Nodding, Clay let a smirk play around his lips. "Yeah. Becca."

Tilley and Becca came out on the back deck. They sat down at the table with glasses of cold lemonade. Clay could see the moisture on the glasses. He knew the sweet taste of Tilley's lemonade.

"Holy shit!" Robby almost crawled through the windshield. "She is hot!"

Slowly turning towards his friend, Clay snickered. "You okay there, sport?"

Robby glared at him. "Don't tell me you didn't notice."

Taking another gulp of beer, Clay lowered the bottle. "Oh, I noticed."

CHAPTER FOUR

When the pick-up trucks rolled in, Becca was already up, showered, dressed and ready to greet Clay. Watching as his sons climbed out, she strained her neck looking through the kitchen window trying to find him. On her tip toes, she almost lost her balance, grabbing the counter, spilling her coffee on the floor.

"Damn!" She sat the cup in the sink, took a towel, bent to wipe up the spill. Coming back up, she came face to face with Clay's oldest son.

Andrew?

"Mornin' ma'am." His smile as electrifying as Clay's.

Giving it her best adult voice. "Mornin'. Andrew?"

He tipped his straw cowboy hat. "Yes Ma'am."

Becca glanced around. "Where's your Dad?"

"He's back at the lumberyard, doing some bidding. We can handle this."

"Oh, I'm sure you can." Letting out her breath, she hoped her disappointment didn't show on her face.

Andrew sounded like a foreman. "We'll be done by midday. Just a few more to put in."

"Thank you. They look real nice." Standing there without anything to say, she waved, turned away.

Damn you Clay. I get all excited about you being here. Now you're a no show. I guess that says how much I mean to you.

Now girl, stop daydreaming, get on with your day.

Becca went to the dining room table, sat down at her laptop. Jon Jr. always emailed her in the morning. She saw the tab telling her she had new mail.

Jon Jr.: Mom, what's going on? I talked to Dad. Said you were at the lake. What lake? Why?

Becca: I have some business of Aunt Tilley's to take care of.

Jon Jr.: I remember her. Her house on the lake.

Becca: She left it to me, so I am doing some repairs.

Jon Jr.: How long will you be there?

Until your Dad divorces me? No, that's snarky.

Becca: I don't know. A while. It's nice and peaceful here. Don't you have a class to go to?

Jon Jr.: Yeah. Later Mom. Love you.

Becca: Love you too.

He was gone. In a way, she felt guilty she didn't tell him the truth, but she wasn't ready yet. Her life was supposed to just go

68

along with no bumps, no potholes. She worked hard to keep it that way.

Damn you Jon.

The pounding of the workers jerked her head toward the studio.

And damn you too, Clay Lester!

Becca pushed away from the table.

Enough of this shit! I need to focus on something.

With her arms still braced on the table, she looked around.

Aunt Tilley's art.

Never did Becca imagine the money Tilley made from her art. Scooting back up to the laptop, she typed in Tilley Young. Her screen became a glow of websites featuring her aunt's art. Clicking on the first one took her to a gallery in New York. The pieces were astounding and the prices matched. Clicking on down the list produced galleries in San Francisco, Chicago...

London? Seriously!

Barcelona, Naples, Sidney...

Wow! All over the world.

Then there is a small gallery in a neighboring town.

Spring Hill. I think I will go check it out.

Checking her watch, it was still early. Going to her bedroom, she looked at her regular clothes, pulled out one of her standard outfits.

Beige slacks, cream blouse, beige shoes.

Jon's requested outfit.

Keep it simple and classy.

Screw that!

Storming back in the closet, she looked at Tilley's clothes. Skirts with splashes of color, brightly decorated shirts, big belts, junk jewelry of silvers, gold, brass and copper. Grabbing items, she picked and chose at will.

Standing over the items on the bed, her hands on her hips, she studied her choices. Before her laid, in its entire splendor, a multi-colored blue skirt, a corn flower blue, cotton top with sparkles, blue leather and sliver sandals. Several samples of silver jewelry, large and obnoxious.

Nodding her head, she gathered up the clothing, went to the bathroom. Removing the jean shorts and her t-shirt, she let the soft skirt fall over her body. The touch of silkiness, the clean feeling of cotton tingled her skin. Slipping the blue shirt over her head, she giggled at feeling so good in this new look. Going back to the bedroom she picked out the silver pieces she felt would go with her new outfit. Long dangle earrings, two, no three chains, trendy bangle bracelets. Looking in the full-length mirror, she twirled around, smiled.

Now she looked like Aunt Tilley's niece.

Sliding her feet into the comfortable sandals, she grabbed her purse, headed out the door. Stopping for a moment, she went to the railing, leaned over.

"Andrew."

Clay's oldest son, holding one of the windows, looked at her. "Yes, ma'am?"

"I'm heading out. And ..." she hesitated. "...can you drop the ma'am? Call me Becca?"

Juggling the heavy window, Andrew shot back. "Yes, Ma'am."

Becca chuckled, walked to the steps. Getting in her car, she felt free and lighthearted.

Road trip.

* * *

Clay decided not to go to Becca's today for his own sanity. She could still stir some hot flames. It had been a long time since he had sex. But being with Becca wasn't just sex. The memories of their sweet love making filtered through his mind. Stopping at the window, he placed his hand on the frame, looked out over Lester Lake.

Yes, they were young, but they could make love. Hot, sweaty love. Slow, leisurely love. Anytime. Anywhere. The lake, her house, his truck. A summer spent awakening Love's greatest passions.

Stop it Clay.

"Hey boss, need your signature." Mae, his secretary, spoke before she got through the door. He loved Mae. She had been with the company since he could remember. His father's secretary, now his. He worried she would retire, or God forbid, die. Mae kept the office running like a fine tuned clock. Everything in its place. Only Mae knew where that place was. Left on his own, he would never find anything. Also, she had been Tilley's best friend. That made her particularly unique. She shared her kindness with everyone. Need something, Mae had or would get it. Her support through his dark days had been his anchor.

Turning to look at her, he narrowed his eyes. "Sure."

Coming in she stood over him as he sat down to sign not one, but several papers. "Am I done?"

"For now. " She took the papers from him. Before turning she asked. "Say, I heard Becca's back in town."

Clay knew a trap when he heard it. "Yeah, she's out at Tilley's place. We're doing a job for her."

Innocently, Mae kept up the facade. "Really? Whatcha doin'?"

"Windows in the studio." His radar went wild. Mae knew the whole story of the Clay and Becca heartbreaking fiasco of a romance, known around the area as the Crawl Bridge tragedy.

Hell, the whole county did.

Most everyone hoped that someday the two lovers would reconnect.

72

"Really?" Mae showed no signs of leaving. "Oh, is she staying?"

Clay his tongue over his back teeth. "Don't know."

"And you are not on the job? Why?"

"Because I have work to do here." He leaned back in his chair. "What's your point, Mae?"

"No point. Just asking." As she left she threw over her shoulder. "Just thought you would be supervising such a valuable customer."

Clay sat there. He didn't want to see her. He really didn't.

Yeah, keep telling yourself that.

Damn! Even the voices in his head argued with him. Slapping the desk, he stood.

Got to get out of here.

Strolling through the open door, he flung his words at Mae. "Goin' for some fresh air."

"Right boss." Her condescending tone followed him out the door.

In his truck, he sat.

Where to go?

Starting the motor, he turned toward Lester Lake. His mind twirling around, he found himself going to a familiar swimming spot. He was glad to see it deserted. Cutting the engine, he leaned back, took several, deep breaths. Then the memories began.

***

After his solo jump into the lake, Clay sat on the bank letting the sun dry his body. His mind still thought of how Becca felt in his arms when they jumped together. Running his hand through his hair, he could feel his loins tightening.

Gawd, that girl can get me aroused.

Glancing over at her, he smiled. One of a kind, the other girls paled in comparison. No, he wanted Becca.

How do I get her? Not just in bed. In my life. I want more from her than I have any other.

"Hey bud. What has you in such deep thought?" Martin, a friend since kindergarten, slapped Clay on the back.

Clay shook his head. "Nothing just drying off. You?"

Going down cross-legged Martin sat across from him. "Just hangin'."

Martin looked over at Becca and Gwen. "Two exceptionally hot chicks over there. I got dibs on Gwen. You got Becca?"

"No. I don't got Becca." Clay picked up a hand full of sand, threw it away from them. When he looked back at Martin, Martin stared back with a smirk. "What?"

"I saw you swing out on the rope with her..."

"Not a big deal. She needed help. I helped." Clay shrugged.

Martin snickered. "Right. Sir Clay to the rescue. How noble."

Clay narrowed his eyes at his boyhood friend. "Don't read something into nothing."

74

"Nothing. Okay." Martin looked back over at the girls. "I'm going over to see 'my girl'. You?"

Desire twisted his gut, adding to his ache. "Later."

Martin towered over him, blocking the sun. "Don't wait too long Clay. Things have a habit of happening."

Clay watched Martin saunter over to the girls. Gwen's face lit up. Becca looked around Martin to Clay. Clay locked eyes with her. Her face stayed straight. Her mouth formed a smirky smile. Then she nodded, looked away. Clay kept his eyes on her. Just watching her made him feel good.

Why is that? How the hell do I know?

***

The evening came, the crowd gathered around a make-shift fire pit. While the temperature remained warm, the dark cover of the night took much of the heat of the day away. Couples started pairing up. Gwen and Martin sat intertwined in each other's arms. These two went through high school as sweethearts. They both just finished college, coming home to rekindle their romance. Clay figured for sure a wedding would happen soon.

Becca sat with Robby. Clay watched their body language. They weren't a couple, just paring together. Her laughter echoed above the talk and cry of the frogs.

A girl came up to Clay, put her arms around his waist. Young, just graduated high school, someone's sister he thought. Cooing,

she pressed against his side. "Clay, let's go off by ourselves..."
Running her fingers up his bare chest. "... and enjoy each other."
The implication was clear. If he wanted to get laid, she was
willing.

Clay still watched Becca. He smiled as he untangled the girl
from him. "Not this time sweetheart." Holding her arms, he kissed
the top of her head. Releasing her, he strolled over to Becca and
Robby, sat down between them. His legs touched Becca's as he
squeezed in.

Looking over at her, he smiled, whispered. "Sorry darlin'. Tight
quarters."

She narrowed her eyes. "Wasn't before you got here."

He grinned in amusement. "You mind?"

He saw her blush. "No, it's fine." Martin and Gwen sat next to
her, further limiting her moving space.

He felt comfortable with her squashed next to him. He was
afraid to move too fast on her, so baby steps. Just being next to
her satisfied him for now.

For several hours, they all sat around. Clay started a
conversation with Becca. "So, you still in college?"

Her eyes mirrored the light of the bonfire. "Yes. This is my last
year."

Lost in the depth of them. "And then?"

She frowned, shrugged. "Get a job somewhere."

76

He wanted to keep her talking, listen to her unbearably sexy voice. "As what? What is your major?"

Shifting her body, she actually moved closer. "Liberal Arts with an Art minor."

His interest spiked. "Art minor? I would think Art would be your major. Considering you're Tilley's niece and all."

Her smile changed her face, becoming softer, adding a touch of directness. "That's a high compliment. She's great."

Clay's mouth eased into a grin he couldn't control. "Yeah, she is." He felt her body relax next to him. The fire reflected in her blue eyes. He kept his on her face.

Lost in the moment, he almost didn't hear her next question. "So what about you? College?"

Jerking his stare away, he picked up a stick, poked at the fire. "Just finished."

Becca crossed her arms. "Your major?"

Still feigning total attention on the fire. "Business. Going into the family business. A lumberyard. I like to work with my hands."

The bluntness in her voice hooked him. "Oh, yeah, Lester Lumber? You're 'the Lester'"

He chuckled. "'The Lester'?"

"Lester County, Lester Lumber, even…" she waved her hand towards the water. "…Lester Lake."

Bowing his head, he looked down at the sand. "Yeah, that's me." Raising his head, he let her see his amusement. "It's where I am rooted. My family goes way back to the first settlers."

She spoke with frankness he welcomed. "That must feel good. To know where you belong, came from."

Tilting his head back to study her face. "Always knew. Don't you?"

She shook her head. "No, we moved a lot. Dad's a professor. We shifted from college to college." A far-off look crossed her face. "Here with Aunt Tilley is the closest I have to a home place."

A sudden feeling of compassion crossed his soul. For, right now, she looked like a lost wanderer.

"Hey dude." Robby slapped Clay's back breaking the moment between them. "How about a skinny dip?"

Clay glanced over at Becca, her eyes narrowed, giving him a look of mischief. Standing, he jerked her to him. "Chicken?"

The rest of the group came to their feet. Shirts and pants flew every which way. Becca darted away from him. Watching her retreat, he smiled as she pulled off her shirt. The darkest of the night covered his view, so he jogged after her. By the time he reached the water's edge, he found her submerged in the black water to her bare shoulders. Dropping his pants, he dove in. Trying to get to her, she teases him, keeping just out of his reach. Finally, he stopped, treaded water, watching her bob.

"Come here." He beckoned her.

Becca shook her head. "Can't. I'm naked."

He advanced towards her.

"Stop!" She moved away.

Oh, gawd.

His passion came hard and quick. She was right. He needed to stay back. Too close, she

would know how she aroused him.

A jolt of sexually charged energy rocked him to the bone.
"Okay, I'll stay back, just don't leave."

Moving her hands around, he could see her smile. "I'll stay. Mr. Lester County."

Raised one corner of his mouth. "That really bugs you?"

"No, honestly. It's kind of cool. Just like to get you going. You're such fun to mess with."

She has no idea how she messes with me.

Hearing a splash, they both turned in that direction. Gwen swam up to Becca. "You ready to leave? Or is Clay bringing you home?"

Becca splashed at her. "No. Clay is not taking me home. I'm leaving with who I came with. You. Let's go. I am freezing."

The two girls swam away. Clay stayed in his spot. He tried to keep his eyes on her, but the distance and the darkness blurred his vision.

A voice sounded behind him. They must have moved silently in the water. "Hey Clay. Just hanging out here?" Martin's words brought a grin to his face.

"Hanging is right."

***

Clay got out of the truck, picked up several small rocks, skipped them across the glass surface of the lake. The beginning of their love affair started that night. He remembered well the feelings she stirred in him. Thing is, she still did. He never forgot his first love. He tried. He probably slept with half the women in Lester County, tried marriage, failed. The best thing that came of that union was his six boys.

No, I am leaving things alone. Better that way.

He walked back to his truck, climbed in. Spinning around, he sprayed gravel for several feet.

***

The art gallery stood, tucked in the southwest corner of the town square, its quaint façade in keeping with the design of it's fellow shops. When Becca stepped inside, she stepped into the bygone era of modern art deco. Many different art forms greeted her-sculptures, paper making, paintings and photography hung everywhere, but Becca stopped in her tracks when an arch over a separate room announced "Art by Tilley Young".

Entering solemnly, Becca stood in awe of all the familiar paintings. She knew Aunt Tilley's style. Each piece told a story of her aunt's life. Walking around the room she could remember when some of the older pieces were created. As the pieces became newer, she frowned. These she had not seen, the years between her last visit to the lake and when Aunt Tilley death. The new art was just as breath-taking, but more controlled, sharper. Aunt Tilley's style had improved, but it was still recognizable.

Becca took her time. Being in this room surrounded by Aunt Tilley's art felt like being in a sacred place. The love and devotion stood apparent as a part of the life injected into the

creation of each piece. Becca could feel her Aunt's love not only for her passion, but for life itself.

When was the last time I felt an excitement for life? Long time.

When she ran from Clay, she also left her enthusiasm for living behind. Even convincing herself it was what she wanted, she pushed the desires and passions of living down deep inside. Life became an easy road of predictable events with unfeeling passages of time. The only real love she honored, her children. The one love she accepted as true. The rest, just intrusions trying to crack her shell.

Guess what? I held tight.

Her hands hung at her sides clenched into fists.

And that got you what, dear heart?

Here, looking at the beautiful soul of an aunt she loved dearly as it jumped off the canvas.

And alone. What did I expect?

Releasing her grip, she hugged her body.

Oh, Aunt Tilley. I was so wrong. You tried to teach me there should be gusto to life. I should have grabbed it. The ups and downs are the joy ride. I just coasted along.

The drawings seemed to mock her. Taking the time to look at each one, she could feel them enter her spirit, blessing her. In one quick thought, she wanted to gather all of them in her arms, take them home. But the world needed to see them. The reason why Aunt Tilley allowed them to go on display.

Continuing her walk around the room, she came to a painting of a young man. Soft brown eyes, a sweet looking face, surrounded by a fading light. Becca leaned in, read the plaque. It simply said. "Jeffery".

Who the hell is Jeffery?

The fact Aunt Tilley never married sometimes bothered Becca, but never enough to inquire. This looked like the portrait of a lover. Painted with soft delicate strokes, it spoke of a lost love.

Jeffery, huh?

Becca chuckled.

So Aunt Tilley had a secret love. How exciting.

Laughing to herself, a male voice behind her shocked Becca out of her daydream. "She did magnificent work, didn't she?"

Turning around to see a distinctive gentleman, dressed in an expensive tailor made suit. Becca nodded. "Yes, she was quite good."

"Ned Shawnmaker, proprietor. Honored to say a good friend of Tilley's." He extended his hand.

Becca slid her hand in his, feeling a comfort from this stiff man. "Glad to meet you. I am…"

Did Aunt Tilley talk about her?

"…Ms Hamilton." She decided she didn't want to give everything away at once.

An old habit? Maybe, but I just wanted to be an observer for now.

"I just admire the style of this artist."

Mr. Shawnmaker released her hand waved it around the room. "Yes, she had a real passion for life."

"As it shows in her work." Becca faked looking at a watch she wasn't wearing. "I must be going. I have a…appointment. Nice to meet you, Mr. Shawnmaker." As she turned he spoke, to her back.

"I hope to see you again, Ms Hamilton."

Turning around she kept moving backward towards the door. "Sure you will. Bye now."

Outside she chuckled.

This is fun. Not having to explain my actions or what I am doing.

Lunch alone. Sounded so much better than lunch with a bunch of rich bitches with nothing of value to say.

This is my new life. Be real. Be me.

Looking around the square, she saw a cute little café across the street. A sidewalk café, shaded with green awnings.

Perfect!

The cute young waiter flirted with her as he took her order of a salad, no a hamburger. Big, thick and juicy. Fries on the side.

Biting into the giant bun, she looked up just in time to see Clay's truck pull up to the art gallery. He stepped out, took a large package out from behind the seat, walked in. Through the window, she saw Mr. Shawnmaker greet him with a smile, a hardy hand shake. Clay slapped him on the back, together they walked to the back, out of her sight.

What the hell is he doing here?

***

Lingering over a cup of coffee, Becca waited until Clay returned to his truck to drive off. Her curiosity piqued.

What did Clay have to do with the art gallery?

Leaving the small rural town a thought came to her.

Why, I need to give a check to Lester Lumber for their services.

84

Directing her car toward the outskirts of town, a few miles later, she pulled in the parking lot, pleased to see Clay's stark black truck sitting there.

After climbing out of her car, she straightened her clothes, wisped her hair with her fingers, put a little swag in her walk, and sauntered in the main door. As soon as she opened it, a cool blast of air hit her. A welcome, refreshing…, then she heard her name.

"Well, glory be. It's Becca." Mae jumped out of her chair, ran around the desk before Becca's eyes adjusted to the dimness of the room. Two arms surrounded her in a giant bear

hug. "Darlin'. It is so good to see you." Pulling back and holding her at arm's length, Mae kept talking so Becca couldn't get a word in.

Becca did notice Clay came to the doorway of his office, leaning against the frame, a cocky smile on his face. Untangling from Mae, Becca stuttered as she tried to explain her reason for being here. It seemed so simple in the car.

"I thought…" Her eyes darted from Mae to Clay. "…I would bring a check by. I left early, so I wasn't there when they finished."

"So how do you know they are finished?" Clay mocked her.

"I… just assumed. They are doing a remarkably good job…." He turned his back to her, walked to his desk to sit down. She looked back at Mae, shrugged her shoulders. Mae tilted her head toward his office. Becca squared her shoulders, marched into the office. "...so I'm here." Plopping down in one of the two chairs before he invited her, she pulled out her checkbook. She laid it on the edge of his desk, grabbed one of the pens in the holder and sat poised to write.

"How much?"

He slid the bill over to her. Finding the total, she wrote out the check, tore it out of the book, handed it to him.

Their eyes locked, a wry smile played around his lips. "No questions. No bartering?"

Becca stood, watching with delight as his eyes widened as they traveled up her body. "No. If they leak, I am sure there is a guarantee you will fix them. Right?" With the last word, she leaned over slightly to give him a glimpse of her cleavage.

He stood abruptly. Becca turned, swaggered out of the room. "Mae. Good to see you."

Mae stopped typing, gave Becca her attention. "So you're living at Tilley's?"

"Yes, it needs some tender loving care. It has always felt like home..."

Mae smiled. "How long are you staying?"

Becca lowered her head. She could feel Clay standing in the doorway behind her.

"I don't know." Part truth. "I just take it one day at a time."

"You look good today girl." Mae smiled, waved her hand. "Don't you think so Clay?"

Becca laughed, hugged the dear woman.

"Yes…"Clay deep rich voice sounded behind her. "Especially good. Where did you go today?"

Becca let go of Mae, moving in front of Clay. "Oh, I went to an art gallery in the next city to check out Aunt Tilley's display. Quite impressive."

This made Clay straighten up. "Spring Hill?"

"Yes, I do believe that is the name of the town. Been there?"

His hard shell returned. "Not lately."

She wanted to scream. *Liar. Liar.*

"Should go. Nice little place. A pleasant sidewalk café across the street. I had lunch there…" She wrinkled her nose. "…very nice."

His body language betrayed him more than his face. "If you say so."

Waving her hand at the two of them, she exited the building, got into her car. Feeling both sets of eyes on her, she deliberately drove off in a nonchalant way.

Out of sight of the office, she drummed on her steering wheel. *Gotcha!!!*

CHAPTER FIVE

Aunt Tilley's Potato Salad.

Yes, I found it.

Tonight was the cook-out over at Sparky and Jilley's. Becca's excitement to reconnect with her long-lost friends grew as the hours passed. The memories of that summer flowed over her all week.

Was it just a week?

It seemed like she found her space in the universe, should have always been here. Sometimes her daydreams took her to the life that might have been. Most of the time she stopped the longing for what never would be. But every once in a while she, allowed herself to indulge in the fantasy.

Tonight she would pretend, no believe, that this is now her real life. Forget about the last twenty years as a robot just going through the motions.

Aunt Tilley always made the best potato salad. Finding the recipe was a godsend. She wanted to do something festive for the friends who opened their arms and hearts to her after so many years. Plus, making an impression wouldn't hurt. Deep down inside she wanted to be one of them. As far away from who she pretended to be for the last years of her life as possible.

Working in the kitchen gave her immense pleasure. The day, a warm late spring day with the feeling of summer creasing its edges, inspired her. The windows stood open letting a sweet breeze blow in from the lake.

The salad finished, she found one of Aunt Tilley's vintage bowls, with bright vegetables painted on the sides. It looked like it was just waiting for a party, she covered it, and put it in the fridge to get cold.

Especially careful about what to wear, she picked a denim skirt with a printed tank and an oversized denim shirt. Warm now, but the evening could turn chilly if the party stayed outside. Going over to the mass assortment of baubles Aunt Tilley acquired over the years, she picked a beaded necklace of turquoise and jade that looked as if it came from a far-away land. Holding it to her chest, she imagined Aunt Tilley on one of her many trips. Once she had stopped by Becca's home.

***

Standing outside, Becca watched the long black limo pull into her circular driveway. When Aunt Tilley called to ask if she could visit the first week of May, Becca was ecstatic. The phone call went something like this:

Becca: Just tell me when to pick you up at the airport.

Aunt Tilley: No need, honey. I will get to your house Sunday afternoon. Do you know the closest hotel?

Becca: Nonsense. You will stay here. I have plenty of room.

Aunt Tilley: Are you sure? I don't want to impose.

Becca: Seriously, I have more than enough room. Just come. I can't wait to see you.

Aunt Tilley: Me too. I'll call later. Love you, honey.

Becca: Back at you, Aunt Tilley.

Hearing the phone go dead, Becca's excitement crashed over her.

Jon came into the room. "Who was on the phone?" He went to the bookcase, ran his finger over the spines until he stopped, pulled one out.

Becca replaced the handset. "Aunt Tilley. She's coming for a visit in May."

"That's nice." Jon's disinterested tone raked on her. His attention stayed on the open book in his hand.

Knowing no reason to discuss it with him, she left the room.

The days seemed to take forever to reach May.

Now the day is here, the limo stopped in front of her. Not waiting for the driver to walk around to open the back door, she jerked it open and squealed.

"Aunt Tilley!" Half dragging her Aunt out of the car, Becca hugged her, holding on like she never wanted to let go.

The driver cleared his throat. The two women parted, looked at him.

"Where would like me to take the bags, ma'am?"

Holding each other by the waist, Becca answered him. "Follow me." Together they walked into the house.

Aunt Tilley stopped when they entered the foyer. "Wow! This is a large house."

"See, I told you I had room." Becca guided Aunt Tilley down the hall to the guest bedroom. The driver followed behind with the luggage.

Entering a sizable room of teal and several shades of brown, Becca released Aunt Tilley to instruct the driver where to put the bags.

He walked over to Aunt Tilley. "I will return next Sunday the same time?"

Aunt Tilley nodded. "Yes, thank you."

Nodding, he exited the room. Becca watched Aunt Tilley's face as she surveyed the room. "Becca this is grand. You have an extremely lovely home."

For the first time, Becca felt pleased with the compliment. Many people said the words, but they evaluated her worth. A stamp of approval from someone who mattered felt good.

"Thanks Aunt Tilley. I'm glad you like it."

"What's not to like?" Aunt Tilley peered into Becca's face, Becca could feel tears coming. Blinking them back she hoped her aunt hadn't seen them.

"Here..." Becca walked to the end of the room. "...is the bathroom and a sitting area and..." Her voice failed.

"You know what I could use?" Aunt Tilley's voice saved her. "A cold beer. Got one?"

Becca laughed. "I do. Come on. We can get you settled later, let's have a cold one and

some girl talk by the pool."

"A pool?" Aunt Tilley chuckled as she took Becca's arm.

Becca shrugged. "It's the closest I could get to a lake."

They both laughed as they headed down the hallway to the kitchen.

The week flew by. Becca and Aunt Tilley caught up on each other's lives. Sort of. Becca didn't tell Aunt Tilley how dull and uninteresting her life had become. Yeah, she knew it. She just convinced herself she wanted it that way.

But Aunt Tilley didn't tell me how famous she was either.

And Becca never asked about Clay. Aunt Tilley casually mentioned he got married. A stab of pain caught Becca's breath, but she pushed it aside. She remembered Aunt Tilley kept looking at her, waiting for some kind of response. Becca couldn't say anything. So she got up, made another drink for the both of them. Someone interrupted them, the subject never came up again.

Becca's father, Aunt Tilley's brother, and mother came to visit for a few days. With her house full, Becca worked on planning activities, meals, whatever anyone else wanted. Jon, the pompous host, and her kids agreed to show up once in a while. Teenagers, their social life was always full.

Sunday came too soon for Becca. Shutting the limo door, she stepped back as it pulled away. Suddenly, she stood alone. She honestly wanted to have a good cry, but Jon already made plans for the evening. She had just enough time to shower to get ready.

***

At a quarter to five, she walked across to Robby and Susie's house. Robby insisted she ride with them. His reasoning was she should not have to show up alone. Stuttering and spitting the words out, Becca got the feeling it was Susie's idea.

Actually, she was grateful for the offer. She dreaded walking in alone, standing there like a lost puppy. Not something she looked forward to.

Knocking on the back door, Susie greeted her.

"Come in. Rob's just about ready." Seeing the bowl in Becca's hand she reached for it. "Here let me put it in the cooler."

Becca followed Susie into the house.

"What did you bring?" Susie spoke over her shoulder.

"I found Aunt Tilley's recipe for her famous potato salad…"

Susie stopped suddenly. "No way. Do you know what a hit her salad was?"

Becca smiled.

Do now.

"You were close to Aunt Tilley?" Becca watched Susie's face.

A look of longing crossed Susie's eyes. "My salvation when I first came here. Strictly, a city girl. I loved it here, but there were some adjustments to living here full time. She took me under her wing, helped me." Looking over at Becca, "She was a remarkable woman. I loved her

dearly and miss her so."

Becca nodded. "She was all that."

I like Susie. I am going to put in the effort to be a good friend.

"Okay lovely ladies, let's hit the road." Robby's booming voice echoed as he walked into the kitchen. "Wow, Becca. You look fabulous! Different?"

Becca could feel her face blush. Glancing over at Susie, gave her a questioning look.

94

Susie nodded her approval. "Your new look wears well on you. It's got some spunk, some fun in it."

The words made her feel good. Maybe being here allowed her come out of the damnable shell she built.

Sparky and Jilley lived on the north side of the lake. The road curved through a majestic forest of tall old trees with striking views of the lake. Becca enjoyed seeing the lake area alive with foliage, the boats at the beginning of the season. A few tourists came to Lester Lake during the summer, for there were cabins to rent. And as always, there were the 'summer people', residents who came from the city during the summer months.

Now this feels like home. A feeling I haven't felt in a long time.

Robby and Susie chatted during the trip, pointing out new structures, businesses, old stomping grounds now taken over by a new generation. Twenty minutes of memories from a different time.

As they pulled into the long driveway, Becca recognized the house. The house had belonged to Jilley's parents. Memories of the sleep-overs, sun bathing on the deck came back. Always the three of them-Jilley, Gwen and Becca.

***

Giggling as girls do, the three stumbled up the stairs to Jilley's bedroom. Just back from the bonfire party, they were full of stories, their young bodies hot with the desires of the boys in their hearts.

"Shhhh." Jilley put her finger to her lips, tossing her blonde hair that was now tangled like a wild lion's mane. Moving down the hall on long tanned legs, she led the other two to her bedroom.

All three, a little tipsy from the heat of the day, the cool of the night and the cold beers. Half-falling into the room, Jilley shut the door behind them. Collapsing on the bed, they laughed for no special reason.

"Hey, Gwen." Jilley's voice low, spiked with mischief. "Where did you and Martin sneak off to?"

Gwen took fake offense. "We did not sneak off." She rose up on her elbows, trying, with a straight face to answer the question. "We are adults. We can go and do what we want."

"So where did you go?" Jilley pursued her question.

"We went to talk about things." Gwen looked away, rolled over on her back. "Then we made love. Damn that man is good!"

All three broke out in a long spell of laughter.

Gwen popped back up. "And you and Sparky?" She narrowed her eyes at Jilley.

Jilley tried to hide the grin, but finally, she gave up trying. Her whole face broke into a big smile. "We're getting there. Right now, I just get him hot, then leave him. He is going to want me so bad when it happens..." She looked between the two girls, paused for effect. "...and it will happen. It will be great sex."

96

Both Jilley and Gwen rolled over on their stomach, stared at Becca.

"What? I didn't go anywhere with anyone." Her sentence ended with a sigh.

"But you wanted to." Jilley winked at Gwen.

"Clay boy." Gwen added an accent on the 'boy'.

"Yeah, well I'm not good at waiting in line." Becca huffed.

"So..." Jilley started. "Go to the head of the line. He is undeniably panting after you."

Becca sat up and crossed her legs. "You think?"

Together in a chorus the other two chimed. "Yes!"

Looking between them, Becca shook her head. "I don't know. I don't need anything going on right now. I have school, besides Clay is rooted here. I'm looking forward to being in the city for a while after graduation. On my own, doing my thing before I settled down."

"So who is talking about settling down? Have a summer love affair." Gwen cocked her head.

Jilley piped in. "Yeah, go for it, girl." Looking sideways at Becca, she smiled a sly pout.

Becca narrowed her eyes and thought.

Why not?

She fell back on the bed.

So help me, I want to make love with that beautiful man.

"Well? " Gwen leaned over her.

"Maybe." Becca rolled her eyes.

Jilley laughed, slapped her leg. "Maybe hell. This girl is going to bring the mighty Clay Lester down."

The thought of it warmed Becca's core.

Why the hell not. It is summer. A good time to have a little fling.

***

A trim woman ran down the front steps of the large Victorian house, her short blonde curls bobbing up and down. Becca jerked opened the car door, jumped out.

"Becca!"

"Jilley!"

Meeting half-way in between, they embraced as long-lost friends do. Hugging and jumping, their squeals of laughter echoed. Robby and Susie came together around the back of the car. Sparky followed his wife down the stairs, nodding at the couple.

"They haven't seen each other for a while." Sparky chuckled as he shook hands with

Robby, kissed Susie on the cheek. The three stood side by side watching the two women.

Finally, Becca pulled back from Jilley. Again, she looked into the periwinkle eyes of a person from the past. She placed her hands on the blushing cheeks, pushing the wisps of hair back from the familiar, welcoming face. "You are a welcome sight. I have missed you." Tears flowed down her cheeks, but she ignored them as she took a long look at her dear friend.

Jilley's eyes, also wet, her voice full of emotion. "Oh, Becca. I didn't think I would ever see you again. You were gone so long..."

"I know. I am so sorry."

Sparky cleared his throat. "Excuse me, you two. We have guests?"

Jilley laughed, let go of Becca, stepped over to hug Susie. "I'm sorry. You know I am always glad to see you...and Robby, you know I love ya'."

Sparky looked down at the cooler Robby carried in his hand. "Whatcha got there, buddy?"

Robby lifted the small cooler up. "Beer, some kind of little sandwiches and..." He winked at Becca. "...Tilley's famous potato salad."

Jilley turned back to Becca. "Wow that will be a treat."

Becca moved up to the group. Linking arms with Jilley and Susie, the three walked up the steps to the house. "I feel like I am home after a very long absence."

Leaning her head against Becca's, Jilley sighed. "You are home darlin'."

Familiar feelings, even smells, greeted Becca as she walked through the door of Jilley's house. Immediately she knew where the rooms were as they headed for the kitchen at the back of the house.

The large kitchen, showing signs of being remodeled, looked like something out of Better Homes and Gardens magazine. The whole north end of doors and glass gave a panoramic view of the lake. The three women broke apart, Jilley and Susie went to the counter, began sitting up the food. Becca, smitten as if in a trance, walked over to the doors, placing her hand on the glass. Closing her eyes, she again saw that summer.

***

The warm sand against Becca's back became as comfortable as her mattress. Wiggling her butt, she found the just-right position. Now to think back on the ride here with Robby and Clay.

The heat of Clay's body radiated to hers as they bounced over the dirt roads to the sacred place known as Copper Beach. Every once in a while she would glance sideways to get a glimpse of his face. His jaw muscles tight, his mouth slightly parted. Then she would look down at her hands in her lap nervously moving. The last time she looked at him, he winked.

So he knows I am watching him.

Copper Beach rose on the horizon. She was glad they were finally there. She needed room to breathe. About to suffocate from the manly smell of him, she slid over closer to Robby.

As the truck came to a quick stop, she nudged Robby to get out. He gave her a surprised look, opened the door, slipped down.

Jumping out of the truck, she quickly half ran, half walked to the sand where Jilley sat. Keeping her eyes forward, she spread out her beach towel to lay down. Her chest heaved up and down as she took small breaths. Finally, feeling her heart slow down, she relaxed.

"Hey girl." The shadow falling over her came with the welcome voice of Gwen. Snapping her large towel as it floated to the sand, she sat down, fluffed her long mane of auburn hair back. Her head bobbed as she checked out the visitors to the spot. "How'd you get here?"

"Clay brought us." Becca watched as Gwen's head snapped back.

Narrowing her eyes, Jilley looked over at Becca. "Clay, the man? Who is us?"

"Robby and I. Clay stopped. Offered us a ride." Becca bit her lower lip.

Gwen lifted her brows lightly at Becca's answer. "How was the ride?"

Becca grinned. "Bumpy, too long. Not long enough. What do you want me to say?"

Gwen crossed her legs. "Well." Gwen leaned back. "Do we need to take a plunge in the lake to cool off?"

Becca looked at the sparkling water beckoning her. "Probably. Wouldn't hurt.

Shouting, the two girls ran to the water, thigh deep they dove under.

***

Jilley put her arms on Becca's shoulder. "Good memories, huh?"

Becca nodded. "Some of my best." She leaned back against Jilley. Feeling their friendship crossing all time, she savored it.

Can I go back and recapture the feelings of the past?

"Make way for the cooks." Sparky's voice broke the spell. Jilley and Becca stepped aside letting Sparky, followed by Robby, pass through the doors. Everyone carried smiles and food. Susie followed the men. Jilley and Becca fell in line.

Soon other couples and stray people gathered on the back deck. The sun soon would set on the west side of the lake. Jilley and Susie trotted her around making introductions. Most of the crowd were strangers to Becca. But they knew Tilley and Tilley's potato salad.

So this is my Aunt's social circle.

Finally, Sparky came over to Becca with a cold beer, guiding her to a lounge chair overlooking the lake. "Sit for a while."

"Thanks, Spark." She leaned back against the soft cushion. Taking her first drink of the cold liquid, she realized just how dry her throat felt. Sparky winked at her, walked back to the large grill which held the many kinds of meats. He and some of the other men stood cooking.

Turning her head to watch as the sun left its trail of dusk light on the lake, she smiled as again that summer popped up in her mind.

***

By two o'clock, the sun started its descent to the west side of the lake. Becca watched

Clay all day as the many girls flirted with him. He stayed to himself mostly. Sometimes she would catch him watching her.

Is he really watching me?

Trying to act coy, she would glance around in the direction of his stare. Most of the time she noticed the only one in his line of view turned out to be her.

"You really should go over there and talk to him. Turn on the Becca charm." Gwen's voice floated over her.

Becca saw Jilley walking toward them.

Becca looked down at the sand, shook her head. "Give me time." Turning her head slightly, she licked her lips. Clay sat, busy talking to Martin and Sparky, she smiled. "I'll let him simmer for a while."

Jilley plopped down on her towel, inclined back. "Let him sweat." She looked over at the other two. "They are so much hotter when they sweat."

The three put their heads together, giggled. Becca straightened up, glanced over at Clay. All three of the boys were looking their way.

Becca put her arms on the other's shoulder, they huddled together. "I think we have been made, girls."

***

Lost in her thoughts it took her a minute to recognize the voice coming across the deck.

Clay

Looking up she watched as he walked in, pretty much taking over the party. Greetings met him at every turn. Slaps on the back, kisses on cheeks, he mesmerized everyone.

And he looked good.

Half-hidden behind a potted plant, Becca let her eyes linger over him. His hair short, styled with one wisp over one eyebrow. His face, a frame for the electric blue eyes she knew lay behind the sunglasses. A five o'clock shadow gave his face character. The navy blue, button down, collared shirt accented his golden tan skin. A silver belt buckle stood in line of his manhood. The tight-fitting jeans gave way to the bulge in the front. Down her eyes traveled over slim, tight thighs to a pair of cowboy boots.

Becca let out a sigh, thought of their first kiss.

***

When the group started pairing up, Becca found herself between Robby and Clay. The usual group for the summer

104

consisted of Gwen and Martin, Jilley and Sparky, Becca, Robby and Clay.

Becca and Robby had played together since they were toddlers. Becca's early years saw her and her dad at Aunt Tilley's. Becca's mom tried to come a couple of times, but the reality remained, she never actually liked the lake or even Aunt Tilley. Soon Becca came on her own during her pre-teen and teenage years. Usually her dad dropped her off, then hurried back to circle the summer social circuit his wife insisted they join. In fact, the first time she drove by

herself became her day of declaring her freedom.

The fire this evening shot sparks into the sky as the dry grass gathered took hold. Becca was sandwiched in between Clay and Robby, and she leaned more toward Clay. Her movements did not go unnoticed. Clay eyed her, casually touched her in subtle ways. Every touch stirred the desire in her. After a few beers, she leaned on him, rubbing his arms, making undercurrent remarks.

When they all decided they needed to break this up, Clay took her hand, pulled her up into his body. Gathering their stuff, he held her hand as he led her to the truck. She turned a couple of times to see if Robby walked behind them.

Robby seemed busy talking to an unknown girl, but then looked up, came running. Going to the passenger side of the truck, he pulled his body into the cab.

Clay walked Becca to the driver's side, opened the door. Taking her beach gear from her, he tossed it in the back of the truck. Becca grabbed hold of the door, lifted herself up. As she expected and hoped, Clay put his hands on her waist, gave her a push. Once seated, she let her leg press against his. Putting the truck in reverse, he winked at her. His eyes stayed on her as he readjusted the steering wheel. Smiling, he turned his attention to driving.

The ride seemed too short. Pulling into Aunt Tilley's driveway, he cut the motor, jumped down from the truck, held out his hand to Becca. As she slipped out of the seat, she heard Robby slam his door.

"Later guys. Thanks Clay."

Her body slid down Clay's as her feet finally found the ground. He held her waist, drew her into him.

"Anytime buddy." His words were spoken close to her lips. Slowly, lazily, never breaking eye contact, he lowered his mouth. The moist heat of his mouth against hers made desire claw at her, hot and sharp. Planting a deep kiss on her mouth, his low growl of delight vibrated her. Returning his kiss, she went up on her tip-toes, ran her hands up his arms, gripping the tight muscles of his upper arms. The kiss continued as he gently, with the touch of fire, let it linger.

When he pulled back, his eyes shot sparkles of pleasure she longed to feel. He stepped back, licked his lower lip.

His words washed over her gently, like a light breeze. "Becca."

Straightening up, she gave him a slight smile, tilted her head. "Clay."

He raised his chin, a smile creased his eyes. "Can I see you tomorrow?"

She slipped out of his reach. "Maybe. What are you doing tomorrow?"

He reached for her. "Working, then I'll be done by noon."

Skirting out of his reach. "I'm going to the lake. Give me a ride?"

His look took on a reserved expression. "Sure."

Becca walked around him, grabbed her bag from the truck bed. Swinging it over her shoulder, she sauntered to the house. Tossing her words over her back. "See you then."

Once inside the door, she heard the tires throw gravel as he pulled out of the driveway

onto the street.

***

Coming back to the present, Becca just noticed Clay watching her.

Shit!

Getting out of the chair, she looked for an escape.

None.

Going to the wooden rail, she turned her back on him, leaned on the sturdy life line.

Maybe he will get the hint.

"Becca." The voice still sent chills down her back.

She turned around. "Clay. Good to see you."

He blocked her view of the other people, so she rested her elbows on the rail, looking into the dancing blue eyes that rocked her world twenty years ago.

Placing his hand on the rail next to her, the slight connection of skin made her breath come in short puffs. Exhaling slowly, she tried hard to relax.

Clay's look bore into her eyes. "So how are those windows?"

Nodding, lost in his eyes. "Windows are good."

"And your life?"

There's that damnable smile.

Standing up, she felt her defenses rise. "My life is fine. Thank you. Yours..."

Before she finished her sentence, a loud, shrill female voice interrupted.

"Clay!"

Becca looked at his face, and it carried an expression of dread. Peeking around his shoulder, she saw a tall, overdressed, underweight woman descending on them. Her long, thick, jet-black hair styled perfectly, accented her china silk skin. Dark piercing eyes set in a contoured face. Clay moved around to stand next to Becca. The woman charged up still talking in the high-pitched voice.

"And who is this?" The woman's glare gave Becca the once over. Extending her hand the woman announced. "Hi, I'm Veronica. Clay's wife."

Becca hesitantly put out her hand as she narrowed her brows to look at Clay. Veronica grabbed her hand.

"Ex-wife." Clay put a heavy accent on 'ex'. "Becca, this is Veronica. Veronica, Becca."

Veronica's grip tightened. "Becca. *The* Becca? The shadow of days past that destroyed my marriage?" Her face dissolved into a wicked smirk. "And here I always thought you were a figment of his imagination."

"Veronica." Jilley came up behind, put her arms on Veronica's shoulder. "I see you are being your normal bitchy self."

Becca jerked her hand from the woman's grip.

The distasteful look on Veronica's face spoke mountains. "Jilley. I see you have retrieved the ghost of the past to haunt me."

Jilley patted Veronica's shoulder. "Roni. It's not always about you." She turned the obnoxious woman around to face away. "Go. Mingle. Make yourself a nuisance to someone else."

With a stomp of her foot, Veronica gave Becca and Clay one last disdainful look, then left.

Jilley turned to Becca. "So…"

Becca looked at Clay. "What is she talking about?"

Clay darted his eyes from one woman to the other. "It's a long story."

"Oh for Pete's sake, Clay. Grow up. Deal with how you feel." Jilley grabbed Becca's hand. "Come on. I'll take you home."

Susie joined them, the three marched out of the backyard to Jilley's car.

All three seated, Jilley turned the car toward the town. Susie, in the back seat, leaned up. "This isn't the way to our houses?"

"No." Jilley laughed. "We are going to Brick's Bar to have a little girl time. And lots of drinks."

"But..." Susie sweet-tempered voice objected to the plan. "...it's your party..."

"...And I can leave when I want to." Jilley winked at Becca.

CHAPTER SIX

The three women strutted into the small bar, led by Jilley, who made a bee line for the round table in the corner. Susie and Becca followed. Becca looked around the mostly empty bar. Some guys playing pool rose up from the table, watching with startled surprise the invasion of their turf. A couple at the bar swirled around on the stools, followed with their eyes the group marching in as if they belonged.

A young man greeted them at the table. "What's your pleasure, ladies?"

The sound of a wooden chair on a tile floor, Jilley plopped down, slapping the table with both hands. "Yes, David. A pitcher of beer, three glasses..." She waved her hands over the table. "...and three shots of tequila, plenty of limes and a salt shaker." Winking at him.

David nodded, gave all of them a quick smile.

Becca and Susie joined Jilley at the table. Becca looked back at the bar, frowned, spoke over her shoulder. "Isn't that one of...?"

Susie finished her sentence. "...Clay's boys."

Becca jerked around. Slightly uncomfortable, she didn't quite understand why.

I'm an adult. I can drink myself under the table. It's not as if he is my son!

Instead, she said. "Heavy drinking? Okay. Why not?"

David placed a tray on the edge of the table. First, he put the pitcher of ice cold beer in the middle, handing each woman an empty glass. Last he set three shot glasses of a clear liquid in front of each woman. A big bowl of cut limes and three salt shakers by each shot glass. He stood back but didn't leave.

Susie and Becca followed Jilley's lead. Licking the side of their hands, they sprinkled salt on the area, licked the salt, took the shot glasses, downed the smooth tequila, then grabbed a lime from the bowl and sucked the bitter fruit.

Throwing the rinds back in the bowl, Jilley looked at David. "Again."

"Yes, ma'am." He showed that damnable Clay smile, went back to the bar.

Jilley poured three glasses of beer. "So, ladies." Lifting up her glass, the other two clinked with her. "To the ladies of Lester Lake."

"Hear, hear." Susie and Becca said in unison.

The cold beer stopped the burning of the shot. Becca sat her glass down, looked at the two sharing her table. Never had she felt so comfortable in the company of other women. First, there was no Jon to interrupt her if he thought she said or did the *wrong thing*. And second, the company she chose to sit with did not come here to judge her.

Three more shots were placed in front of them. Becca smiled as she picked up her glass first. "To the divas of Lester Lake."

Jilley and Susie clinked glasses with Becca. Jilley threw back her head, laughing. "I like that."

Sitting the glasses down, in unison they licked their hands, sprinkled the salt, downed the shots, bit into the limes.

"Damn!" Becca shook her head. David stood guard. "Again?"

Raising one brow, he chuckled. "Okay." Went back to the bar.

"So…" Becca felt her resistance fall away. "…who is that woman?"

Jilley slipped her beer. "Clay's ex, Veronica."

Becca breathed a sigh of relief. "So it is his ex?"

"Oh, hell yeah. They've been divorced for what…?" Looking over at Susie. "…five years?"

Susie shrugged. "At least."

Becca nodded toward the bar. "Isn't she his mother?"

"If you want to call her that. Clay raised those boys. She hated it here in this small town."

Becca frowned. "So where did her meet her?"

Jilley chuckled. "A convention in the city. They only dated for a month or so, then they got married."

Susie cut in. "That's when the fangs came out. The wedding, the most god awful production this county has ever seen."

Becca sucked in her breath. "What?" Her heart felt a strong compassion for him.

Jilley took hold of Becca's hand. "Clay was in a bad way after you left. What with the accident and all, he sort of went off the deep end. Didn't resurface until Veronica became pregnant with Andrew."

Letting all of Jilley and Susie's words sink in, she looked from one to the other. David placed three more shots on the table. Without speaking, the three raised their glasses, clinked them.

Looking over the table at Jilley, the words came out before Becca realized. "To Gwen." Every day for twenty years she thought of her friend, but *never* did she say her name out loud.

The shock in Jilley's eyes told Becca she hit a nerve. "To Gwen." Her voice low, controlled.

Susie looked at each of them. Holding her glass up, she echoed their toast. "To Gwen."

Downing the drinks, they slammed the glasses upside down on the table together. David, who stood next to Becca, remained

114

silent. He picked up the nine shots glasses, retreated without a word.

Biting her lower lip, Becca raised her eyes to Jilley. The pain she buried for all these years cut into her heart. Tears burst from her eyes as if they were just waiting for the chance to flow.

Jilley stood up so quickly she knocked the chair over, causing everyone in the bar to turn to look at them. Becca jumped to her feet. Each moving toward the other, they met half way, embracing. Becca didn't know if the alcohol, the scene at the party or her own pent up

heartache forced her to release her feelings, but there they were. Clinging to Jilley, she kept repeating. "I am sorry. I am so sorry I left."

Jilley's comforting words sounded in her ear. "It's okay. I understand."

Becca drew back. "Do you really?"

Jilley chuckled. "No. Why did you leave?"

Shaking her head, Becca had nothing for her. "I don't know. I honestly don't know. I was scared, hurt." Looking into Jilley's eyes. "I was with her when she let go."

Shock reflected in Jilley's eyes. "Let go?"

Becca nodded, tried to speak between sobs. "Yes. I just told her Martin didn't make it. She saw him and she...left me."

Jilley drew Becca back into her arms. "Oh honey. I didn't know that."

Becca blubbered on. "It hurt so badly. I just ran...married the first uninteresting man I met."

Laughing, Jilley broke the spell. "Jon?"

The flood of tears started again, but this time Becca laughed. "Yes, Jon. Dull, always predictable, live-by-my-rules, Jon."

Jilley let a smirk play about her mouth. "Oh, sounds marvelous! Not."

"Oh, it isn't. The stories I could tell." Becca shook her head.

Picking up her chair, Jilley waved at the other customers. "It's okay. Just a girlfriend thing."

Taking her chair back, Becca chuckled as she sat down.

Persistent as always, Jilley raised her hand to David, leaned over the table, spoke low. "So tell me about this man, Jon."

David set three more shot glasses in front of the women. This time he left.

Susie remained quiet through the whole crying thing, but now Becca raised her glass to her. "To Susie. Who walked into a group of misfits, married the best one of the bunch and is now a good friend."

Susie blushed as Jilley shouted. "Hear, hear!"

Clink. The glasses came together, lick, salt, drink, lime.

The three laughed as they slammed the glasses on the table.

"So tell us about Jon." Jilley leaned back, smiled. Susie scooted around to face Becca and nodded.

***

The cocktail gathering for the new members of the firm did not impress Becca. Wearing a stunning black cocktail dress, her slim body looked almost too thin. Six months ago she fled Aunt Tilley's. The time passed without any major events, which suited her just fine.

Several handsome young men strolled through the crowd in tailored tuxes, a drink in hand, flashing pure white smiles for the benefit of the single women. Becca felt bored. Taking a champagne glass from a passing tray, she nursed it. She found, during the last few months,

alcohol did not dull the pain as promised. In fact, it brought feelings to the surface she wanted kept down. So her drinking stayed limited to social only because, if she didn't there were always questions.

"Do you come to these often?" A male voice spoke at her side. Turning to see who talked, she found a nice-looking man. His dress and manners spoke of good breeding.

Giving him a slight smile, she put out her hand. "More than I want. Becca."

"Jon. Jon Hamilton. One of the many new VPs." His hand shake firm, impersonal. "Do you work here?"

"Not quite. I provide the artwork for their buildings."

Jon glanced at the towering watercolor Becca knew hung behind her. "Nice job. I like that one."

Everyone likes that one. It's an extremely expensive piece.

But instead. "Good eye. One of the new up-and-coming artists."

Interrupted by a group of fellow co-workers, Jon's co-workers, Becca worked alone. The evening ended with a promise to call from Jon.

***

Answering her cell phone two days later, she heard his voice. "Dinner? Tonight?"

Tired of eating alone. "Sure, I'll meet you."

She heard the surprise in his voice. Not knowing if it sounded because of her acceptance or her statement that she would meet him, she shrugged it off.

Arriving on time, she found Jon already there. He greeted her at the door, nodded to the maître d'. They were shown to a table. No small talk, right to Jon ordering dinner for both. For some reason, Becca didn't mind. The fewer decisions the better as far as she was concerned.

She felt safe with this guy since there no physical attraction to distract her. Dinner stayed quiet and uneventful. Conversation consisted of him gloating over his outstanding accomplishments. Still she didn't mind, it kept him off the subject of her.

118

After a month, she accepted she could live with Jon, share an uneventful life. So, two months later when he went down on his knees to offer her a ring with a trouble-free life of bland, she said yes.

Her mother, thrilled at the idea, took over the plans. All Becca needed to do was show up in white. Walking down the aisle, she knew she would never love the man waiting for her. That spoke of a good future for her. Now she would never need to feel.

Only problem, the day her daughter burst into the world, a feeling of an immense love rose in her soul. Try as she may, to the contrary, she loved this human being more than anything in the world. She never told anyone except Haley, the name she picked all on her own.

Two years later they had a son, Jon Jr. Quietly in her heart, she loved him as much as Haley. Always careful not to show anyone else how strong her love for them grew she played the dutiful mother role. Except when she and the children were alone she laughed and played with them. The children soon realized there were two sides to their mother. The fun-loving

companion and a woman who acted as everyone else expected.

***

Three hours later, the three women had drank more than enough. Giggling at Becca's miserable life Jilley choked on her laughter. "Oh, I don't believe you left hunka-hunka Clay to marry a dud like Jon."

Becca laughed loud and long. Once she faced the truth, the humor hit her in the face. "Oh, hell yeah." She swigged a generous gulp of beer, wiped her mouth with the back of her hand.

Quiet Susie spoke with an air of authority. "You, Becca were avoiding...life."

"No shit, Sherlock." Becca chuckled.

Susie's serious face swam before Becca. "So you knew you were in the arms of the wrong man."

Raising her glass, Becca announced. "Knew it. Didn't want to change it."

Jilley piped in. "So what brought you here now, dear friend?"

"Jon decided he didn't want to be married anymore." Her sarcastic laugh echoed in the now empty, except for David, bar. "Go figure." She could hear her words slur, didn't really care.

"So what is keeping you from jumping Clay's bones?" Straight to the point Jilley.

Becca leaned back. The thought at this time made her tingle. "I don't think he wants to be jumped...well, not by me."

Jilley tried to stand up. Swaying, she grabbed the table's edge. "We need to go see Clay." Turning to Becca, squinting her eyes she tried to focus on Becca. "Come on."

120

Susie stood up, her dark green eyes paling as they rolled. "Let's go sistas." Raising one arm, she fell down.

Becca and Jilley reached her together, took an arm and pulled. But instead of picking Susie up, they slipped, fell down also. Clawing their way back up to stand at the table, all three were laughing so hard, they decided to loop arms to support each other, so they could walk out of the bar. Becca saw David hang up his cell phone, coming over to help. Jilley draped her arm over the boy.

"David, we need to talk to your father."

Becca slapped her lightly. "No, we don't. I made my choice, I have to live with it. Right Susie?"

Susie's head hung listless her chin on the chest.

"Susie are you okay?" Becca looked at her new friend with fogged over eyes.

No answer.

At the door, as Becca pushed on it, she tightened her grip on Susie. The brisk night air cleared a small part of Becca's fog. Adjusting her eyes, she stopped, stared at the two policemen leaning on their squad car, arms folded across their chests.

Becca's sudden stop jerked Jilley back. Jilley gave her a frown, but Becca nodded her

head toward the officers.

Jilley tried to focus. "Ben Cooper. Is that you?"

One of the men answered her. "Yes, Jilley. It's me."

"Good night to you officer. We ladies are going home." Jilley turned toward her car.

Ben stepped in front of her. "Not a good idea, Jilley."

Jilley stopped, looked at him. "Excuse me." Drawing her head back.

Ben took her arm away from David, nodding. David let go of Jilley, grabbed Susie.

The other officer came up to Becca. Becca handed him Susie, stepped back as he maneuvered her to the squad car. Ben got Jilley to the other side, pushed her in.

"I'm calling your husbands." Ben leaned down, spoke to the two in the car.

Becca decided she would walk home. Pointing her body toward what she hoped was north, she carefully started to stroll off.

A hand on her arm stopped her. "Sorry, Becca. You're coming too." Officer Cooper spoke in his police voice.

"But I don't have a husband. Well, not one that will come get me. He is far, far away." The movement of her head set the ground to spinning. She fell against the officer.

Ben chuckled. "I know who to call for you, Becca." He nodded to David.

She took a deep look at him. "Do I know you?"

"Not really." He let her rest on his arm as he took her to the car, pushed down her head for her to get in. The slamming of the door made all three of them jump. As the car pulled away, David stepped back, letting them pass. Becca waved at him, smiled.

"They aren't really arresting us, are they?" Becca talked across Susie to Jilley.

"They wouldn't dare." Jilley said in a smug, confident way.

However, the word 'JAIL' stood out on the building they pulled up in front of. The two officers stepped out of the car, opened the back doors.

One reached in to help Jilley, she smacked his hand. "You are fucking kidding me, Ben." She jumped out, fire shooting from her eyes.

Becca allowed the officer who offered her his hand to assist her. Then the two of them propped up Susie as she half fell out.

I can't believe I am going to jail. Son of a bitch. I haven't had this much excitement for twenty years.

A small jail, remarkable clean and tidy. Two cells stood on the far end of the room. Ben led a fussing and fretting Jilley to the bunk in the first cell.

His voice barked the order. "Sit. Jilley."

He walked out, shut the door. Motioning to the other officer, he ushered Becca and Susie to the other cell. Becca took Susie, laid her on one of the bunks. The door slammed behind them.

Looking around she saw Jilley clutching the bars screaming. "Ben Cooper, are you fucking kidding me?"

Becca flopped down, chuckling.

Yes, this is funny.

Leaning to her right, she felt the mattress on the cot meet her face.

Just a small nap.

The rattling of the bars, the loud voice of Jilley filtered through Becca's cloudy mind.

"Carter, get me the fuck out of here."

Becca rolled over watched as Sparky walked in to try to calm his wife. "Okay, Jilley." Becca could see his attempt not to laugh.

Jilley's anger flared. "Don't you laugh at me."

The door behind Becca now rattled.

Good. Robby is here to get us.

"Well, well, well." Not Robby's voice.

Becca rolled over to see Clay standing over her. Sitting up too quickly, she grabbed her head as the room went spinning out of control.

"What the hell are you doing here?" Looking up into the blue eyes and the damnable smile.

"I came to help Sparky and Robby get the drunk ladies home." He snickered.

124

Becca, trying to get up, finally took his outstretched hand so she could stand. His tight grip pulled her to her feet. Still quite wobbly, he steadied her with his body.

Pushing a mass of her hair out of her eyes, she glared at him. "So they called you for backup?"

"No. My son called. Said a friend of mine was in trouble."

David! Sweet kid. Good bartender. Snitch.

"I can manage on my own from here on, thank you." She pushed him away, started to walk toward the open cell door. As he released her, she found walking straight a difficult task. Nevertheless, she grabbed hold of the bars, proceed out the door.

Robby's arm around Susie, she looked back. "Coming Becca?"

"Right behind ya'." Becca felt Clay next to her, but she ignored him, strolled as best she could into the now cold night air. The sky carried tints of pink and gold.

Dawn?

At the car, Robby put Susie in the passenger seat, ran around and opened the back door for Becca. Slipping, more like falling, she touched the warm seat with her hip. Curling up in a ball, she felt the door close.

Becca spoke out loudly, hurting her eyes. "Susie? Are you okay?"

Susie's voice muffled her answer. "I don't know. You?"

Becca lowered her voice. "The jury's still out on that one."

Together they snickered. Robby got in the car, it started moving.

Home. Just get me the fuck home.

No one talked all the way home. Becca swore she could see Robby's body shake with

laughter. The crunch of gravel told Becca they turned into the driveway.

"Susie, stay put. I'm going to get Becca in her house, then I'll help you. Okay?"

Even though Susie didn't answer, her head nodding on the seat made a faint sound. Becca forced herself to move as Robby opened the door.

"I'm good, Robby." Her foot stepped hard on the ground. Followed by the other foot. Robby took her arm, waited while she steadied herself.

Together, they trod lightly over the uneven ground. At the door, Robby guided her in, down the hall, to her bedroom. When she collapsed on the soft quilt, she knew she was finally home. With her head buried in a pillow she murmured. "Thank you, Robby.

"You're welcome, Bec. See you later."

The last sound she heard was the sound of his footsteps echoing down the hall.

***

Clay stood in the parking lot of the jail watching Robby's car leave. A chuckle escaped as he thought of Becca drunk on her ass. Turning toward the lake, the taillights vanished in the early morning fog.

Remembering how hard it had been to get over her, the turning point in his recovery came the night he learned she married another man.

***

Clay could not shake the haze in his head. Since he had been in it for six months, it became more normal to not feel the ground under his feet. Finding a chair, he plopped down in it, poured another beer. A female hand stopped its journey to his mouth.

"Enough Clay." The voice sounded familiar, but he couldn't shake the confusion long enough to figure out who.

Raising his head, he narrowed his eyes to focus. "Tilley?"

"Yes. We need to talk." Tilley's commanding voice told him this would be serious.

Trying to find his feet, he braced his hands on the table, stood. On shaky legs, but he stood.

One of the girls hanging at the bar slithered up to him, rubbing her breasts on his chest. Tilley grabbed the girl's arm, pulled her off of him. "Excuse me. We are talking."

The bimbo girl giggled. "Clay talks? Not much talking when we're together." She started for him again. Again stopped by the strong arm of Tilley.

"Go away, little girl." Tilley hissed.

The young girl blinked, backed up. "Fine old lady. Just save some of him for me later."

Tilley lunged, Clay caught her around the waist. "Whoa, Tilley." Swinging her around he walked her to the door. Tilley raised her voice as she shouted back over their shoulders. "Is that the kind of trash you've been bangin'?"

Clay picked up speed. "Shhh. Tilley."

As soon as the night air hit him, he felt a wave of dizziness. Swaying, he released Tilley to grab his head. Tilley switched places, now she held him by the waist, his arm over her shoulders.

"Tilley. What are you doing here?" He knew his words slurred, but he couldn't stop.

"I came to talk some sense in that thick skull of yours."

Directing him to her car, she opened the door, shoved the large body into the passenger seat. Clay rolled his head on the back of the seat, shut his eyes. Hearing the click of the seat belt, then the slamming of the door.

Oh, gawd. This is fucked up.

He felt the car move as Tilley got in, click of her seat belt, the start of the motor. No idea where they were going or why. Seriously, he didn't care. Nothing mattered since Becca walked out

128

of his life. No explanation, no contact. He had waited. But the more the days passed, the more he knew she was not coming back. He moaned as Tilley hit a bump. Surprised she wasn't lecturing him about his wayward ways.

The car jerked, then stopped. Clay lifted his head, focused on the house in front of them.

Tilley's house. Becca's house.

He shook his head.

You have to stop thinking about her. She's gone.

Tilley jerked open the door, unfastened his seat belt, hauled him out. Supporting him, she dragged him up the steps, into the house. He saw a hallway wall pass by. He recognized it. It led to Becca's bedroom. Sharply, Tilley turned him into a room.

This is the guest room. Did Becca and I ever make love in this room? I can't remember. Don't think so.

Once in the room, Tilley threw him on the bed. He groaned, started to roll over when he felt Tilley tugging on his clothes.

"What are you doing woman?" *He raised up to look at her.*

She kept removing his shirt. "Getting these smelly clothes off of you. When is the last time you took a shower?"

He plopped back. "I don't know. Days."

"Smells more like weeks."

His pants were being jerked down his legs. Too exhausted to fight her, he just laid still while she undressed him. Finally, she moved him under the covers. He snuggled down, letting his beer soaked brain relax.

Sleep. Beautiful, peaceful sleep.

***

Morning came long before Clay felt ready. A faint idea of what happened last night rocked his head, but the particulars were blurred. Tilley, the bar, the bed. He felt the silkiness of the sheets against his bare skin.

My clothes. Where the hell are my clothes?

Sitting up, he saw them folded on the table next to the bed. Holding still until the room stopped spinning, he swung his legs over the edge. The clean clothes carried the smell of fresh linen. Grabbing his boxers, he stood to pull them up. His jeans felt fresh and soft as he stepped

into them. Throwing his t-shirt over his shoulder, he went out the door.

Still barefooted, he padded down the hall to the kitchen. The aroma of fresh coffee directed his attention to the maker on the counter, a cup stood waiting for him. As he poured the hot brown liquid he saw Tilley outside on the deck. Letting the screen door slam shut as he walked out, Tilley turned toward the sound.

"Mornin' Glory." *Tilley's tone had a sneer to it.*

Clay grumbled. "Mornin' Tilley." *He sat down on the steps, looked out at the quiet lake. By the position of the sun, it was mid-morning.*

130

"She's not coming back is she Tilley?"

"No, Clay she's not." He heard her sigh. "She's getting married."

The words hit him like a punch in the stomach. He had no response. The silence between them hung like a fog.

"Clay, you need to get on with your life. She is."

No words. More silence.

"Who is she marrying?"

"Some guy she met at college."

"Did she know him before...before us?"

"No. He's some kind of a businessman. Her mother is thrilled. Her father, my brother thinks she is just making a choice to avoid facing what happened here. I tend to agree."

Clay stood up. "Doesn't matter. It's done." He stepped up on the deck, turned to face her. "Thanks for the coffee, Tilley."

"Do you need a ride to your truck?"

"No, the walk will do me good."

Going into the house, he put the coffee cup on the counter, went back to the bedroom, sat down on the bed to put on his socks and boots.

No, they never made love in this room.

He remembered thinking of it last night. Didn't know why it seemed so important then or even now. Leaving the house he headed for the town.

The longer he walked the more he resigned himself to the fact that he would never have Becca back. A wall of indifference started to form one block at a time.

This ends here.

As his truck came into view, he made up his mind. He needed focus in his life and he knew where to find it. Jumping into the cab, he started the engine, turning toward to the outskirts of town where his father's lumberyard sat.

CHAPTER SEVEN

"Hey Dad." David's voice sounded behind him.

Without turning around. "Yeah Son?"

"So that's Becca?"

Clay looked down at the ground, never realizing everything had been so obvious. "Yeah. That's Becca." Looking at David he put his hand on the boy's shoulder. "Thanks for calling." He walked over to his truck.

His son's words triggered memories he hoped would never surface again. "Do you wish it was her you married?"

His hand on the door handle, Clay decided now he needed to tell the truth. The boys were grown men in their own right. He didn't need to hide anymore. Anyway it didn't seem like he had hidden anything.

"I do. I always thought she would be my wife from the first time I saw her."

"So what changed?"

"Things happen, alters one's decisions."

With his back to his son, Clay heard the chuckle in his voice. "She's funny. I like her."

Clay licked his lower lip.

So do I.

Opening the door, he climbed into the truck. Starting the motor, he remembered why he picked Veronica for his wife. And it had nothing to do with love.

***

The convention for lumberyard owners smelled of saw dust and paint. Clay walked around looking at the displays. His dad and uncles decided, since he stood next in line for ownership, he should get acquainted with the world of home improvement.

The vendors hawked their wares, some better than others. Taking pamphlets and business cards he listened to them, shook their hands, promising to get in touch.

Finally he needed a break. Going to the makeshift bar in the corner of the event center, he ordered a light beer.

"First convention?" Her voice echoed low and gravelly.

Turning to his right, he found an attractive woman standing in a sultry pose next to him. Dressed in a red business suit, it showcased her endless legs, hugged her generous breasts. He had never seen such a stunning woman in one package.

"Does it show that much?" Her look pushed all his buttons in a very big way.

"No." Her body language spoke volumes. *"I would just remember someone like you."*

"You come here a lot?" Clay leaned against the bar, took a sip of beer.

Moving so close to him her chest nearly touched his. "Every year for the last five. Where are you from, cowboy?"

Clay chuckled. "Lester Lake. Heard of it?"

Her tongue stroked her red lips with a sharp, sensual lick. "Oh yeah. You must be one of the younger Lesters."

"The son."

She leaned her body against his arm. "Well son, let me teach you about conventions."

And teach him, she did. The rest of the afternoon they hung out in the hotel bar. When he felt no pain, he took her to his room.

She came to him with no reservations. He welcomed her as he did all women, with a strong, vigorous eagerness.

As he pushed her against the wall, his hands slowly and deliberately removed each layer of clothing as his tongue probed her mouth deeper and deeper. Freeing her ample breasts, he took one at a time in his mouth. She groaned, arched for him. Letting his tongue follow down the valley of her breasts, he tasted her honeyed skin. Her perfume, Chanel No 5, filled his head.

She clawed at him, sending the buttons flying as she ripped open his shirt. He felt her heat as he unfastened her skirt, pushing it to the floor.

Peeling her off the wall, he took her to his bed. Tossing her down, he admired her body as he removed his jeans. One fine looking woman, silky, creamy skin, flawless to a fault. Her dark hair fanned out above her head. Her eyes closed, a look of anticipation on her face. Her legs bent at the knees exposing her womanhood, coiled, ready for him.

Not yet.

As she waited for him, he knew her desire built to the point of unbearable sweet pain. Slowly he moved up her legs with his mouth. Her hands gripped his hair as he brought her to the edge of her climax. A screamer, she begged him to finish. Lowering into her, he pushed a little at a time, watching her face as the ecstasy overtook her body, sending spasms of pleasure.

On his last thrust, she screamed as she grabbed the bedding, a shudder jiggled her breast.

His climax came at the same time, sending waves of satisfaction as he let go. Holding his body rigid as he let the tide of desire finish, feeling the rush he groaned, burying his face in the valley of her breasts.

Rolling off of her, he felt the sweat on his forehead. Still under the influence of the alcohol, he took small breaths as he waited for the room to stop spinning. Sleep overtook him immediately as it always did, to block the image of Becca from his mind.

Awakening with the stroking of her mouth on his body and the hardening of his manhood, he relaxed to let her have her way. Veronica knew how to please a man. Every inch of his body reacted to her touch. She moved over him, sitting on his thighs as she massaged him. Her eyes closed as she lowered herself on him. He placed his hands on her tight ass, riding out the exhilaration of being pleasured to the height of rapture.

Her body was made for sex. Her finish left him breathless and satisfied. Few women stopped his craving for sex. Since Becca, he never considered it making love, just the hunger to

feed an empty, maddening need.

As she lay in his arms, sleeping peacefully, he uncontrollably thought back to Becca.

Gawd, will I ever forget her? I have to. She left and never looked back. She's married. Some other man is laying with her right now. Get over it!

Sleep didn't come until four in the morning. The good smells of coffee and bacon awakened his mind to open his eyes. Veronica, wrapped in the hotel's white robe, dewy fresh from a shower, fretted over the table of food. Laying there watching her, he sighed. *Tired of one night stands, meaningless relationships. Even though he thought he was done with all the nonsense, he realized he still let his needs rule his actions.*

Veronica turned around with a cup in her hand. A smile crossed her face. "Good morning Luv." *Her voice carried a slight east coast accent.* "How do you like your coffee?"

Clay pushed his body up to sit with his back against the pillows. "Black."

Walking toward him, her robe slightly open to reveal her creamy, perky breasts, her long black hair still damp, feathered around her face. Even without make-up, her skin radiated a flawless beauty. Handing Clay the cup she sat on the bed, the robe gaped showing long legs, a teasing glimpse of her pussy. Clay felt his manhood harden. This time, cold sober, he wanted this woman.

Setting his cup on the night stand, he grabbed the lapel of her robe, drew her to him. Kissing her deeply he ran his hands inside the robe to cup her breasts. She moaned in his mouth as she opened her body to accept him. This time he took it slow, enjoyed seeing her squirm with impatience begging him for the release of her orgasm. He teased her, brought her to the brink, then stopped to let her shudder with pleasure. She clutched and clawed at him, her screams rising in volume as he let his actions entice her, pursue her, keep her fighting for more.

Pleasing a woman came easy. He loved watching them bloom under his guiding hand. His professor lover directed and tutored him on the important spots of the female body.

Sweat beaded up on her body, Clay licked at them, tasting the sweet salt. Rolling his tongue down her legs, he felt the shudder of her nerves as her core prepared for the climax. When he brought her finally to the peak she screamed, scratched at his back. The pain urging him on, to go deeper and deeper until her hips arched, took him all in. In sync, they moved jointly harder, harder and harder. Cresting at the same time, Clay felt the mighty release of a long absence of sex.

Lying on her, waiting to catch his breath, he rose up to look at her. Her dark eyes open. A wide smile on her face.

"Damn Clay. You are a great lover."

He laughed as he slapped her bare butt, rolled off. "Not so bad yourself."

On one elbow she traced his pleasure trail with a fingernail. "So can we meet up every so once in a while?

Searching her almost black eyes, he figured why not.

"I think we can arrange that." He put his hand behind her neck, pulled her down to his

lips. Tasting the coffee, he pulled back. "What's for breakfast? I am famished."

***

Returning home, he felt ashamed to tell his dad he didn't get much work done.

"A woman?"

Clay casted his eyes down. "Yeah."

"Are we going to start this all over again?"

Raising his head to look the man in the eyes. "No. I...fell in love this time."

A small white lie.

What he didn't expect his dad's overwhelming approval. "Good son. Time you settle down."

Okay go with it.

"Thanks Dad."

"So get her up here so we can meet her."

Damn!

"She pretty busy and...all." The disappointment crossed the elder Lester's face. Clay stood up. "But I'll make plans."

A wide smile told him this would not go away quickly. Stepping outside, he dialed the number Veronica put in his contacts.

"Veronica?"

Her voice picked up a notch. "Clay. So glad to hear from you."

"Listen, My father wants to meet you. I kind of implied we were serious..."

"I'd love to. I'll drive up this weekend. Can't wait to see you, Love."

140

Clay stared at the disconnected phone, then back at the building where he knew his dad waited for his answer. Walking back in. "She's coming up this weekend."

"Great son. What's her name?"

"Veronica."

Please don't ask me her last name. I have no idea.

"Sweet name. I'll call your mom." *He pick up the receiver from the phone on his desk, punched the buttons.* "She'll stay at the house. We'll have a big family gathering…Edie, our son has a guest coming this weekend…Yes, a girl…too soon for that, but we can hope."

Clay silently left the office and the building. Walking across the lumberyard, he met his Uncle Horace.

"What's going on, kid?"

"My life up shit's creek."

"What's wrong?"

Clay waved him off. "Never mind. I am going to check inventory."

The rest is history. Veronica made a big splash with the family, so it became assumed they would marry. Clay just accepted it. Better than trying to explain or rationalize that his heart never wanted to love again.

What the hell! The sex was good. No, great! It always seemed to be when it stayed sex and not making love.

He could do worse. At least he thought so at the time.

No sooner did he propose than shit hit the fan. Veronica and his mother planned this elaborate wedding. The event to end all events of Lester County. Whatever they wanted, the Lester family, so glad he accepted marriage, granted them. Clay just sat back, let it ride.

All but the night before the wedding. Sparky, Robby, Ben Cooper and a couple other close friends gathered at the only bar in town. Clay started to drink his feelings away.

This is it. I am letting go of Becca. Going for the gold in Veronica. Okay maybe I don't love her, but I will make it work.

"You don't love her?" The guys were all looking at him.

"Did I say that out loud?"

Robby nodded. "Yes. Dude, you don't have to do this."

Clay glanced at each one of them. "It's okay guys. I know what I'm doing." Raising his glass, he drained the cold liquid, poured more.

The memories of the day were foggy and vague. He remembered saying 'I do' to something. Dancing and drinking. Lots of drinking.

Life became work, then he went home to a whiny, bitchy wife who went through money like water. He didn't care. For him this would be his future.

Until three months after the wedding, Veronica announced at a family dinner she expected a child in six months. A cold slap in the face, Clay felt a joy seep up from his stomach. When they placed his son in his arms, he then knew he found love. So he made a deal with Veronica.

Produce me children. I'll stay with you.

She held out for five more sons. Then she declared she was done with being a breeder. Clay said fine, moved out.

Being a father became his greatest joy. So he told her lawyers, she can have whatever she wants, I get the boys. Not surprisingly, she agreed. The big house, the place in what stood as Lester Lake society, alimony until she moved on. Which she never did.

Clay didn't care. He raised his boys, worked hard for the family business, accepted life as good.

Until Becca walked back in his life.

***

Opening her eyes slowly, Becca realized some kind of covering held her down. Clawing at the layers of fabric, she fought her way to the surface. Gasping for air, she lay back, exhausted from the battle with her bedcovers. Her head felt on fire with a foggy, pounding pain.

What the fuck did I do last night? Last night?

Focusing on her bed side clock it read: 10:32.

AM or PM?

Since the room seemed encased in darkness, she surmised it must be PM.

How long ago did she fall into the bed?

Let's see by the time Robby bailed us out of jail...Clay!

Fuck!

Coming up too quickly, the rush felt like a sledgehammer hitting her face. She plopped back down. Raising her arm, she laid it easily over her eyes as the memory of the night before smashed over her carrying a roll of the stomach embarrassment.

Did I say anything stupid?

Did I say anything...nice...mushy...get-out-of-town humiliating?

Clay's face became all she could recall, towering over her with a smug look.

Now why did that make her all warm and tingly instead of boiling mad?

Because he came. His son called and he came.

Dropping her arm to her side, she smiled.

He came.

Rolling over to her side, she thought about getting out of bed. Finally her body moved, painfully and stiffly, but move it did.

Her feet hit the carpet on the floor not with a thud, but first her toes, then the fullness of her feet. Standing shakily, she pushed the mop of hair out of her eyes. She must look a sight.

Oh, well.

Padding to the bathroom, standing over the sink, she reluctantly looked in the mirror.

144

Oh my fucking god! I look like I was rode hard, put up wet. Whatever the hell that meant.

Even in her disheveled state she had no desire to rectify it now. Quick potty break, she stumbled back to bed. Curling up in the covers, she snuggled down, fell asleep smiling.

He came.

***

Jilley's eyes did not want to open. The darkness could be felt through her eye lids. She must have passed out because nothing registered except leaving the jail house. Truth be known, she couldn't conceive any ideas on how she got to bed.

It must have been Sparky. When was the last time she got wasted? Try never.

Okay, I need to get out of this bed. At least go to the bathroom.

Her body rebelled with all of its strength not to move, but she demanded it did.

I have not taken ten years of yoga for you not to move. Now move!

Shuffling to the bathroom, she avoided the mirror, just splashed water on her face and ran her fingers through her hair. Ready to leave the room, she hesitated at the doorway.

Do I go back to the bedroom and my comfortable cocoon or downstairs to face the day.

The day? Since it is dark and I turned on the light, it must be night.

The unanswered question, what day?

Grabbing the handrail, she stepped easily on the carpeted steps. Moving slower than a tortoise, she lingered as her head caught up to her body. The bright lights from the family room shot sharp pains between her eyes.

Pain killer. Need a pill. No, this is a seven or ten pill headache. Shot? I actually did shots?

As the memories came flooding back, she chuckled.

If I admit the truth, several shots of tequila. What the fuck were you thinking?

At the bottom of the stairs she paused, adjusted to who sat on the couch.

My husband. My dear sweet husband, who bailed me out of jail...oh shit, jail!

Her back hit the wall, Sparky turned around.

"Well, well. Look who is up and walking. Dear..." Rising off the couch, he walked over to her, put his arms around her shoulders, pulled her to him. "...you had quite the reunion with Becca." His arms guided her war-torn body to sit. She curled her legs under her as he sat next to her. She laid her head on his chest.

"I really had a night, didn't I?"

"That would have to be the understatement of the year."

"Did you know Becca was with Gwen when she died?"

"We were all there." His confusing sounded in his tone.

"No…" she raised her head, looked him in the eyes. "…in the room. She said Gwen let go."

"Let go? What do you mean?"

"Gwen saw Martin and let go. Died."

Sparky's eyes clouded over. "And Becca was there?…No wonder she ran. Must have been hard."

"I think it must have been really hard." Jilley felt the sadness in her heart. She put her head back on his chest. "I wish she hadn't of run…but I guess I understand better why."

Sparky chuckled. "I for one was surprised to see Clay at the jail."

Jilley sat straight up as the memory hit her. "Clay was there…" She smacked him lightly. "…he came for her. Damn straight."

"What are you thinking?"

"They need to be together."

"That's ship pretty much has sailed." Sparky shook his head.

Jilley leaped up on her knees. "No!…no. That ship is back in the harbor. Anchored and ready to be boarded."

She almost laughed at her husband's expression. He didn't hear the undertone in Becca's voice last night when she talked about Clay.

***

Susie stumbled from the bathroom to the kitchen. Going first to the sink, she turned on

the faucet, filled a small glass with water. Tipping the glass, she drank the cool liquid without coming up for air. Feeling a person come in the room, she knew Robby stood behind her.

"Hey, honey." Susie put the glass in the sink, leaned over. Filling her hand with cold water, she splashed her face. Taking the towel from his extended hand, she wiped off the left-over moisture.

Two hands massaged her shoulders. "Are you okay?" The voice of her concerned husband swept over her. She leaned back against his body.

"I can't believe I did that. And…" Covering her eyes with her hands. "…jail! You had to bail me out of jail."

His chuckle vibrated against her back. "There really wasn't any bailing. Ben just put you there to keep you safe. You were really going to let Jilley drive you home?"

Susie shook her head. "Not home. To Clay's house."

Robby turned her around. "Clay's house? Why were you going to Clay's house?"

Turning her deep green eyes on her charming husband, she cooed. "Well, darlin', it seems your friend Becca buried her feelings for Clay in a loveless marriage for twenty years."

"I knew it!" He jumped around like a kangaroo.

148

"Quite proud of yourself aren't you?" Susie laughed, leaning against the counter, her arms folded.

Robby locked a huge bear hug on his wife. Releasing her, his face glowed with pride. "I just knew they would at some time, somehow get back together. You didn't see them that summer. They were so in love…"

CHAPTER EIGHT

Becca had just stepped out of the shower when she heard the phone ring. Hastily wrapping a towel around her, she skidded into the bedroom to answer her cell phone. She heard it. Couldn't find it. Following the sound she found it wrapped in the bed covers.

"Hello?" Her towel started slipping, she tried unsuccessfully to keep it up.

"Becca?" Jilley's voice carried a welcome tone.

Becca plopped down on the bed, her towel falling to her lap. "Jilley. How are you?"

"Recovering."

"Ditto."

"Hey, if you're up to it, how about brunch tomorrow at the Club?"

"Sounds good. What time?"

150

"Meet us there around noon."

"Us?"

"Susie and I. The three lushes of Lester Lake!" Her laugh echoed through the phone.

Becca laugh also. "So are we scarlet lettered in town?"

"Probably. You know the gossips around here." Still chuckling.

The light-hearted tone relaxed Becca. "I'll be there. Thanks for the invite."

"See you then."

Becca tossed the phone on the bed. Her spirit felt lighter, she actually moved from under the fog to the light of day. Gathering up her towel, she went to the closet. Picking out a flop-around-the-house outfit of jean shorts and a tee, she hummed as she finished dressing.

Maybe the night of drinking did me some good.

* * *

The Club, considered 'the social gathering place' of Lester Lake, sat on the east edge of the lake. A golf course, swimming pool and restaurant welcomed the people as spring turned to summer. The days became longer and warmer. Becca strolled up to the main entrance, nodded at the smartly uniformed young man.

"Here with Jillian Carter."

The young man looked down the list on the stand. He looked up with a smile, which looked vaguely familiar to her. "Ms Young?"

Becca chuckled at Jilley using her maiden name. "Yes."

The young man's smile made his eyes twinkle like...

He waved his arm for her to go ahead of him. "You will be lunching on the terrace."

Studying his profile, Becca narrowed her eyes.

He's...

Reaching the table, he pulled the chair out for her. "Ma'am.

He's another one of Clay's sons!

Jilley came around the table to hug her. Watching the back the young man as he walked away, the same strut as his dad, the same form, Becca whispered. "Which one of Clay's son is that?"

"Matt."

Pulling back, Becca looked over her shoulder at the departing figure. "They are everywhere."

The two women felt a third set of arms hugging them, then Susie's soft voice. "Fellow cell mates. Glad you got paroled in time for lunch."

Chuckling with their heads together, they pulled apart, sat down.

Susie picked up her napkin, laid it in her lap, "So how is everyone?"

152

Becca put her head in her hand. "How did I go from tipsy to pole dancing wasted in sixty seconds?"

Laughter broke out around the table.

A young girl sat salads in front of the women. "Drinks for anyone?"

This made the giggles start again. Jilley waved her hand over the table, barely able to speak. "No. Water is fine."

The confused look on the girl's face started the laughter again.

Digging into the salad, Becca observed the other two women. The easy feeling of the lunch, the long history with one brought back good feelings. Something she had not felt for several years. The warm sun on the lake reminded her of the summer to come. The terrace set over the lake allowed an impressive overview of the splendid scenery.

Jilley raised her glass of water. "To my fellow felons. May we only room together when arrested!"

Susie and Becca chimed in. "Here, here." Clinking the glasses, each drank.

"I guess it wasn't an actually arrest." Susie set her glass down.

Jilley's voice was full of annoyance. "I can't believe Ben put me in jail."

"Robby said there was no bail. So I guess, in fact, we were just detained until our husbands came to get us."

"Or Clay." Jilley's eyes shot sparks of mischief at Becca.

Becca could felt the blush on her face. "Yeah...well..."

"Well hell." Jilley's tone cut to the chase. "He came for you. You still have feelings for him. He must care some. He didn't want you rotting in jail."

"I was far from rotting."

Susie chuckled. "I wasn't part of that summer...I can still feel the tension between the two of you. There are still feelings. Admit it Becca."

"Yeah, admit it." Jilley chimed in.

Becca looked from one to the other. Like a deer in the headlights, she felt stunned, caught. Shaking her head. "I don't know...I am still married...It's water under the bridge...I don't know."

"Well..." Jilley leaned back with the know-it-all look on her face. "...water under the bridge or ship has sailed...you and Clay belong together. Always should have been."

Becca studied her old friend's words. Nodding her head. "We'll see. After the drinking night, anything could happen here in Lester Lake."

Susie raised her glass this time. "Hear. Hear. To anything and everything happening. And all that's in-between."

Jilley's cheer sounded the loudest. "Hear. Hear."

"Hear. Hear." In truth, the though made sense to Becca. She spoke low, with a smile on her lips. Her two companions winked at her.

154

***

After lunch Becca parted from Jilley and Susie, decided to go on into town to get some groceries. The one supermarket stood alone at the edge of town. Parking her car, she entered the store, grabbed a cart, headed first to the produce.

Surprised at the great selection of fresh fruit, she became totally involved in picking a honey dew when the voice behind her caused her to drop the round fruit.

"Are you going to eat it or drink it?"

Clay!

The honey dew hitting the others caused an avalanche. Grabbing desperately to stop the rush of fruit to the floor, she felt frazzled, embarrassed.

"Whoa!" Clay started helping her. Picking up the rolling, awkward melons from the floor, he brushed her arm as he leaned over to replace them on the stand.

Becca wished the floor would just open up and swallow her. Once all the honey dews were back on the shelf, Becca raised her eyes to focus on his face.

"Hi, Clay."

His knee-dropping smile creased his eyes. "Becca."

She wiped her hands down her shirt more from nerves than anything else. Pushing her hair out of her face, she looked into his eyes filled with sexuality. She took a deep breath. "Look, I meant to thank you for coming to ...the jail...that night..."

"I would do it for any friend."

The words surprised her.

Friends. We are at least friends?

"Sorry you had to come out at night for nothing."

"Nothing? Being in jail is nothing to you?" She saw how he tried to not laugh. "Do you do that often? You have changed Becca Young. Excuse me, Hamilton."

Narrowing her eyes, she glared at him. Getting his chuckle for the day at her expense pissed her off. "No. That is my first and will be my only time."

He still smiled at her.

"Look..." she turned her back to him. "...I need to finish shopping." Grabbing the closest honey dew, she tossed it in her cart. Giving the cart a hard shove, he stepped back as she pushed it forward to the tomatoes.

Not bothering to look back she felt his eyes on her.

Why does he unnerve me so? I am acting like that young girl who twenty years ago would spit fire when she became mad.

***

A barely clad girl surrounded Clay, blocking his path, rubbing her boobs on him. Becca's insides fumed with jealousy and exasperation. Clay kept pushing the girl away, stepped aside to get around her, but that did not bring Becca's boiling blood down.

156

Waiting for him on her towel on the beach, she found it hard to be in this position. Since he kissed her, Clay always came to be with her. His subtle touches sent waves of desire down her body. Ready to sleep with him, she kept a cautious distance because of what she witnessed today. There were just too many girls after him. She couldn't ask him to be faithful to just her. She had no claim on him.

Biting her lip, Becca changed her line of vision, looking out over the lake. As Clay sat down behind her, he straddled her with his legs, wrapped his arms around her shoulders. Resting his chin on her neck, the warmth of his breath only made her want him more, fueling her anger.

Without thinking she shrugged him off, moved away from his embrace.

Opening his arms. "What's wrong?"

"Nothing." She hated saying that. Such a trite statement. Everything felt wrong, except the feelings developing for Clay. That felt right.

"Something's wrong. You're tense. Are you mad?"

"No."

Liar. You just don't think you have a right to be mad.

Glancing over her shoulder, she saw him recline to lean back on his elbows. A wry smile played at his lips. His body enticed, mocked her. Her imagination flowed with thoughts of them together. A heat seared her thighs.

Damn it stop!

With one hand he stroked her arm. "What's wrong baby?"

Becca kept facing front, her back stiffened. "It's just... the other girls..."

Shut up Becca.

"I just..."

A small frown slipped across his face. "Other girls? What other girls?'

Oh, don't even act like you are clueless.

"Oh, I don't know. Maybe Miss Boobs over there. Rubbing against you..."

"Her? Give me a break. I like my women with some brains."

"Oh, so you want me for my mind?"

His grin widened. "Your mind..." He came back up to circle her with his arms. Laying soft kisses on her bare shoulders. "...your body...your charm...your spunk."

Try as she did, he did not let her get away from him. Instead, he pulled her back to look into her face. His mouth tipped into a lazy, sexy smile. "I want you Becca Young."

In a swift move he eased her down to the towel. His lips barely touched hers in a light teasing kiss, just enough to melt her reserve. Running his hand down her side, she went into his arms. Sliding her hand to the nape of his neck, she planted a searing kiss

158

on his mouth. He groaned, kissed her deeply, sending shots of
flames to her central part. The hungry swipe of his tongue took
her breath away...

***

"Ma'am? You're next." The check-out girl looked at Becca, waiting for her reaction. Lost in her daydream, leaning on her cart, she was startled, then noticed the next people in line were waiting for her. The girl nodded toward the conveyer belt for Becca to place her items on it. Straightening up, she started placing her food.

When did I pick this up?

Becca looked questioningly at the jar of olives.

The cashier cleared her throat. Becca placed the olives on the belt. Empting her cart, she pushed it out of the way. Looking up, she saw Clay standing in the door, with some woman fawning all over him.

Some things never change!

Turning back to the lane, she swiped her card, gathered up her groceries, went for the other door. Juggling three plastic bags, she did not notice when Clay stepped up behind her.

"Here, let me help you." His voice made her jerk around, clutching her bags to her chest.

With both of their hands on the bags, she slightly snatched them toward her. "No, I'm good."

Clay's jerk was stronger as he pulled them to him. "Really, Becca? You can let me help."

His eyes were sincere, so she released her hold. "I'm over here." She spun around looking for her car, when she realized she stood next to it. "Here." Hitting the button on the key, all the buttons popped up as if she had called them to attention.

Clay switched the bags to one hand, opened the back door, put her bags in. Becca stood frozen in her spot as she watched him. He still moved with strong movements, graceful strides. Age had been kind to Clay Lester. If anything he improved in looks and manner. No longer the cocky young stud, he could still make a woman's heart beat faster.

Shutting the back door, he turned to her. His eyes locked with hers as, with one hand, he opened the driver's door. They stood there for a moment in silence.

He leaned his hand on the door frame. "Is there something you want to say, Becca?"

Shaking her head, she came back to the present. "Thank you." She lowered her head, then raised it back up. "Really. Thank you for everything." She crossed in front of him, slid into the seat.

With one hand on the door, the other still on the frame, his face broke into a smile. "Let's not bicker. We are still old friends. I can help you without there being an alternative

reason."

160

Ashamed of her thoughts, she nodded. "Yes. You have been very helpful with the windows, carrying my bags and…" She knew she blushed "…jail."

Their laughter echoed together.

"Really, Becca? Jail?"

"It was Jilley's fault!" She chuckled at the thoughts.

Clay shook his head. "Jilley. She really is a case."

"But a good one. She and Susie have helped me a lot since I got here."

Clay touched her cheek lightly. "I'm here too, Becca."

She could feel her good emotions starting to surface. "Thanks Clay."

He shut her door. "Take care Becca."

Putting the car in reverse, she nodded. Backing out, she glanced over at him, saw him still watching her. Shifting into drive she pulled away.

***

Clay spotted Becca when she first walked in the store. He debated approaching her, but the thoughts of seeing her in jail made him chuckle.

Oh what the hell.

Coming up behind her, he couldn't resist his line. He didn't expect it to startle her, he remained motionless, stunned as all the honey dews fell to the floor. When she stood up, she blew him away with eyes that could make a man forget to breathe.

Too close Clay. Back away.

So he baited her, she responded in typical Becca way, taking no prisoners. Watching her walk away, his mind went to another time when her spunk cold cocked him, and he fought like hell to keep her.

***

Clay just arrived at the bar to gather with the gang. "Hey baby."

"Don't you fucking 'hey baby' me." Becca's words came at him in a fury of fighting fire.

Clay took a step back, looked at her with puzzlement. "What?"

Becca slide off the stool, punching on his chest with her finger. "I saw you do the once over on Sally Brown over there."

Clay looked back at the door, thinking back to when he came in, his one consuming thought only to find Becca. Spotting her at the bar with Jilley and Gwen, he ignored Sparky and Martin at the pool table, made a bee-line for her.

He had waited all day to see her.

His dad gave him some last minute thing to do made that him late. Vaguely he remembered Sally coming up to him, cooing something. He nodded, moved her out of his way.

Now he had a fighting mad, wild woman in front of him and his level of desire rose quickly. Try as he did, he couldn't hide his smile. That made it worse.

"Don't laugh about it, you shit." *Becca's eyes flashed sparks as she returned to the stool.*

Gawd, I love her this way!

"I'm not laughing. I…" *He reached for her. Her arms went stiff, her eyes narrowed. If he could he would take her right here, right now.* "…am sorry. I didn't think."

He felt her arms relax, her body language change, soften. A small smile played at her lips.

"I'm sorry. I overreacted." *She turned around on the stool, took a drink of her beer. Clay encircled her with his arms, nudged her neck.*

"You know you're the only girl for me. I can't help it if I'm irresistible to other woman." *He chuckled as he kissed her neck.*

She elbowed him, in a joking way. "Don't get so cocky." *She spun around on the stool, wrapped her arms around his neck, spoke on his lips.* "I can take 'em, you know."

"Of that I have no doubt." *His lips captured hers in a deep, passionate kiss.*

***

Getting to the house, Becca unloaded her bags. The day was a warm first-of-summer day. She enjoyed the feeling. Even seeing Clay, made the day brighter. Peace in her life is a good feeling.

I think I will enjoy it.

Dumping the bags in the kitchen, she unpacked them as she hummed. Pulling out a bottle of her favorite wine, she put it in the fridge to chill. Maybe not the proper thing to do, but she liked her wine cold, red or white. Jon always did the room temperature thing. His idea of a good wine was bitter and dry. This evening she would enjoy her wine her way.

Thank you.

Late that afternoon, Becca looked out the window at the calm lake. Dragonflies swooped down to gather the water, their colored, translucent wings catching the sunlight. Grabbing her camera, she hurried out to snap some pictures. All of a sudden, she felt the urge to paint.

Returning to the house, she walked to the studio. The memories assaulted her. All good. The best. The day she and Clay made love for the first time.

Searching around she found a clean canvas, dusted off a stand. Opening several new bottles of paint, she loaded her palette. A set of new brushes were in the drawer of the big table. In a chest she found clean painting smocks. Slipping into one, she set all her elements up, drug a stool from the corner, hopped up.

Ready to paint, she let her mind wander. The place it went? To Clay and her and the new table.

***

The light summer rain bounced off the windows. It came as a warm refreshing break from the summer heat. The sound soothed Becca's mind. Her thoughts now were completely consumed by Clay. His body. His lips. Her day and night dreams of them together. Just thinking about it made her feel sexy.

Coming out of the shower, she wanted to feel light and free. Slipping into her silkiest

panties, a fresh painting smock that hung to her knees, she fluffed her hair, strutted down the hall to the kitchen.

Aunt Tilley left for the day to go to the city for an art thing. Since the forecast said rain all day, she knew there would be no beach time. And Clay worked during the day, so she wouldn't see him until tonight at the bar.

Taking her cup of coffee into the studio, she watched the drops of water fall into the lake. Even the dark dull day didn't dampen her mood.

I am falling in love.

An overwhelming passion crashed over her, sending a wave of longing to feel Clay's arms around her. Picking up a brush, she started letting her feelings guide her hand. Lost in the world of creativity, she sat, painting for over an hour.

A hard rap on the front door knocked her back into the present.

Who could it be?

Going to the sound, she cracked the door, saw Clay standing on the porch.

"Hey, darlin'"

Becca realized she stood there half dressed. "Hey?"

His smile intensified her discomfort, but also her desire. "We have Tilley's new table." He pointed his thumb over his shoulder.

"We?" Becca looked around him to see one of his uncles emerging from the delivery truck. Hearing the rattle of the truck's door slide up made her feel more uncomfortable.

Clay cocked his head at her. "Are you going to let us in?'

"Yes. Yes of course." She opened the door wide. Clay's eyes skirted down her body, his mouth tipped in a lazy, sexy smile.

"Hey Clay." His uncle yelled at him. "Tell her to clear a path. Does she know where it goes?"

"Do you?"

Becca titled her head. "The studio."

Reluctantly Clay peeled his glazed from her, turned back to the truck. "Yeah, she knows."

Pulling the door open as far as she could, she hid behind. What she really wanted to do was run down the hall, pull on a pair of jeans.

166

Clay and his uncle huffed as they brought the table through the doorway. Clay walked backwards, his arm muscles bulged as he lifted the long, heavy table. He winked at her as he passed. His uncle, an older version of Clay, did an exceptional job of holding up his end. He paid little attention to Becca as he passed.

Once in, they stopped and Clay looked at her. "The studio?"

Oh, yeah. They don't know where it is.

Coming out from behind the door, she slid past the table, as it took up most of the hallway. The tight space made her shirt twist on her body, she could feel it hiking up. Finally pass the table, she tried to bring the shirt back in place without drawing attention to herself. A

hot blush rose on her face as she straightened up, walked like everything was just fine.

Entering the studio, she stepped aside, crossed her arms over her chest. Stepping out of their way, she watched the two men put the table in the empty spot.

Clay looked remarkably handsome today. His plain tee shirt plastered to his body from sweat and rain. Becca could not stop the sharp heat curling inside of her. His gaze snared with hers, her pulse flickered, leaped.

"Is this good?"

Becca nodded.

Clay leaned his butt on the table, his slow, appraising gaze aroused her as no man ever had.

Without looking away, he talked to his uncle. "Uncle Horace, this is Becca. Becca, this is my Uncle Horace, the master crafter of this fine table.

The older man turned, put out his hand, Becca had no choice but to walk over to him. "Glad to meet you...Uncle...uh...Mr. ...Horace." Now standing next to Clay she could feel his body heat. Running her hand over the polished wood. "Nice work."

Uncle Horace nodded. "Clay. We need to get back to the shop."

Clay's voice washed over her as he spoke next to her back, sending vibration deep into the core of her body. "I think I will take my lunch break now, Uncle Horace."

"But it's only nine thirty?"

Becca could hear the edginess in Clay's voice. "I'm hungry now."

She turned to look at him over her shoulder, steadying herself with her hands on the table as her knees were going weak.

Uncle Horace sighed, walked out of the room, murmuring to himself. "Well... okay."

Becca and Clay stood still as they waited for the front door to close. Eyes locked, her hunger for him possessing her.

"How long is Tilley gone for?"

"'Till tomorrow morning."

168

When the click echoed back to the studio, Clay's eyes flashed devilment. Her gaze snared with his, the throb in her flickered and leaped.

Without a word, he moved toward her. Her hands went to the front of his jeans, pulled him to her. Without breaking the stare, she unfastened the large silver belt buckle. The jingle of its looseness moved her hands to the snap. Tugging at the snap, she felt it open in her hand. Clay's look told her to continue. Running her hands around his slim waist, pushing them deep into the seat of his pants, she grabbed his tight ass cheeks, pulled him closer.

With one swift move, he lifted her up to sit on the table. His hands worked at her shirt buttons. With skills, he removed the barriers blocking his mouth from licking and tasting her. Becca grabbed his hair, leaned into him, her eagerness to have him as close as she could.

Lifting her up slightly, he slid her panties off. Her bare butt, touching the quilt, slightly damp, sent a heat wave through her legs. Clay took her lips into his as he kissed her with all the

pent up passion they both needed to release. She could feel his intensity. Hers matched it.

Driven by her own needs, she clawed at his shirt to remove it from his body. The dampness and coolness only fired her excitement. The sight of a set of perfect abs covered by glistening skin produced a fire such as she'd never imagined searing her feminine center.

A hungry, insatiable look in his eyes, melted her last stage of resistance. She wrapped her legs tightly around his waist pressing her eager womanhood against him.

"Easy baby. We have lots of time."

His words made her relax her grip. He scooted her back on the table, moved his lips slowly, torturously, over her stomach, to her thighs. The sensations caressed her, sending shock waves up to her breasts. His mouth took over her mind as he probed and teased her.

Grabbing the blanket with both hands, she arched her back, moaned with the ecstasy encompassing her. His hands stroked her hips as he continued to excite the pleasure in her. Feeling a climax coming she prepared for the excitement.

Like he sensed her coming orgasm, he pushed her backwards, dropped his pants, climbed up on the table with her. Her eyes begged him to finish, but his lip curved in a treacherous smile.

"Not yet darlin'. You need to feel everything. Relax, enjoy. I am here to please you."

Even his words twisted her desire, adding to her ache. Everywhere he touched burned. He looked at her as if nothing else in the world mattered.

The rain hitting the skylights above her sparked her higher. His mouth on her breast stirred her libido in all the forbidden ways.

170

Her hands slipped off his damp skin. Adjusting her curves to fit the hard plane of his body, the feel of him moving over her sucked the breath out of her.

Just when every nerve in her body ignited, she felt his hardness. Teasing, he mounted her, with a push and pull rhythm brought an orgasm. He smiled as he entered her deep, brought another orgasm crashing over the first. Her screams echoed in the room, again, he pulled out, put his mouth on her. She squirmed and twisted as one after another orgasm drew her legs up to vibrate with desire. He held her down as she fought to accept the sensations crashing over her. Sweat dripped into her eyes. Her heart pounded against her chest.

She begged for release. "Please! Clay!"

Just when she believed she could not take any more, he entered her, pumped hard. Another sensation flooded her whole body as satisfaction and pleasure brought tears to her eyes. This orgasm grew to be the biggest she ever felt. Never had she screamed or experienced any such rush.

His coming coincided with her last one. Together they climbed the height, peaked together. The gratification of each collided, creating shudders wracking their bodies, tumbled over the last edge of pleasure.

He'd awakened hidden pleasures of her body. Swamped with emotions, she buried her face in his chest.

"You, okay?"

Becca couldn't speak. She nodded.

He kissed her gently, sweetly. "Becca, I..."

***

The hard knock on the front door, jarred Becca back to the present. Looking around, it took a moment to get back to now.

Who the hell is this?

Standing up, she smoothed down her shirt. Glancing at the canvas she'd been working on, she is shocked to see a beautiful couple embracing each other.

The pounding continued.

Still disorientated, she went to the door. Opening it, her shock almost knocked her back.

On her porch stood her daughter, Haley and her son, Jon Jr.

"Hi, Mom."

CHAPTER NINE

"Kids!" Becca swooped them into her arms.

The feel of their physical presence was something Becca did not realized she missed, until she got hugs from each child. Pulling back, she touched her oldest child's face, "Haley, darling."

Jon Jr., her baby, is a man standing in front of her. She ruffled his curly mop top, took in the facial hair. "No barbers at Berkley?"

"It's the style Mom." His face broke into the crooked smile she loved from the day he was born.

Linking arms she guided them into the house.

Haley looked up and around. "Wow, I remember this house. It was always so comfortable and inviting." She turned to Becca. "Why did we stop coming?"

Becca bit her lower lip. "Long story."

Jon Jr. "We have a month. And we're not leaving until we know what's going on with you and Dad."

So the time has come to face the music.

"Okay." Becca would just as soon get it over with. "Look, are you hungry?" Both kids nodded. "We'll talk over lunch."

Directing them to the kitchen, she pulled out the chairs at the table for them to sit. Jon Jr. went to the back door.

"Wow, what a great lake." He turned to Haley. "I remember this too." He looked back outside. "Do you have a boat, Mom?"

Becca stopped in mid-air putting things on the counter. "I don't know."

Haley chuckled. "You don't know?"

Laughing, Becca turned back to her task. "I guess I never thought of it." Chopping vegetables, she titled her head. "We'll check it out after lunch."

Setting salads on the table, Becca finished. "If not, we'll buy one."

"Mom?" Haley stopped halfway to sitting on her chair. "We'll just buy one?"

Flippantly, Becca tossed her hair back. "Sure. Why not?"

Jon Jr. rubbed his hands together. "Cool. Mom you have changed."

When all three were seated, Becca broached the forbidden subject. "So let's talk about the elephant in the room."

Haley snorted. "You mean Dad?"

Becca found it funny, but fought to keep a straight face. "Well, yes. In a way. But I wasn't calling him the elephant."

174

"Then how about a jerk." Haley's vehemence was obvious.

Jon Jr. sat looking back between his mom and sister, not saying anything.

Haley picked up the wand. "So what happened?"

Becca dabbed at her mouth with her napkin. "I guess your Dad wants a divorce."

"And you?" Haley pointed her fork at Becca.

Taking a deep breath, she only wanted to speak the truth. It was time. "I didn't think so at first, but now..." she raised her head, looked at both of her children. "...Yes. I think a divorce is a good idea."

"Finally!" Haley dug into her salad.

Laying her fork down, Becca took a large gulp of water. Her mouth became very dry. "Why do you say that?"

"Because you have let Dad run your life far too long. I'm glad you grew some balls."

The sentence bothered Becca. Swallowing hard, she tried not to choke. "Why, I didn't know I needed to."

"You know what I mean Mom."

"No, explain it to me."

"Dad is a tyrant. He runs all our lives. Why do you think Jonny and I went to colleges so far away? To get out from under him." Haley shoved a forkful of greens into her mouth, raised her eyebrows at Becca.

Searching the faces of her children, Jon Jr. shrugged.

So it is true. While I lived in my cocoon, my children lived under a controlling man who made their lives miserable.

"I'm sorry. I guess I didn't realize." The guilt weighed heavy on her heart.

Jon Jr. broke his silence. "It wasn't that bad, Mom. We always had you to even things out." He leaned back in his chair. "Besides, I like this new Mom. You look happy, relaxed. Also diggin' your funky look. Hair all over your head, your clothes not so uptight."

"Uptight? I wore very nice clothes…"

Haley chimed in. "…for a rigid woman with no life."

Becca became defensive. "I had a life."

"Really?" Haley leaned forward on her elbows. "Tell me about it."

"I worked…"

"…at a part time job where Dad could still have you at his beck and call…"

"…and a social life…"

"…with a bunch of bitches who biggest achievement is a sale at Macy's…"

Becca plopped back. "Was my life that lame?"

Haley's look softened. "Sorry Mom, but Jonny and I knew the other side of you. The creative, fun side. No one else got that."

"You saw that?"

Jon Jr. took Becca's hand. "Of course we did. You are the greatest Mom. You just sucked at being a person."

Becca gave them both her best disgusted look, then laughed. A deep releasing laugh.

"You're right. I sucked..." Hitting the table with her palms. "...but no more. I have found my wings."

Haley took hold of Becca's other hand, also Jon's. "Good. It's nice to see you fly."

Jon Jr. squeezed Becca's hand. "And we get a boat."

***

Together the three cleaned up after lunch. As they went outside to the deck, Becca saw Robby down by the lake.

Taking the arms of both of her children. "Come on. I want you to meet someone."

Guiding them over the sand, when Robby saw them his face broke into a smile. "This must be Haley and Jon Jr." He extended his hand.

Haley took it first. "How did you know my name?"

"Your Mom talks about you all the time." He released her hand, took the boy's. "Jon...Jr.? Is what you like to be called?"

"Just Jonny. The junior was meant to keep from confusing me and my Dad. I don't think it will be problem here."

Robby raised an eyebrow at Becca. She nodded back. Her pride in her two children overflowed into her soul. They took the circumstance of the situation as adults.

"Robby..." Becca interrupted. "...the kids were asking about a boat. Did Aunt Tilley have one?"

Robby smiled. "Why, yes she did. A pontoon. Tootled around this lake all the time, taking pictures, painting. Lester Lake Marine has it. I'll call them, have it delivered. But..." Robby turned his attention to Jon. "...if you want something with some power, try my speed boat." He pointed over his shoulder with his thumb.

Jon stepped aside, whistled. "Nice."

Robby put his arm across the boy's shoulder. "Want to go for a ride?"

Jon jumped at the chance. "Sure!"

Robby turned to Becca and Haley. "Want to go?"

Becca chuckled. "I'll pass this time. Haley?"

"I'll pass too. Seems like it is a male bonding thing."

"Your loss." Robby and Jon tore down the beach to the dock to jump into the shiny, black, magnificently slick boat.

Susie yelled from their deck. "Becca!"

"Come on. Meet my new BFF."

"BFF?"

"You sound surprised."

"I am on two accounts. First you use the term BFF. Second you say it with such affection."

178

Becca hugged her daughter. "It's different here."

"Good, Mom."

Reaching the deck, Susie came down the stairs to greet them. "Is this Haley? Glad to meet you, I'm Susie." Susie hugged a surprised Haley.

Becca watched as her daughter relaxed, returned the hug.

"Nice to meet you, Susie."

A young girl came out from the house. Susie motioned her down. "Becca, Haley, this is my daughter Franny." Franny looked like her mother, with soft delicate features, compassionate green eyes. Reaching the bottom of the stairs she went to her mother. Susie put her arms on the girl's shoulders. "Franny, this is Becca, Tilley's niece, and Becca's daughter Haley."

Franny put out her hand to both of them. "Nice to meet you." Franny, about three years young than Haley, making her still about a year young than Jon Jr.

Susie put her hand up to shade her eyes. "So is that your son with my dare-devil husband?"

Becca and Haley chuckled together. Becca turned to face the lake. "Yes, it is."

Susie guided the other three to the gazebo. "Come have some tea and chat."

Becca looked at Haley, gave her a silent 'well'? Haley took her mother's arm. "Yes."

Relieved, Becca wanted her children to get to know her friends. They seemed to have understood more of her former life than she did.

The four ladies gathered and chatted. Every once in a while the speed boat would fly by, Robby and Jon Jr. would wave, yell, then disappear leaving a large wake trailing behind.

Susie tapped Becca's arm. "Say, most of the kids from the lake are coming home from college for summer break. Let's throw a beach party, introduce your kids?"

Haley spoke up before Becca even had a chance to think about it. "Sounds like fun. Mom?"

Becca nodded. "Sure." She hoped she didn't sound too surprised at Haley's enthusiasm.

Franny jumped up. "I'll get the phone. We'll start calling." She ran up the deck stairs, into the house.

Haley looked over at her Mom. "You just call?"

Becca shrugged. She had no idea.

"No engraved invitations?" Haley gave Becca a smug look.

Becca chuckled, knowing where her daughter was going with this.

Susie saved her. "No, honey. You're on the lake now. We just give a call, people come, usually bringing food and drinks."

"Potluck?" Haley's voice rose an octave. "Seriously!"

The roaring sound of the speed boat saved Becca from answering. Cutting the motor, it floated into the slip. All turned

180

to watch as Jon Jr. jumped out, tied the ropes to the pillars. Once secured, Robby jumped out and the two men walked up the dock. Reaching the gazebo, the sound of the screen door slamming turned all eyes to Franny as she walked out. Stopping at the railing, she looked down at Jon Jr.

Becca watched as her man-slash-boy took in a quick breath. Haley got up, walked over behind her brother. While she spoke low, Becca heard her words.

"Little brother. You're drooling."

***

The sound of a huge vehicle, brought all three of the Hamiltons out of the house to the back porch. A tow truck with *Lester Lake Marine* on the door backed a pontoon boat down the ramp into the lake. As the boat broke water, the tow line jerked as the truck stopped. A young man emerged from the cab, slipping on leather gloves as he walked to the chains holding the boat. Another man jumped into the boat as the chains were released. The pontoon slid easily into the water. Starting the motor, it sputtered, then hummed as it glided backwards. The man at the wheel turned the boat toward the dock with grace and ease, he cut the motor, guiding it in. The other man caught the ropes as they were thrown to him, tied off the boat. Sitting there proud and beautiful, the sparkling navy blue boat welcomed her new owners. The two men walked up the dock to the three, handed Becca the keys.

"There you are ma'am. She's fit, ready to go."

Becca cocked her head. "She?"

He pointed his thumb over his shoulder. "Tilley named her 'My Girl', so she."

Becca chuckled. "Thank you..." She held out her hand.

"Kevin. Kevin Lester."

But of course!

"Glad to meet you. I'm Becca. These are my children, Jon Jr. and Haley."

Each shook hands.

So this is the fifth son of Clay's I have met. One to go.

"Is that okay, Mom?" Jon Jr.'s voice interrupted her thoughts.

"What honey?"

"I said, Kevin invited me to go back with them to look at the speed boats. Is that okay?"

"Sure honey, check them out."

As the three guys walked away Becca heard the unnamed third guy say. "Jet skis. They are the best."

Haley walked down toward the dock, tossing her words over her shoulder. "Mom? You know how to drive one of these?"

Becca is surprised she knows the answer. "Yes? Yes, I do. I think Aunt Tilley had a boat when I came here. Not this one..."

182

Becca caught up to her daughter, laid her arms across Haley's shoulder. "...this is a beauty."

Juggling the keys, Becca, with a little jiggling, got the small metal door open, stepped on the front deck. The boat stood gleaming. It couldn't be very old. Everything looked brand new.

Haley still stood on the dock. Becca started giving out orders like the captain of a ship.

Grabbing one of the pillars. "Haley, untie the rope."

Haley leaped into action. Throwing the rope onto the deck, she skipped over to the

second one.

Becca held the boat steady, as she waited for Haley to untie the second rope, then hop on board.

As the boat started to float, Becca went over, started the motor. It purred like a kitten. Putting it into reverse, she backed it out. Clear of the dock, she put it into neutral to idle, then shoved the handle into drive.

The boat cut through the still water. All of a sudden, Becca remembered the feeling of riding on the water. The wind blowing her hair, the mist touching her face. Feeling the freedom of flying. The beauty of the water's edge. The familiar feeling of being where she belonged. She turned to look back at Haley, resting on the back seat, her arms spread out on the back, with her youthful face gathering the sunlight and smiling. Becca loved her smile.

Becca cut the motor, letting the boat drift. She turned to Haley. "Do you want to drive?"

Haley jumped up. "Sure. Is it hard?"

Becca moved from the driver's seat. "It's just like driving a car." Leaning over she explained how to shift. "Push in the button, it will move forward."

The boat started to move slowly. Becca patted Haley's shoulders. "Just take it easy."

Passing Copper Beach, Becca saw a dozen or so kids mingling around. The old rope swing still hung in the trees.

"What's that?" Haley asked as she glanced toward the beach.

"Copper Beach. Good hangout for the young."

"Did you hang out there, Mom?"

Becca smiled at the memories. "I did. When I was younger. Before your Dad and you and Jon Jr."

Haley looked back at her. "Wild parties, Mom?"

Becca could feel the blush. "Some. I was young..."

"...and in love?" Haley finished for her.

"What makes you say that?"

"Oh, come on Mom. Dad could not have been your first love. Surely you had a hot summer romance at some point."

When did my daughter start reading me so well?

"A slight one."

"And who is it? Is he still here?"

"It doesn't matter. I don't know." Becca switched her gaze from the beach to a house on the lake. "Look there's Jilley's house."

Haley swung her head in the opposite direction. "Who's Jilley?"

"A long lost friend I have reconnected with."

"Like Susie?"

Becca shook her head. "Susie's not an old friend. I just met her. Her husband and I were part of 'the gang' one summer."

"Sounds like there's a story there."

"Not really.   Just kid stuff."

***

After Clay and Becca made love for the first time, they couldn't stay apart. They met every day at Copper Beach to make the six, Gwen and Martin, Jilley and Sparky, Clay and Becca. Robby dated several girls that summer, but he always came back to the group to hang. So sometimes there were seven of them.

"Hey gang!" Martin's voice echoed down to where everyone sat. Reaching them, he slid down in the sand landing next to Gwen. "There's a concert in the city at the Sandbar Ballroom. It's Vinnie and Will's band."

Becca leaned back against Clay. "Who's Vinnie and Will?"

He leaned into her. "Two guys from school who formed a band."

"Are they any good?"

"Not bad. It would be worth going to see." Clay addressed Martin. "We're in. When?"

Martin smiled. "This Saturday. Great. Everyone else?"

Jilley and Sparky chimed in. "Sure."

Robby got excited. "I'll get a date. How do we get tickets?"

"We can buy them there. It's all GA. I'll get a hold of Vinnie, make arrangements to meet up."

As the evening crested, Clay and Becca moved closer. Touch and kissing, her fire flamed as soon as she felt his touch. Teasing her with kisses, words of sexual desires, she knew she was in love with this man.

Pulling her up, he took her hand, leading her to the truck. Throwing their beach stuff in the truck's bed, he would kiss her as he lifted her up into the seat. His hand roamed down her legs, giving her sweet sensations. To wait until they were away from everyone became torture. Sitting as close as she could to him, she allowed him to tantalize her skin with quick touches, long strokes. Pulling up in back of Aunt Tilley's property, they were secluded behind the giant trees growing along the lake's edge.

As she fell into his waiting arms, he lifted her, put her in the back of the truck. Spreading the blanket out together, they knelt facing each other. Kissing him, luscious anticipation together with the slow burn of desire curled through her. Raking her hair from her eyes, he pressed her body into his.

186

His fingers untied her bathing suit top at her neck, each of his touches sent sparks to her breasts causing her nipples to harden. He rolled his hand over them, his eyes letting her know every ember of desire would be ignited, flamed, finally would devour her. Getting there sometimes felt as if it would kill her, but she knew it was worth the wait.

"You, Clay Lester have made me a sex animal. I can't get enough of you." Nibbling on his ear she whispered. "You have spoiled me for any other man."

He whipped her around to be pinned underneath him. "There better not be any other

man."

Looking into his blue eyes, her body melted. "There will never be another man."

His mouth covered hers, his tongue darting, swiping hungrily. Moaning, she formed to his body. Feeling his hardness, her fever for him spiked. Grabbing the cord of his swimming trunks, she pulled, releasing the waist band. Shoving her hands down she gripped him. He groaned.

"Listen to me Clay Lester. Same goes for you. I find you with any other girl..." Just the thought became unbearable to her. She knew in her heart of hearts she could never give this man up.

The wicked smile she so loved crossed his face. "...believe me. You are woman enough for me."

His hands traveled down her side, to her thighs. Petting the inside, a tiny moan escaped as her body prepared for the pleasures he always gave her. Opening up to him, his tongue did magical things to her desires.

Looking over his shoulder, she saw a million stars against the dark night sky. Relaxing her body she allowed his mouth to do the wondrous things that would spike her. Stroke after sensuous stroke, a small orgasm shuttled her core.

She clawed at the blanket beneath her, begging him for the sweet release. "Oh my god, Clay!"

"Say it again." His voice like a smooth whiskey, burning in a delightful way.

"Clay!" Her voice rose, her body arched.

His teasing only created endless vibrations to crash over her. When speaking, his breath tickled and stimulated. She ran her hands over his tight ass, around to the front, closing her hand over him. She watched the pleasure on his face as she toyed with his manhood.

"You're treading water baby."

She intensified her grip. "How so?"

His mouth took her in, she screamed with pleasure. A pounding orgasm exploded sending shock waves through her. She guided his rock hard steel into her. He gasped as she took him in.

Their passion triggered an avalanche of orgasms as they peaked together in one explosive climax. Together they tumbled over the cliff of ecstasy.

Clay dropped soft kisses on her face and throat. She wrapped her arms around his neck, pulled his head down, pressing a kiss against the pulse of his neck.

Raising his head. "Woman. You know you have captured my heart."

"Not any less than you have mine." She released him as he rolled to her side. Running her hand over his damp skin, she couldn't think of anything that could top Clay's love making.

His heavy sigh alarmed her. "Is everything alright?"

He laid his arm over his eyes. "That's the problem. Everything is so right."

She quivered with happiness. "So what's the problem?"

He lowered his arm, locked his eyes with hers. "You know I want to do this for the rest of my life."

"I know."

"And..."

"So do I."

His arms grabbed her as he rolled her on top of him. "Then let's do it."

"Are you asking me to marry you, Clay Lester?"

"Not yet. When I do it will be a proper, down on my knees, once in a lifetime event. With a ring, all of it."

She laid her head on his chest. "You know 'all of that' doesn't matter. It's you I want."

"I know. But it's what I want to give you."

His sweetness and her contentment swelled her heart with all the love the future could provide.

As they untangled from each other to redress, she felt light, ready to be what now became her one desire. Clay's wife.

Walking up to Aunt Tilley's house, they trod softly on the gravel walkway. At the back steps, Becca stepped up one to be eye level with Clay. Giving her his final kiss for the night, she glowed as she walked into the house. Tip toeing down the hallway, she slipped into her room. Going to the window, she waved at the waiting Clay. Nodding, he turned, walked away. Leaning on the window sill she watched his figure disappear into the woods.

***

"Oh my lord! Mom do you see what Jonny did?"

Becca shook her head as the walk down memory lane disappeared. Turning her direction towards the boat launch, she chuckled as she witnessed Jon Jr., Kevin Lester and Robby putting two jet skis in the water.

As Becca maneuvered her boat into the slip, she cut the motor. Throwing the lines to Haley on the dock, she turned to watch the boys.

190

Haley shouted back over her shoulder as she ran for the house. "Wait for me. I'm getting in my swim suit."

"Hey Mom, look at these beauties. Kevin said we could try them out."

Becca looked over at Kevin, smiled. "That's nice. Setting me up, Kev?"

Kevin's smile erupted into a full body laugh. "I know how to win over a customer."

The roar of the motor drowned out his words. Becca just nodded. The streak of a body flew by her. Haley waded out into the water. Kevin helped her into her life vest. Holding the Jet Ski for her, he helped her on. Then her two children sped off, a tall gusher of water spouting behind them.

Becca walked off the pontoon, down the dock, over to Kevin and Robby. The three stood, watching the water crafts fade into the distance.

Robby slapped Kevin on the back. "Nice choice." With his hands in his pockets, he

moved in front of them. "Listen Kevin. We're throwing a cook-out tomorrow night to introduce Becca's kids to the lake people. Tell your dad and brothers. Say around fivesh?"

Kevin nodded his acceptation. "Sure we'll come." He walked to his big tow truck, climbed in. "See ya' all tomorrow night. Can I bring a date?"

Becca and Robby spoke at the same time. "Sure."

They watched the truck pull out onto the road. Robby winked at her, then ambled off toward his house, whistling. Becca stared at his back, narrowed her eyes,

Clay will be coming. I guess I never thought about it.

Made sense though. Clay had a hoard of kids the same age as hers.

CHAPTER TEN

Becca sat at her kitchen table writing a to do list for the party this afternoon. If she admitted it, she was excited about entertaining. Oh, she had thrown parties before. Formal, stiff affairs with caterers, stuffy people afraid to laugh too loud or too long. More for networking, being seen in the right place with the right people. Becca chuckled. She always got a kick out of the fact that she became one of the right people.

No, it was more Jon.

He worked at being the right person. She just provided him the backdrop to seek the movers and shakers, as he called them. She thought of them more as superficial and dull. If anyone of them realized the façade she hid behind, they would have applauded, handed her an Oscar.

Tonight would be different. This would be a party of grilled steaks, baked beans and cold beer. Lots of laughter and good times Becca had no doubt.

Jon Jr. shuffled into the kitchen. Going to the coffee pot, he poured a cup, sat down at the table across from his mom.

"What ya' doin'?" He strained his neck to look at her list.

"Making a list for the food tonight. I need to go to the store in town." She looked up at him. "You want to go?"

"Sure. What is this town? Lesterville?" His light blue eyes sparkled with humor.

Becca leaned back, laughed. "You'd think? No, it's called Somerset."

Haley bounced in the room. "Where are you going?"

Jon Jr. stood, put his thumbs in the front belt loops of his jeans. "We're goin' to town Sis."

Haley's face broke out into a huge smile. "I wanta go."

Becca was surprised but glad. "Okay get ready. I have lots to do before this shindig tonight." She grabbed her list, her purse. "Meet you in the car."

Somerset was one of those quaint little towns hidden among the trees and lakes of the countryside. Since Lester Lake was a major summer draw to the little town, the locals worked all winter fixing and sprucing up the town square. It stood clean, colorful, charming.

194

Becca always loved the little town. It seemed to welcome her as she drove down Main Street. Pulling in a parking space in front of the one and only grocery store, her two kids bounced out of the car.

Becca could tell they were chomping at the bit to explore the square. "Go." She waved them off. "Be back in an hour. I'll be done shopping by then."

In unison. "Thanks Mom. Later." The two spilt ways.

An hour later with a cart filled to overflowing, Becca stood in the check-out line. Jon Jr. came in first. Spotting his Mom, he walked over to her line, helping put the sacks in the cart.

"Wow, this is a lot of food. Who's cooking?"

After Becca paid, she locked arms with him. "I am." She knew where this was coming from. They always had a cook. Or a caterer for big doings.

Jon Jr. snickered. "You cook?"

Becca nudged him playfully. "Yes, I can cook."

"Didn't know that about you Mom. Learn something new every day."

Jon Jr. pushed the cart to the car, opened the rear hatch. Haley reached the car at the same time as them.

As the three loaded up the back of the SUV, Becca looked at the two loves of her life. "So what do you think of my little town?"

Haley cocked her head as she opened the passenger side front door. "Your little town? Are you going to stay here?"

Becca didn't know what can of worms this would open, but she decided she didn't want to walk softly anymore. "Yes. I have a home here. And I think I can build a life here." Becca slid behind the steering wheel. Glancing over at Haley she waited for her response.

"I can see that." Haley shrugged her shoulders.

Becca swallowed. "Really?"

Jon Jr. piped up from the back seat. "Yes, Mom. You must not see it, but you have come alive here in lake country."

Haley chimed in. "You look happy."

Starting the car, Becca nodded. "I am. I really am."

"So be happy mom. It's okay."

Becca had never been so proud of her kids. She could feel love surrounding them.

***

Turning into the driveway it looked like the circus came to town. The space between the two houses was filled with white canopies, tables, chairs and men setting up. Becca quickly spotted Clay with three of his sons. She thought hard, Andrew, the oldest, worked with Clay. David the bartender. Feeling the heat come to her cheeks.

I still haven't told my kids I got thrown in jail!

And Stephen the youngest.

196

"What the fuck!" Haley shrieked. "Who the hell are all these cute guys?"

Stopping the car, Becca chuckled. "The boys of Lester Lake. Most of them are Clay's sons."

"Who's Clay?" Haley asked as she got out of the car.

Shit! I hope my voice didn't betray me. Stay cool.

"An old friend."

The three walked to the back of the car as the hatch opened. Haley gave Becca a sly look. "An old flame did you say?"

Becca put her hands on her hips. "Friend. I said friend."

Jon Jr. nudged Haley. "I think you made Mom blush."

Becca grabbed three bags, turned, headed for the house. Now she could feel the blush on her cheeks. Since lately she had decided to be honest with her kids, she wasn't quite ready to explain Clay.

Careful, girl.

Lifting the bags to the kitchen counter, she heard them coming behind her. Pushing her hair out of her eyes, she glanced out the window, spotted Clay. He looked so damn good in his tight jeans and cowboy boots.

Haley's warm breath on Becca's cheek announced her presence. "Which one's Clay?"

Becca turned away from the window. "The older one." She quipped, slipping a little sarcasm in her tone.

Haley chuckled. "Good, cause I want one of the younger ones."

Becca snickered at the quirk of fate if Haley fell in love with one of Clay's sons. Then a sobering thought hit her, she jerked her head to look at her daughter.

What if?

Jon Jr. interrupted her thoughts. "Hey, Mom, what do you want me to do to help?"

Becca turned her attention to Jon Jr. He was looking at the bags, trying to figure out if he could be helpful.

"You know what, go help the men outside." The relief on her son's face was almost comical.

Haley came up behind Becca, hugged her shoulders, kissed her cheek. "I'm going to see what's all going on out there. I'll be back to help in a jiff."

Becca followed Haley with her eyes. "Be easy on them honey. They're just small town boys."

Haley laughed. "I'll try."

Becca watched the two leave by the back door. A smile crossed her face and her heart. The freedom to enjoy her children, her friends, made her all warm and tingling inside.

Lord help the Lester boys!

***

The inviting essence of grilling meat seemed to bring swells of people to the cook-out. Jilley arrived first, bursting through the

198

kitchen door. Becca and Haley were putting the final touches on their cooking.

Both turned at the sound of Jilley's voice. "Girls!"

Becca saw a surprised smile flash across Haley's face. She looked over at her mom. "Jilley?"

Wiping her hands on a dish rag, Becca smiled, nodded. "Haley this is Jilley." Turning to Jilley. "Jilley, my daughter Haley."

Jilley hugged the young girl. "You are beautiful darlin'. Look just like your mother twenty years ago."

Haley pulled back. "You knew Mom way back right?"

"Sure did, honey."

"So who's Clay?" Haley shot Becca a sly look.

Jilley looked at Becca. "You told her about Clay?"

"Just that he's an old friend." Becca narrowed her eyes at Jilley.

Haley leaned in to loudly whisper to Jilley. "There's more isn't there? I met Clay. He's hot."

Jilley and Haley let go of a hardy laugh. Becca tried to act miffed, but she had to smile. She had never seen Haley talk to any of her 'before' friends. But she and Jilley seemed to hit it off.

Becca swiped her dish rag at them. "Enough. Let's get this food out."

All three grabbed what they could carry, headed out the door. Jilley almost bumped into Jon Jr.

"Oh my! And who would you be?"

With her arms full, Becca swung her body. "Jilley, my son Jon Jr. Jon, Jilley an old 'dear' friend."

"Wow. Glad to meet you." Jilley could only nod.

"Nice to meet you, ma'am. Need any help Mom?"

"There's some things left on the counter."

Jon Jr. held the door as the three women scooted through. "Got it, Mom." The screen door slammed with a bang.

Jilley nudged Becca's side. "Nice lookin' boy. Take after his dad?"

"Pretty much. But in looks only."

"You failed to mention Jon is good-lookin'."

"I never said he was ugly, just an idiot."

The two women laughed as they approached the table set up for the food. Offering their wares, Susie took the dishes, placed them on the table.

"Nice work girls. It all looks good."

Becca noticed Haley beaming. "Haley helped. Actually…" Becca looked at her daughter. "…she seemed to enjoy it."

"I did. I guess I forgot to tell you, I changed my major to culinary arts."

"You want to be a cook?"

"Chef, Mom. I want to be a chef."

A young man walked up behind Haley, took a piece of bread, dipped it in the rich cream sauce, popped it in his mouth. "This is good." He spoke close to her cheek.

Andrew. Got this one.

Haley giggled. "Thanks, glad you like it."

Andrew took her hand. "Let's get a beer."

Watching them walk off, Becca spoke back over her shoulder to Jilley and Susie. "I think

I could use one of those beers."

Jilley placed her hands on Becca's shoulder. "Like history repeating itself?"

Indeed.

***

At dusk, small sparkly lights came on to give the cook-out a fairy-land appearance. Everyone was having a great time. Becca, amazed that, when all of the younger generation got together, years dropped away. The lost years of weddings, births, school days now college. The gang from that summer stood on the sidelines, watch the next batch of their families emerge as adults.

Becca sat alone at one of the picnic tables, sipping an ice cold beer. The day had been warm, but not the stifling heat that was yet to come. The evening brought a refreshing chill. Enjoying the coolness, she wiped the moisture from her face with a napkin.

Haley and Jon Jr. seemed to fit right in. As she expected, Jon Jr. was smitten with Franny. They made a cute couple. Franny may look petite and fluffy, but she gave Jon Jr. a run for his money when they mounted the jet skis.

Haley and Andrew? Becca was unsure of how she felt about that. Becca always thought of Haley as more like her dad. The sure, social figure, standing aware of people around her. Becca knew her as the fun-loving girl with a fascination for life. But to see her take to the lake crowd like it was her place to belong; Becca liked her new daughter. The one no long keeping two lives separate, but joining a third life to relish the taste of living.

And her change in majors.

What is that all about?

Becca had no idea. Sad she didn't know about it, but the last four years put a void in her life. The day she and Jon left Haley at college had scared the hell out of Becca.

***

The flight to San Francisco took only a couple hours. Jon secured the company plane, so there were no lay-overs, baggage checks or crowds to deal with. Becca swiped at her grey Chanel pantsuit. Proper in its presence, but a statement in style. It spoke of money as did everything Jon touched.

Haley had been super excited about the college of her choice. Berkley. Her major was business. Jon would have preferred she go to one of the top ten, but on this Haley held her ground.

202

Becca remembered picking up the catalog for Berkley. "This is where you want to go?"

Haley stood from her desk, leaned her chin on Becca's shoulder. "Yes. It has a great history with a kind of an artsy atmosphere. It just sounds like fun."

"You know your Dad will pay for you to go anywhere."

"I know. And this is where I want to go."

Becca shrugged. A pain stabbed at her heart, her only daughter would be hundreds of miles away. Still, Becca would not refuse Haley anything she set her heart on.

A black limo waited in the parking lot of the charter hangar. A driver opened the back door for the three. Haley slid in, Becca followed. Jon gave instructions to the driver, then crawled in.

Watching the buildings of the city pass by, Becca leaned her chin on her fist. The silence hung like a fog inside the car. Jon was on his phone, checking messages. Haley had the brochure spread across her knees, looking at different pictures, writing in a notebook.

Crossing the bay, Becca could understand why Haley chose this place. It was not only different from home, it carried the feel of adventure.

"The moving van will meet us there." Jon's words cut though Becca's thoughts. She turned her head to look at him. They were always following a plan, she thought.

Haley's eyes lit up with excitement. "Good."

Becca went back to watching the scenery. Trying to keep a handle on everything, she reminded herself she still had Jon Jr. at home. But, in two years she would be sending him off to college. Never had the emptiness of her life exposed itself so cruelly.

The limo slowed down, wound its way through the narrow streets of the campus. Stopping behind a moving van, the driver of the limo came back to open the door on Jon's side. Haley jumped out first. Jon followed her, then turned to offer his hand to Becca.

Instead, Becca opened her door. Standing on the sidewalk, she looked up at the large dorm building in front of her. Haley ran around the car, grabbed Becca's hand.

"Come on, Mom. Let's find my room." Haley pulled Becca beside her.

Up several fights of stairs, they found her floor, finally her room. The décor was stark, the room bare. Haley picked out her own furniture and colors. Bright and cheerful, it would give this space an upgrade.

For the next four hours, Jon, Becca and Haley emptied boxes, set up furniture. The moving men did most of the assembly. For a price.

Finally the room was complete. Becca gave Haley a thumbs up on her choices.

So this will be her home for the next four years.

"We need to get going Becca. We are scheduled to fly out in an hour."

Becca bit her lower lip.

It was time.

Pulling herself up, she raised her inner wall, walking stiffly to her daughter. Haley smiled to acknowledge she understood her Mom's demure countenance.

Haley whispered as she hugged Becca. "Are you going to be all right?"

The words almost brought Becca's wall crashing down. But she recovered, kissed Haley's cheek. "Yes. I will be fine. You have a great time here. Keep in touch as I will miss you terribly. But I still have Jon Jr." Becca pulled back to look into Haley's hazel eyes. The two women laughed and put their heads together as if they were sharing a deep secret.

Letting go of Haley was like letting go of her heart. She patted her daughter's arms, moved away.

Jon came up to Haley, hugged her quickly. "Call if you need anything."

"I will daddy."

Jon stuttered. "See you later."

"Bye."

Becca stood watching the scene. It seemed cold, forced to her. Jon quickly released his daughter, moved to take Becca's arm.

Guiding her out of the door, Becca glanced over her shoulder quickly stealing one last look of her daughter in her new home.

I love you. Becca mouthed.

Haley smiled, mouthed back. "Back at ya'."

***

"Hey, Mom." The soft touch of Haley's hands on Becca's shoulders ended her thoughts of days gone by.

Becca covered Haley's hands with her own. "Hey baby. How's it goin'?"

"Great." Haley sat down next to Becca.

Andrew sat down across from the two women. Becca smiled at him. "Hi Andrew."

"Ma'am." He tilted his head.

"Okay, we need to stop this ma'am stuff. Call me Becca, will you?"

"Yes, ma'am." A broad smile creased his face as they all chuckled.

"You know Andrew?"

"Yes, he helped put the new windows in the studio. I think I've met all your brothers, except one..."

"Thomas."

Becca looked over the crowd. "Is he here?"

"No, he stays pretty much away from any kind of gathering."

Becca wanted to probe, but decided against it. "Maybe I'll run into him one day."

206

"Run into who?" Clay's sexy voice cut into the conversation. He sat down next to Andrew.

Becca had spent most of the day staying as far away from Clay as she could without being rude. Watching him from a distance, she felt old flames lick at her core, but she didn't want the kids to ponder the likelihood that anything could be going on.

Andrew answered the question. "Thomas. Becca hasn't met him."

"Probably won't." Clay rubbed his forehead. "He pretty much avoids us as much as possible."

Again Becca wanted to ask questions, but stopped herself. She just didn't feel like now was the right time

Instead, she changed the subject. "I for one think this is a great party?"

Haley stretched her hand across the table toward Andrew. His hand met her half way, took ahold.

A band started playing some upbeat country song. Andrew nodded at Haley.

"Yes." She stood up, looked down at Becca. "Mom?" Haley's glaze darted over to Clay.

"No, honey. " Becca felt caught between a rock and a hard place. She shook her head. "I'm not really good at dancing to this kind of music."

Clay's outstretched hand made her silently gasp. She looked up into his electric eyes that sparked with mischief.

"Come on, Becca. Let's trip the light fandango. Show the youngsters how it's done."

Either the beer or the lack of common sense made her take the challenge. "You're on cowboy."

Slipping her hand into his, her heart leaped in her chest. He led her to the dance floor, pulling her into his arms. While everyone else was rocking, he led her into a light two step. The years fell away, they were young again. As if none of the past years happened.

Clay, with a light pressure on the small of her back, drew her into him. Becca's chin was at his shoulder height. Memories of her face nestling in his neck surfaced, bringing a sweet familiar feeling. His smell of musk and leather always pleased her senses. It still remained, so did the feeling.

Their bodies moved together to the soft beat of the music. She had not danced in years. Surprised by how she flowed into it so easily, the hardness of his body only excited the long dead feelings of intimacy.

Relax girl. It's only a dance with a good friend.

Bullshit!

This is me recognizing the biggest mistake I made in my sorry life.

Running her hand along his shoulder, she cupped the back of his neck. A low groan in his chest gave her chills. He pulled her closer. Willingly, she molded to him. Her bare legs brushed against the rough fabric of his jeans.

Becca was not surprised she responded to him. He would always be the love of her life. Her first true love. For once, Becca accepted that her feelings for Clay never died. She just buried them so deep they could not fight to the surface.

Now, Becca's wall came crumbling down. Brick by brick it fell from the moment she accepted her marriage was over. She could make a new life, especially now that the two most important relationships in her life came to be with her.

The contentment of finally being able to be herself after so many years of the false Becca, caused her to moan, snuggling into the comfort of Clay's arms.

"Becca?" He whispered in her ear.

"Mmmm."

"The music stopped. The band is taking a break."

Stunned Becca pulled back, looked at him, then glanced around the crowd. Everyone was standing around staring at them.

Becca hid her face in his chest. "I am so embarrassed."

The sweet vibration of Clay's chest told her he was chuckling.

CHAPTER ELEVEN

The morning sun streamed through the open window of the room where Haley slept. The light breeze caressed her cheek, she smiled. Stretching out, she welcomed the morning. Looking over at two walls of windows, she caught a glimpse of the lake. The memories of the night before washed over her.

Andrew!

Haley moved her legs as if she was running under the covers.

What a great night.

***

Haley followed her brother out the door, all heads turned in her direction. Stopping short, she glanced at the young men working so hard. There was one older guy, about her Mom's age. She had a feeling it was Clay.

Haley walked straight over to him, held out her hand. "Are you Clay?"

The man straightened up, looked her in the eyes.

Damn, he is mighty good looking for his age. And those eyes!

"I am. And who would you be darlin'?"

"I'm Haley. Becca's daughter." She pointed her thumb toward the house.

Clay pushed back his cowboy hat. Looking toward the house, he smiled. "You're as pretty as your mother."

Haley blushed.

This man is a charmer. If her mother didn't have a fling with him, she is crazy.

"Thanks. Mom said you and her were old friends."

Clay wrinkled his brow. "Becca told you about me?"

Haley caught the wry smile. "Not nearly enough. Is there is a story?"

Clay ran his tongue inside his cheek. "Only if Becca says there is."

The mystery behind the smile intrigued Haley.

I have a feeling there is a lot more than I'm getting from either of them. Hummm!

One of the younger boys walked up to them. His eyes traveled down her body, making her skin tingle just by his look.

Clay stepped back. "Andrew this is Haley. Becca's daughter."

Andrew stretched out his hand. She slipped her hand in his. His skin was warm and she could feel the calluses on his palms and fingers.

His smile was lopsided, a dimple creased his cheek. "Glad to meet you. Going to be here long?"

Haley shifted from one foot to the other. He still held her hand. "I don't know. I haven't decided yet."

"W e l l..." Andrew's eyes shot sparks of wickedness. "Let me see if I can convince you to

stay. Come meet the rest of gang."

Haley let him guide her. Watching the muscles in his back, the way his jeans hugged his firm ass, she smiled.

This might be the best summer ever!

***

The smell of freshly brewed coffee opened up Haley's senses. Throwing back the covers, she felt the soft area rug hug her toes. Standing, she adjusted her boxer shorts, straightened her tank top. Padding down the hall, she passed Jonny's door and smiled. He had a good time last night. She was glad. This parent thing hit him hard, as her baby brother she worried about him. Always Jonny to her, never Jon Jr., she felt the Jr. put him as a second to the Sr. Jonny was never second to anything, especially their father. Jon Sr. was a cold, calculating businessman who displayed his family as trophies. Jonny was a sensitive soul with a compassion for life and other people. He had a creative side few

212

knew of, especially their parents. Haley visited him at his college, saw his art work. She didn't know where it came from, but he made the canvas come to life.

Entering the main room, Haley found her mother on the laptop at the dining room table.

"Morning, Mom."

Becca looked up, smiled. "Morning sunshine."

Haley looked around for a clock. "Is it still morning?"

"It's only ten. You're still safe. What gets you up on this fine Sunday morning?"

"The smell of your divine coffee." Haley turned toward the kitchen. "I'll be right back."

Moving into the kitchen, she was warmed by the sight of the lake from all the many windows. Searching for the coffee pot, she just followed her nose. Grabbing a cup out of the cupboard, she poured the rich brown liquid, savoring the aroma.

What a view! This is certainly better to wake up to than the manicured garden behind the house at home.

Walking back to Becca in the dining room, Haley took a chair across from her mother. Taking the first sip, enjoying the rich flavor, she cocked her head, watching Becca type. Her hands stopped, a small smile creased her lips.

"What are you doing, Mom?"

Becca looked over the lid, smiled. "Your aunt Tilley was a very good artist, but more than that a famous artist. She had pieces of work all over the world. I am tracking them. Some of the canvases are breath taking." She turned the screen towards Haley. "Look."

Haley took in a quick breath. On the screen was a scene of rain falling on a lake. Vibrant colors captured the warmth and softness of the showering mist. For a moment Haley was standing in the picture, the tepid drops hitting her skin like a sweet caress. So real, Haley could almost feel the spray on her face. Transported to the special scene, the elements came alive, the feelings of being alive and content washed over her.

"Man, she is good." Haley could hardly pry her eyes from the picture. "I saw the studio.

Jonny would like it."

Becca frowned. "Our Jon Jr.?"

Turning the laptop back to Becca, Haley shrugged. "Yeah, our Jon. He quite the talented artist."

"Really?" Her mother's surprise did not shock Haley. Since Jonny went off to college, life had been rough for Becca. Then this separation thing.

My dad is such an ass.

"Yeah, Mom. He is awesome when he gets a paint brush in his hand."

214

A crackly male voice interrupted their conversation. "Who are you talking about?" Jonny stood in the doorway in his pj bottoms, his mass of hair tousled, twice its size.

"You little brother."

"Oh, okay. Gotta gets some coffee." He turned, shuffled toward the kitchen.

Haley watched her mom suck on her lower lip. She stretched out her hand, placed it on her mother's forearm. "Don't beat yourself up. He isn't really forthcoming about it."

Jonny came back to the table. "So what about me?"

Haley turned the laptop screen toward him. "This is some of Aunt Tilley's work. I can see where you get your talent."

Jonny, in the middle of a sip, narrowed his eyes, swallowed hard. "Oh, my... that is beyond words." He squinted, looked closer. "Where is it at? It says Madrid Spain."

Haley took up the conversation with enthusiasm. "Yes, she has her work all over the world."

Jonny leaned back. "Wow she is good."

"And so are you. Tell Mom your plans."

Jonny looked from one to another, frowned at Haley, then softened his scowl, finally looking at his Mom. "I changed my major to art. My teacher said I had a real gift. I am also studying commercial art to make a living, but my real passion..." He paused as if not sure of his position. "...is fine art." He nodded towards the laptop. "Like this."

Haley watched Becca's face for her reaction. They just dropped two bombshells on her about their majors.

The silence was long and painful. Becca looked from one to the other. Taking each one of their hands, she spoke in a soft, gentle voice. "I'm proud of both of you. You have chosen your paths based on your heart's desire." Haley felt the squeeze of her hand. "Does your father know?"

Haley and Jonny replied in unison. "No."

***

Andrew drove his 4x4 silver truck in silence. Stephen sat at shotgun. Andrew's thoughts were on the girl with hair the color of a fine polished wood table. Oak, light blonde with streaks of brown. Hazel eyes that could hypnotize a man into surrendering.

Not that I would mind.

Never before had he been so taken with a girl. Going home with the worst hard-on, he writhed in his bed, struggling to not think of her. Little good it did. When sleep finally did come, she invaded his dreams. Waking up wringing with sweat, he took a cold, very cold shower, begging his over aroused body to please settle down.

Turning down the one lane road with the sign reading *Copper Beach*, they bumped along until the road peaked, then opened up to a sandy beach surrounded by trees. It was a cove off of Lester

Lake. A hang-out for the young'uns and had been for a long time, if the stories were true.

Pulling to a stop, he swung out, down from the truck. Wearing only swim trunks, Ray-ban sunglasses, his tousled good-looks turned the heads of every female on the beach. Always wearing a cowboy hat, he knew his effect on the women.

Yells acknowledged his arrival. He scouted the people on the beach, not seeing the one he wanted. His disappointment hit him in the stomach. A low pain gripping him in his loins, felt unbearable.

Before he got half-way down to where most of the people gathered, he heard the crunch of gravel under tires. Out of curiosity, or just plain hope, he turned to see the new arrival. He was not disappointed.

The white Mercedes-Benz convertible held three people. The driver was the one bringing a big smile to his face.

Haley.

Whipping around, he sauntered up to the car. Whistling low, he ran his hand over the fender, like stroking a lover. "Damn, this is some car, lady."

Haley opened her door, stepped out, damn near dropping him to his knees. Her fine body barely covered with a small swimming suit, wearing Coach Sunglasses. He couldn't see her eyes, but he knew they all but snapped with a challenge.

"Like her do you?"

His look traveled down Haley's body. "Not as much as the woman driving it."

"Good answer." She ran her fingernails down his bare chest. "So what's happening cowboy?"

A deep robust laugh echoed from him as he took her in his arms. "Everything good, now that you're here."

The sound of the other two people getting out of the car, made him turn his head.

"Hey, Franny. Jon. Good to see you guys." Speaking to them, his eyes went back to hers.

Giving him a sexy, half-smile. "So show me what you locals do around here for fun."

She so makes me smile.

"Not much. We swim, play volleyball, drink cold beer. What did you have in mind, darlin'?"

Moving her arms around his waist, she pressed against him. "Sounds good to me."

***

Summer was at its peak, the scorching hot days only heated up young bodies already at their boiling point. Days were spent at the beach, nights gathered around in a circle.

Jonny hung during the day with Franny, Kevin from the boat shop and Jilley's youngest daughter, Wendy.

The four would meet at Copper Beach around noon. The sizzling afternoons were filled with water sports to stay cool. Jonny loved his jet skis. Franny could keep up with him, sometimes even whipped his ass in endurance.

As soon as the sun went down, the four would gather around the fire pit to roast hot dogs, indulge in ice cold beers. There was never any drinking other than water when on the lake. The drinks in the evening were to refresh, to enjoy, never to become sloppy drunk. To the group it was lame.

Some days Kevin didn't show until almost dark. And on rainy days, Jonny went to the marina to help, shoot the shit with the guys.

Jonny and Kevin were working on the motor of a large, beautiful speed boat. Jonny was sitting on the side of the big motor, working under the cover.

Deep in thought about his task, Jonny half listened to Kevin's chatter. Then two words together in the same sentence, brought his head up.

"Your Dad and my Mom? What?"

Kevin narrowed his eyes. "They had a thing years ago. I know Dad never got over it. Your Mom never told you?"

Jonny shook his head.

That explains a lot.

"So what happened?"

"There was a bad accident on Crawl River Bridge. I don't know exactly what went down, but your mom left."

Jonny was totally baffled. "How do you know this?"

"My parents argued about it all the time." Kevin's eyes reflected his indifference.

"Is that what broke them up?"

"Not so much. My Mom is a piece of work. The rumor is she married Dad for his money and name." Kevin minimizing the importance of the subject, puzzled Jonny.

"Do you think that?"

Kevin looked up from his work. "Wouldn't surprise me."

The conversation took a lull. Jonny was trying absorb the information just dropped on him.

Jonny cocked his head. "So who is this mysterious brother that never comes around?"

"Thomas. Oh, he comes around. When he gets into trouble he runs home to Mama, she rags on Dad until he pays to make it all go away."

"Little bitterness there?" Jonny was taken back at how Kevin's malice as he spit out the words.

"Somewhat. Dad's a good man. He loves all his sons. Thomas just breaks his heart." Kevin ran his hand over his hair. "I think he's buried all the pain of losing your mom by switching to raising his sons. His way of moving on."

"Wow. I never would have thought." Jonny shook his head. Quite the too much information day.

"Your mom never mentioned it?"

"No. But she hides a lot." Jonny turned the wrench to loosen a nut.

"I like her. David said she was funnier than hell the night she got put in jail."

Jonny jerked his head up so fast he hit it on the motor cover. "She what? In jail?'

Kevin chuckled. "Yeah, her, Jilley and Susie. They got smashed at the bar then wanted to drive home. Ben Cooper stopped them by putting them in jail. My dad went down to bail her out."

"Really?" Jonny went deep into thought.

So Clay came to her rescue. I doubt my Dad would.

No way. He would have a fit!

"Sorry dude. I guess I said too much." Kevin's word cut though his thoughts.

Jon Jr. shook his head. "No. You just explained a lot about my mother I didn't know."

***

Arriving home, Jonny found his mom sitting on the porch, sheltered from the rain, reading. Haley came out the door carrying a drink, looked like iced tea.

"Hey, Jonny. Where you been?

Becca looked up, smiling as he walked up the stairs.

"At the marina helping Kevin. You, sis?"

A look of pleasure crossed her face. "Roaming around the town."

"With Andrew?"

Haley shot him a look. "Yes, with Andrew. He couldn't work today, because of the rain."

Jonny stopped in front of them, leaned on the railing, folded his arms across his chest.

"So, Mom. When were you going to tell us about your night in jail?"

Haley busted out laughing, looking over at Becca. "Jail? Mom? You were in jail? What the hell did you do? Rob a bank? Or..." She looked over at Jonny with a big smile on her face, raising her eyebrows. ...kill someone?"

Jonny noticed the deep blush creeping up Becca's face. He cocked his head. "Well?"

Becca took a deep breath. "It wasn't anything like robbing a bank, nor did I kill someone. Jilley, Susie and I got slightly intoxicated. We were put in jail until someone came to take us home. That's all."

"Not quite." Jonny smiled a wicked grin. Keeping his eyes on his mother, he spoke to Haley. "Guess who came to get Mom?"

Haley looked over at Becca. "Who?"

222

Becca shot him a sharp look. Jonny couldn't resist being the bearer of such news. "Clay

Lester."

Haley was properly surprised. "No!"

Jonny watched as the color drained from his mother's face.

Bingo!

***

Andrew picked Haley up from her house promptly at five. She emerged dressed nice, but definitely sexy. The dress long, sheer, and black, flowed around her body like melted chocolate. The halter top accented her perky breasts to their best advantage.

A low whistle came from Andrew as she opened the door to him. "Gawd girl, you are beautiful!"

Slithering by him, she gave him her best smile. "Like what you see?"

"Love what I see." He followed her to his truck, reached around to open the door. Putting his hands on her waist, he lifted her into the cab. Haley watched him run around the truck to get in the driver's side.

Once seated, he started the motor. "Where to lovely lady?"

Haley unfolded a piece of paper she had hidden in her hand, reading the name. "Do you know of a little town named Spring Hill?"

Andrew hesitated before putting the truck in gear. "Yeah. It's about thirty-minutes from here. Why?"

"There's an art gallery there called, Shawnmaker's?"

"Yeah?"

"Can we go there? It stays open until seven?" Haley searched his eyes.

Andrew shrugged. "Sure. But why?"

"They have some of my Aunt Tilley's work. I want to see it."

"You've never seen her work?"

"Just on the internet. I'd like to see it in person."

Andrew shifted the truck. "Okay, darlin'. Anything for you."

Haley slid over next to him, tucking her arm in his. "Thanks."

***

Jonny entered the studio like it was a sanctuary, with reverence and awe. It was equipped with everything an artist would want. The windows gave the most natural light.

He stopped at the canvas on the easel. A stunning couple in a loving embrace, done in shades of blue. It couldn't have been painted by Aunt Tilley. It was too new.

Mom?

He couldn't think of anyone else.

"You like?" Becca's voice sounded behind him.

Turning he smiled at her standing in the doorway. "Yes. You?"

Walking into the room she went to the painting. "Yeah. It felt good to pick up a paint brush after all these years."

224

"Why did you hide it? I never saw you paint."

"There wasn't a place for it in my life. Plus, it brought back painful memories."

Jon Jr. put his arms around her shoulders. "All kidding aside, Mom. What happened here all those years ago? Was Clay part of it?"

He felt her take a deep sigh. She kept her face away from him. "It was the summer before I graduated. I fell in love with a boy. Clay. Then my world came crashing down."

"The accident at Crawl River Bridge?"

Becca turned to look at her son. "You've done your homework. How do you know about that?"

"The kids around here talk."

Becca moved away from him, went to stand by the windows. The rain did a dance on the lake. With an underlying bitterness. "It was a turning point in my life."

Jonny put his hands in his pockets, watching his mother's body language. Never had he seen her so vulnerable. It must have been an awful incident for her to never mention it. His unemotional mom was filled with all sorts of baggage.

Becca wiped her eyes, turned to look at him. "So, tell me about this interest in painting."

Jonny recognized the wall he hit. Not wanting to cause her pain, he allowed her to change the subject. "I always liked to draw. So when I went to college, I dabbled in painting. I found it opened up a world of emotions and joy." He finished with a shrug.

His Mom smiled at him. "It does do that, doesn't it?"

For once, Jonny felt he was on the same wave link as her. "Yeah. So I switched to Commercial Art."

"And how is that working for you?"

"Good. I have some clients I do work for. It would pay the bills if need be."

Becca walked over to her son with a look of pride on her face. "Then follow your heart honey."

"Do you wish you followed yours?" He nodded toward her painting. "You're pretty good."

A sadness crossed her eyes. "I don't know. Things are what they are."

"Mom. It's not too late for you to change your direction."

Becca chuckled. "I think it has already changed for me. Pretty much by someone else."

"Then this time do it your way."

"You know I don't regret everything. I have you and Haley. You both are so worth it." She patted Jon Jr.'s cheek.

He grabbed her hand, held it. "You will always have us. But go your own way, Mom. You deserve it."

Becca nodded. He could see the tears at the edge of her eyes. Without saying anything else, she left.

226

Jon Jr. looked around the studio. Finding a fresh canvas, he lifted it to an empty easel.

Picking out the brushes, mixing his paint on a palette, he escaped into his own utopia world of colors and shapes.

***

Andrew parked his truck in front of the art gallery, walked around to open the door for Haley.

Taking her hand, he led her inside. Haley stopped, looked around until she saw the banner "Tilley Young". She led Andrew into the room filled with the style and color of her aunt's work. Starting just inside the door, she stopped in front of every painting. The colors were muted yet energetic. The style unmistakably Tilley.

She loved it. "She's quite good. I never knew."

Andrew's breath warmed her neck as he spoke. "She's our local celebrity."

Haley leaned back against him. "Did you know her?"

His body vibrated as he chuckled. "Yeah I knew her. I grew up with her. She and Dad were great friends. I guess she hauled his ass up when he was drowning the pain of losing your mom in liquor." Andrew put his arms around her waist. "Your mother never said anything about it?

Haley shook her head. "No. I didn't know anything about Clay until I got here. Why do you know so much?"

"It's been the talk of the town for years. The tragedy of Lester Lake."

"Tragedy? Them breaking up was considered a tragedy?"

"No, the accident on Crawl River. Two of their closest friends died. Your mother just left. Never told anyone why. Not even Tilley."

The sadness of the story touched Haley's soul. For mom to carry it all these years and never tell anyone.

Moving on around the room, Haley studied the paintings. The things she was finding out. Her great-aunt was a famous artist and her mother loved a man before her dad. Now some kind of tragic accident had changed the course of her mom's life.

Haley reached the painting of the young boy. His intense eyes and youthful face looked back at her. She stepped forward to read the title.

"Jeffery." She spoke out loud. "Who's Jeffery?"

"No idea. I never saw Tilley with anyone. There were stories..."

Haley turned, narrowed her eyes at him. "Stories? What kind of stories."

Andrew laughed as he drew her to him. "Let's just say art wasn't Tilley's only passion."

"Aunt Tilley?"

"She was quite the woman. You are a lot like her."

"How so?" She tickled his ribs.

Jumping at her touch, he grabbed her hands. "You're warm, passionate and sexy."

"Thank you for the compliment, but Aunt Tilley. Sexy?"

"Oh, lord yes. She could give every guy she met a hard on. Young and old."

Something else I didn't know. This has been a very enlightening summer.

A man in a dark, expensive suit entered the room. "Andrew, I didn't see you come in. "

Andrew took one of his hands off of Haley to shake the man's hand. "Mr. Shawnmaker." He gently pushed Haley forward. "This is Haley, the great-niece of the artist." He waved his hand at the portrait of 'Jeffery'.

The man took Haley's hand into both of his. "So nice to meet you. Tilley was a great lady as well as a good artist."

Haley looked back at Andrew. "Yeah. I hear as a lady she was a little on the shady side." They both snickered.

"Excuse me?" Mr. Shawnmaker frowned at her words.

Haley smiled at the clueless man. "Nothing. Private joke."

Stepping away from Andrew she circled the room. "Yes, I am just finding out..."

The last painting made her stop. The picture of a bridge on a dark, eerie night, the moon the only light. A haze blurred the picture even though the lines were sharp.

Without turning around, she motioned to Andrew. "Andrew? Is this the bridge?" Then the plate with the words, 'Crawl River Bridge' jumped out at her.

Coming up behind her, Andrew stood silent for a few moments as he studied the painting. Finally he spoke on the back of her neck. "Yes. That's it. Funny I never knew she painted it."

Mr. Shawnmaker interrupted. "That painting just came into our possession. Matter of fact, your dad brought it in just a few months ago."

Haley turned to look at Andrew's face. It radiated his surprise. "He did? I never saw it before."

Mr. Shawnmaker shrugged. "He said something about it was time to let the world see it. He enjoyed its beauty long enough."

"When was this?" Andrew held Haley's shoulders.

"This spring. Just before summer."

The words hit Haley hard. When her mom came here.

Andrew gripped her tighter. "Thank you Mr. Shawnmaker." He lifted his left hand up even with Haley's face. "Oh, look darling. It's almost time for our reservation." Spinning Haley around, Andrew nodded at the man. Grasping her hand he half drug her away, Haley took one more look at the bridge. For some reason it haunted her.

With her mind swirling from too many new facts, not enough information, she was surprised when Andrew stopped. They were inside a little bistro. Andrew requested a 'quiet' table. The dining room was dimly lit, decorated in shades of gray and maroon. Not real full, the host stopped at a booth in a corner.

"Will this do Sir?"

Andrew nodded. "Yes. Nice. Thank you." He stepped back to let Haley slide in first.

"Could we have some water, please?"

"Certainly." The man snapped his fingers, a young boy came with a pitcher of iced water, filled the empty glasses.

Sitting down next to Haley, Andrew picked up the nearest glass. "Drink."

Without arguing, Haley let the cold liquid bring her back into focus. In a hoarse voice she looked at Andrew. "Thanks. I needed that."

"Look, I'm sorry I am the bearer of bad news. I just grew up with the stories. I guess I figured you knew."

"It's okay." Haley shook her head. "I guess I never thought about Mom having a life before Dad."

"Were they happy?"

"I don't know. I mean they never seemed unhappy. They just got along. Went through the motions." She titled her head, looked at him. "Your parents?"

Andrew leaned back, put his arm on the back of the seat behind her. "Fought all the time like banshees. Dad finally left after Stephen was born. Built him a house, raised all of us except for Thomas. He is Mama's boy."

"Does that bother you?"

"Only that Thomas is a leach." The words sounded more like a hiss.

Haley had to smile. "You don't get along?"

"It's not that. I barely see him. He's just…"

"Just what?"

"Different than the rest of us I guess. My brothers and I like to work. Thomas likes to play. Never worked a day in his life."

Haley snuggled into his side. "Different strokes for different folks, I guess."

He kissed the top of her head. "You and your brother seem to get along."

Haley smiled at the thought of Jonny. "He's a peach. We always have each other's back."

Andrew stiffened. "Speak of the devil."

A polished version of the Lester brothers entered the room. Talking to the waiter, he stopped cold, then smiled when he saw them. Patting the man's back, he sauntered over toward them. "Andrew, my brother." His tone like his hair is smooth and oily.

"Thomas. What are you doing in Spring Hill?"

232

Thomas pulled a chair from a nearby table, sat down. "Having dinner with our mother."

Haley felt Andrew jerk. She put her hand on his leg, felt his thigh muscles tighten.

"Mother's coming here?"

"Yes, dear brother. Would you and your lady like to join us?" His eyes focused on Haley. She squirmed under his direct stare.

I don't like him. There's an undercurrent of mean.

Andrew took her hand under the table, squeezed it, his manner cool and controlled.

"We'll pass."

"And who is this lovely lady?" Thomas cocked his head.

"Tilley's great-niece, Haley."

There was a slight pause. "Nice to meet you, Haley."

Haley nodded. Looking up she saw a stick thin woman coming up behind him. She carried a powerful presence. Immediately she disliked this woman.

As the woman approached, Andrew slid out of the booth. "Mother." He leaned in, kissed her cheek.

No, wait. This is Andrew's mother.

The woman glared at Haley as she accepted Andrew's kiss. "And who is this Andrew?"

Andrew sighed, looked over at Haley. "This is Haley, Mother. Haley, my mother Veronica Lester."

"She's Tilley's great-niece." Thomas piped up.

Veronica narrowed her eyes, sending a chill down Haley spine. "Becca's kid?"

Haley couldn't speak. She reached for Andrew's hand. Once she felt the warmth, she nodded.

Andrew stood up to his mother. "Yes, mother. Becca's daughter. Got a problem with that?"

"Don't let her get her claws in you. You know they never let go."

Andrew went into a defensive mode. "Mother, I think your table is ready."

The anger rose in Veronica's face as she debated whether to accept his dismissal or not. Thomas broke the standoff by standing up from his chair.

"He's right Mother."

"Will you join us?" Veronica's words were full of insincerity.

Thomas took her arm. "Already asked and answered. They want to dine alone."

Haley could tell Veronica only allowed Thomas to manipulate her to avoid a public scene. Pushing his mother ahead of him, Thomas spoke back. "Nice seeing you brother. Haley, another time."

Andrew stood, watching the couple leave. Biting his lower lip, he frowned. "Sorry about that."

Haley let out a long breath. "So that's your mother. Nice."

234

Andrew sat back down. He put his arms around her. "I was hoping you wouldn't meet her until the wedding."

"So I couldn't refuse."

"Something like that."

Haley realized this was a hard thing for him. "Look, how about we head for home. I could use a good hamburger from Brick's.

The big smile on Andrew's face told her she said the right thing. He kissed her cheek. "Thanks babe."

CHAPTER TWELVE

Haley took a big bite of the huge, juicy hamburger. The grease rolled over her fingers, dribbled down her arm. She started to laugh as she looked over at Andrew, saw him also covered in hamburger juices, with mustard on his cheek.

Still gripping her sandwich with both hands she leaned over, licked his cheek. He quickly turned, planted a sloppy, hamburger-flavored kiss on her lips.

Haley licked her lips. "Mmmm. My favorite flavor. Onion, pickles and meat on a bun."

Andrew smiled, nodding with his mouth still full.

David came over, turned a chair around, plopped down, leaning his elbows on the back. "So what brings you two here tonight? Really Andrew, I thought you would treat a class-act girl like this to a fancy dinner somewhere special."

236

Taking a swallow, Andrew shrugged. "I tried. But she wanted to come to this joint."

"Where did you try?" David chuckled.

"A restaurant in Spring Hill."

"So what happened?"

"It seems it's Mother and Thomas's date night." The hostility hung in the air.

"Oh, I see. Why Spring Hill?"

"We went to see Tilley's art in the gallery."

David turned to Haley. "What did you think?"

"I was blown away. Especially the bridge."

David looked over at Andrew. "The bridge? I don't remember a bridge?"

"I hadn't either. Evidently dad gave it to the gallery a few months ago. "

Haley chirped in. "About the time my mom arrived."

David's eyes lit up, a sly smile creased his mouth. "Yeah. Dad has done a lot of different things since Becca showed up."

Leaning back in her chair, Haley wiped her mouth with the paper napkin. "Mom's changed too. For the good, but it's like she has emerged from a shell to be free."

"Dad whistles a lot. And walks with a lighter step."

"Did he really come to bail her out of jail?" Haley leaned forward, resting her elbows on the table.

Andrew and David chuckled together.

"Yes, she was madder than a firecracker. I could see he was getting a kick out of it." David shook his head. "I don't think I have ever seen the old man so intrigued by a woman."

"My mother gets all giddy when we mention him."

"Your mom's still married?"

"Not for long. When I was home I saw the divorce papers on my dad's desk."

Andrew put his hand on her arm. "I'm sorry. We've been through it. Not fun."

"Did you feel guilty because you felt it was a good thing?" Haley searched both faces.

David patted her shoulder. "Yes. At first you feel you are betraying them by wishing they would stay apart."

Andrew squeezed her arm. "But when you see them come to life and be happy, you accept it as the best thing. Some animosity remains between them, but it's not an all the time ugliness."

Haley hesitated to speak the next words, but they were burning inside her. "Do you think your dad and my mom will ever get together?"

David and Andrew exchanged looks. "I think it would be the best thing for both of them." Andrew smiled.

David nodded. "There is a chemistry there."

Haley took hold of both of their hands. "Then let's help this along."

The three smiled. There would be not a blockade strong enough to hold them back.

**

The truck bumped along a narrow dirt lane. The sun set, darkness surrounded them. Andrew wanted Haley to see this. Tonight. Tonight was the right night. He needed to say what was in his heart. As the trees parted, the headlights hit the water of the lake. Andrew stopped the truck, shinning the headlights on a clearing. Putting it into park, he leaned back stared straight ahead. This was something new. Something so important it scared him.

"Let's walk."

Haley remained quiet. She took his hand, slid down from the cab. Letting him lead, she walked over the uneven ground, grabbing him when she stumbled.

Finally he stopped, stood still. "Haley."

"Yes?"

Andrew took a deep breath. "I wanted you to see this."

Haley looked out over the lake, the full moon made the small ripples sparkle. The night animals created a melody. "It's beautiful, Andrew."

Andrew paused then continued on. "Would you ever want to..."

Haley turned to look at him, grinning. He knew he needed to finish. "...live here?"

A look of confusion crept across her face. "You mean Lester Lake?"

"Yeah. But no, I mean here on this spot with me?" There he said it.

Haley gave him a sly look. "Are you proposing?"

"Yeah. No. When I propose there will be a ring. A nice dinner and... I just want to know how you would like the idea."

Haley put her hands on her hips. "I think I would like it just fine." Then she broke out into a huge smile.

Andrew shook his head, cocked it to one side, laughed. "You had me there for a minute." Sweeping her into his arms, his mouth all but consumed her in a rush of frantic kisses. Her body melted into his as she returned the kisses.

Andrew buried his face in the hollow of her throat where he could drink in her scent. Everything about this woman set him on fire. He felt her stir in his arms as she unbuttoned his shirt, laying soft butterfly kisses on his chest.

He moaned. "Be careful baby. I don't know if I can stop once the launch sequence is activated."

Haley took his ear lobe in her mouth, whispered. "So don't."

He pulled back. "Seriously?"

Haley smiled. "Why not? Isn't this where we want to spend the rest of our lives? I think it is only right we make love for the

240

first time here." She went down on him with sweet kisses and a tongue lapping fire. He shivered at the sensation of her lips on his flesh. When she reached his belt she undid it, pulling down his zipper. She slid her hand inside to cup his warm, hard, flesh.

He wrapped his hands around her buttocks, lifted her up. As she wrapped her long legs tightly around his waist, he went down to his knees, easily laying her on the cool grass.

His fingers moved over her blouse, one by one undid the small buttons. Even though he was ready, he wanted the first time to be complete. She needed to feel how much he wanted her.

Haley moaned as his mouth traveled down the valley of her breasts, to her belly button. Sucking on it, he moved his hands to her thighs. Removing her panties, his tongue took a sweet, enticing journey to her sweet spot. Her body arched as she screamed with the first orgasm. When he felt her body escalate up again, he entered her. Slow at first, but her tunnel grabbed his member drawing him in deeper and deeper.

Together they climaxed. Crying out, Haley's screams of pleasure matched the call of the night birds, echoing across the lake. Andrew groaned as he never felt such a release, such satisfaction from making love.

His sweat dripped on her skin, she smiled at him. Burying his face in her neck, he licked the moisture from her.

"Gawd I love you." His words came in a quick whisper.

Wrapping her arms around him, she answered in his ear. "Not as much as I love you."

Never wanting to move he did roll off of her, to lay next to her. Looking up at the star-filled sky, he felt a connection with the universe. Taking her hand, she squeezed his.

"Andrew."

"Yes, darlin'"

"I'm glad you love me."

"I'm glad I love you too."

Her laugh vibrated across him as she tickled his ribs.

***

Mid-morning, Becca sat at her computer checking on the art world. Since she inherited Tilley's art, and her son was on his way to becoming an artist, she figured she needed to be up

on things. Jon Jr. left early to go boating with Franny. Becca smiled. She saw a good friendship building. Then there was Haley and Andrew. Becca picked up her coffee cup, took a long sip. A serious relationship could happen.

Thinking about what it meant to her, she smiled.

We Young women can't resist those Lester men.

***

Once Becca and Clay became a couple, the summer took a romantic turn. While it was fun hanging with Gwen and Martin, and Jilley and Sparky, it was the moments they were alone she enjoyed the most.

242

Clay was interesting and fun. While he could knock her socks off with just his look, his love-making brought out the animal in her. Somehow he guided her to enjoy her sexual side. Opening up new feelings, stimulating pleasures, she discovered his body as he explored hers. Every inch of him had been kissed, licked or sucked. He more than returned the gratification.

But it wasn't all sex. Clay worked with his hands in more than one way. He was a master craftsman. He loved making furniture, building houses, anything to do with wood.

Becca bounced against his side as the truck took the rough road to a secluded spot. When the water came into view, he slowed down. The last shades of the day hung across the peaceful lake. Brilliant colors of oranges and reds crested along the horizon.

Stopping the truck, Clay bound out of the cab, dragging Becca with him. Going behind her, his hands on her shoulders he guided to a spot with stakes, string and flags.

"What do you think?" He wrapped his arms around her waist, drew her into his body.

Becca looked around. "What is it?"

"Our home. I'm building it for us." He hugged her, rocking back and forth.

Stunned, Becca had no words. The thought that he believed in them as a couple was so beautiful, so touching. Her eyes misted as her love for him engulfed her.

Turning her around, he wiped the tears from her eyes with his thumb. "I hope those are happy tears."

Nodding, she buried her face in his chest. She loved how they fit together.

"Look, I know you need to go back to finish college. By the time you come back, I'll have it completed, ready to move into."

His love for her surrounded her spirit, giving her a sense of security and peace. How she loved this man.

Clay took her face in his hands, capturing her lips in a searing kiss. She responded with her whole body and soul. Pulling him down with her they both went to their knees on the soft sand.

***

"Mom." Haley's voice put an end to Becca's thoughts.

Becca blinked as her daughter's face came into focus. Haley sat across from her with a steaming cup of coffee.

"Haley. Mornin' honey."

"Where were you?" Haley smiled over the cup's rim.

"Lost in thoughts." Becca looked down at her laptop. The screen was black. Looking back up, she smiled. "So what's new?"

"Look, Mom, I want to talk to you about something."

Becca closed the lid, crossed her arms. "Go."

"Well...can I come back to live here with you for a while?"

"Come back?"

"I need to finish this one class. Then I can graduate."

"That's important. Your Dad would have a fit if you dropped out when you were so close."

"Dad." Haley snorted.

Becca felt guilty she found comfort in her daughter's attitude toward Jon, but... "So what are you thinking, hon?"

"I am thinking of coming back here to marry Andrew." The big smile on Haley's face warmed Becca's heart.

"What? Did he propose?"

Haley blushed. "Kind of. Not formally, but we are thinking about it."

"And the plans are?"

Haley smiled shyly. "He's building us a house. A home." She grabbed Becca's hands. "Oh Mom, I love him so much."

Watching the sparkle in her daughter's eyes made Becca smile. "Then do it. Yes, you can live here. Whatever you need."

"I'm going back to the house, pack my stuff. Anything I need to get for you?"

Becca shook her head. "I have all I want from the house."

"Mom." The seriousness in Haley's voice alerted Becca. "I saw the divorce papers on Dad's desk. Just FYI."

Becca nodded. "I expected them. Sparky will handle it for me."

Haley hesitated. "Look, I don't mean to pry, but get him for all you are due. You need to think of yourself."

"I'm good. Aunt Tilley was a very wealthy woman. She left it all to me. Plus, I own all of her paintings. So..." Becca shrugged.

"Good for you Mom."

This moment with her daughter was priceless. She saw a bright future unfolding for Haley.

Maybe she can have the happiness I threw away. Odd how history repeats itself.

"Mom!"

Again Becca zoned out. "Yes?"

"What about Clay?"

"Oh, honey..." Becca stood, looked around for a way to retreat. "...pretty much water under the bridge."

Haley met her at the end of the table. "Build a new bridge, Mom. I don't know what happened, but I think you would have a better life with Clay, than Dad."

Becca touched her sweet daughter's cheek. "But then I wouldn't have you and Clay wouldn't have Andrew. Things work out for the best." Patting Haley's cheek, Becca gave her a weak smile. Walking into the kitchen, Becca leaned on the counter, looked out the window.

What if? Don't beat yourself up. What's done is done. Just make the next part of your life better.

***

Finishing what she started on the computer, Becca stood and stretched. Checking her watch she saw it was noon already.

Lunch. Lunch would be good.

Having no idea where Haley made off to, Becca walked to the studio. There she found Jon Jr. working on a colorful painting of long brush strokes with simple shapes. Not knowing where it was going, she liked the feel of it.

"Looking good. What is it?"

Jon Jr. turned, smiled. "It's feelings."

Did he actually blush?

Becca leaned against the door frame. "Good feelings I hope. Hungry?"

Jon Jr. still putting brush strokes on the canvas. "Yeah, I could use some food."

"Okay, I'll fix it. Let you know when it's ready."

Working efficiently, with her thoughts flying everywhere, Becca tried to reel them in.

Oh forget it. Life needs to flow. Go its own way.

The song stuck in her head.

You can go your own way

Moving to the music in her head she hummed, not knowing the rest of the words. Swaying her hips, she finished the lunch with a flare of hand gestures. Turning around with the two plates in her hands, she stopped short, Jon Jr. was standing in the doorway.

He smiled that knowing smile. There was always a silent connection between them. An awareness of the souls. Becca stopped gyrating, walked ladylike to the table.

Placing the lunch plates carefully down, she smiled at her son. "Lunch."

Jon Jr., still with a grin, pulled the chair out to sit down. "So Mom, what makes you so happy these days?"

Becca pondered the question. Simple answer. "Life. Life makes me happy. You and Haley being here. Watching you paint, her cook. Just life."

Jon Jr. took a bite of the sandwich, chewed, then spoke. "Mom. I'm going to ride back with Haley. I have two more years of school. So does Franny..."

Becca smiled as she interrupted. "...so Franny is...?"

Jon Jr. smiled. "Yes, she is. We both need to finish school, but if we are still together when we graduate, we will be together the rest of our lives. Is that okay?"

"Darlin', whatever makes you happy. I can see you have thought about this, are making good choices. Carry on."

"My wayward son?" Jon Jr. sang back to her.

Together they laughed. Becca took in a breath. "We are musical today aren't we?"

***

Jonny finished up painting for the day. Taking a shower, he sang under the spray of water. *Carry On* stuck in his mind. The time here with his mom and Haley made the summer great. And, of course, Franny. Her hot young body had him taking lots of cold showers. Getting ready for his date with her tonight, he whistled.

Hurriedly he dried off, slipping into clean jeans. Pulling the fresh white tee shirt over his head, he shook his hair, letting it fall where it would. Going barefoot to his room, he sat down on the bed, put on his socks, grabbing his first pair of cowboy boots.

Cowboy boots! Who would have guessed?

But everyone wore them here. Plus he liked the statement they made. Raw, male magnetism. Strong and bold. Anyway that how they made him feel.

Picking up his pocket change, keys from the dresser, he walked into the hall. A horn sounding told him Franny was waiting. He left his car at home, since he rode here with Haley.

Rushing to get out the door he ran into Haley. "Hey Sis. Goin' out tonight?"

Haley shifted to the side to avoid being mowed down by him. He grabbed her arms to stop.

"Yeah. Andrew and I are going to Brick's. You?"

"Same place. I'll see you there." Out the door, bounding down the steps. Franny stood in front of the car, leaning back on the hood. His eyes traveled over her half buttoned shirt revealing a tank top stretched to its limit by her round, supple breasts. Her denim mini shirt barely covered her long, slender, tan legs. Red cowgirl boots finished his journey of visual pleasure.

"'bout time." She threw her head back, laughed as he grabbed her, swinging her around, topping to kiss her, deeply and hungrily.

"Sorry to keep you waiting. But it's worth it isn't?" He moved his hands down to her butt, squeezing he nuzzled her neck.

Franny laughed. "You are so worth the wait, cowboy."

The words he wanted to hear. "Come on woman, let's get going."

Separating, Jonny went to the driver's side, Franny to the passenger's. Franny drove a cute little Mustang convertible, silver with black interior.

The summer evening carried the feel of fall. Soon, the days would cool and the nights turn cold. Just at the peak of cross-over, the smell of falling leaves mixed with the lingering heat of summer.

Pulling into Brick's parking lot, the place was filling up quickly. As they both jumped out of the car, meeting in the front, Jonn-grabbed her hand, pulling her into his side. Arms around each other's waist, they strolled to the door, greeting several people as they passed.

Once in the dim space, they looked around. Seeing a hand in the air they waved. Weaving their way to the table to join Kevin and Wendy.

"Howdy, folks." Each took a chair and sat down. A half full pitcher of beer sat in the middle of the table. Jonny grabbed two glasses, pouring the remaining. Setting the empty pitcher down, he signaled the waitress for another.

Kevin leaned over to Jonny. "A new boat came in today. Real honey."

Jonny nodded, smiled. "Sent me a pic. I am going home tomorrow. I'll hit the old man up for the money."

"Dude. You're leaving so soon?"

"I need to take care of some things. When do you leave?"

"Couple of weeks. We aren't far from each other. I'll let you know when I get settled."

Wendy shouted over the noise of the crowd and band. "You're leaving?"

Jonny shouted back. "Tomorrow."

Wendy glanced at Franny. Franny nodded. Jonny pulled her head to him, kissed the tip of her nose. "Let's dance."

Leading her to the small crowded dance floor, he took her in his arms. In sync they two-stepped to the music. The feel of her body swaying with him only confirmed how good they were together.

Since coming to Lester Lake, Jonny had the time of his life. He always hated the uptight life of his childhood. The only thing that made it bearable was his Mom. And Haley. As soon as the two of them got away to college, they spent many weekends meeting half-way to enjoy join activities. The relationship between father and son was strained, to say the least. He sometimes wondered if his dad had any feelings at all. Jonny could count on one hand the number of times Jon Sr. said the words, I love you.

The music stopped. Still holding Franny, Jonny looked down into her kind brown eyes. If they didn't stay together, he would always love this girl. She showed him how to love. For that, he would forever be grateful.

Jonny smiled, tenderly kissed her. A slap on his back interrupted the kiss. He smiled at her as the intruder walked into view.

"Jonny boy." It was David Lester.

"Yeah, David."

"Hear you're leaving tomorrow."

"I'll be back."

"Good, because we feel like you are a good addition to our group of locals."

"Well, thank you. It's an honor."

"Come on. Have a drink on me." David pulled Jonny away from Franny. Guiding him to

the bar, David went around to the other side, poured a shot of tequila, set it in front of Jonny, with one swallow, he drained the glass.

Slamming the shot glass upside down on the bar, he winked at David. "So, I am approved."

David leaned on the bar. "Only 'cause you're Becca's son."

"Sometimes I feel like my mother is a legend around here."

David looked around. "Let's just say she left her mark." Patting Jonny's arm, "Go back to your girl. Just stay in touch."

"I plan on it. Thanks for the drink."

Going back to his table, he took the empty seat next to Franny. "Sorry, babe."

Franny took his hand. "Now that the male bonding is over, you're mine."

"Fair enough."

They closed the bar down at 2:00 am. Franny drove home as she always drank less than Jonny. Pulling into her driveway, as they both got out, she stopped him at the front of the car. Wrapping her arms around his neck, she brought his head down to her lips, giving him an inviting kiss.

He wrapped his arms around her waist, lifting her up. "You, my darlin', are a sexy woman."

"Yes." She moved her body to fit into his.

He groaned. "Oh. Baby."

"Yes." She ran her hands over his ass.

"Do you know what you are doing?"

"Yes." Grabbing his ass in a tight squeeze.

He pushed her away. "What are you doing to me?"

Franny pulled him back to her. "Showing you what I want."

"Where?"

Her tongue circled his ear. "My room."

"Your parents?"

"Gone for the night."

He laughed as he swung her up, carried her up the steps to her house. Franny turned the handle of the front door. It swung open, Jonny carried her in, kicking the door shut with his foot. At the stairs he put her down. One step up from him, she kissed him, then turned to run up the stairs. He followed close behind.

Once in her room, she grabbed him, threw him to the bed. Removing her skirt, she straddled him. Tightening her thighs on his ribs, she removed his tee shirt. Taking his hands, she raised his arms above his head.

He wiggled, but her strong legs held him tight. Her mouth went to his chest, licking her way down his pleasure trail. He felt his member hardening, his body arousing to her touch.

Franny rose to her knees, grabbing hold of his jean's waistband. With one sharp pull she

released him. Jonny could take no more. Flipping her to her back, he entered her. Her channel gripped him, pulled him in farther. As they climaxed together, she laughed with pleasure causing him to explode.

254

Coming down from the high, both were bathed in sweat. Rolling off of her, Jonny took hold of her hand. Unable to speak, he squeezed it. Franny squeezed back.

Lying in the quiet, the sound of tires on gravel brought both up off the bed.

"My folks!"

Jumping, he pulled up his pants. "I thought you said they were gone for the night?"

Haley threw his tee shirt at him. "Something must have changed. Get out of here." She pushed him out the door.

"But your dad likes me." He protested as she pushed him toward the stairs.

Giving him a quick kiss. "Not in his daughter's bed."

"Good point." Jonny stepped quickly down the stairs to the back door. Slipping out, he carefully went down the steps of the deck. Pausing at the corner of the house, he heard Franny's folks talking inside. Running, he got to his back door, carefully opened it so it wouldn't squeak, slithered in.

Once in his room, he saw the lights go out on the house next door.

Leaning on the window frame, he smiled.

Night Franny

CHAPTER THIRTEEN

Clay sat on his dock with his legs dangling in the water. With a swift snap, he threw the fishing line into the clear morning water. The art of fishing involves patience. Holding the pole firmly, but with a light grip, he picked up the cup of coffee sitting next to him.

Looking out over the water, he let his mind wander. This was his quiet time. Usually he thought about the business. It was a good time to clear up all the loose ends thrown at him during the day.

The seasons were changing, summer was winding down, fall barely on the crest ready to jump in. He could smell it in the air. Live here long enough, you know when nature transforms to a climate switch.

It was at this time of the year he lost Becca. He had such high hopes of beginning a life with the woman he loved. In one moment it all changed. And all that remained was the pain. He bowed his head, watching the ripples in the water grow outward.

***

Clay watched the tail lights of Sparky's car disappear. Running his hands through his hair, looking down he saw he was covered in mud and blood. A noise made him look over at the ambulance. The gurney with a black body bag on it came up over the embankment.

Martin.

A shudder went through Clay. He had known Martin since grade school. All the times of their lives flashed before his eyes. He could not remember a time without Martin as a pal.

A policeman came over to Clay. "Can you tell me what happened?"

My friend died.

Clay sighed. "A car came from the left." He pointed in the direction the car had appeared out of nowhere. "Slammed broadside into Mart...in's car." He took a deep breath. "Martin's car hit the bridge and dove into the river. It happened so fast."

"This your truck?" The policeman pointed at the black Chevy.

Clay turned around to look, like he didn't know it was behind him. The front was smashed into a large pole. He didn't remember the impact or getting out. Becca was his first concern, then Martin and Gwen.

Clay grimaced. "Yeah. It was."

258

"And did you have a passenger?"

Clay frowned as he looked at the man.

Why does it matter?

"Yeah, my girlfriend."

"Her name?"

"Becca. Becca Young." Impatience made him grit his back teeth.

"And yours?"

"Clay Lester."

"And where is Miss Young now?"

A muscle jumped in Clay's jaw. "On her way to the hospital. Gwen was her best friend."

All the while the policeman wrote in a small book. "And who is Gwen?"

"The girl in the car that landed in the river."

Clay's sharp words made the cop look up. "I'm sorry. I am supposed to ask questions." He put his hand on Clay's shoulder. "You need to be with your friends. I'll get you to the hospital. We'll do this later."

The policeman motioned to an officer standing by the squad car. "Will you take Clay to the hospital." It was a command, not a question.

Nodding, the young rookie opened the passenger door. Clay slid in, shut the door. Silent for the whole ride, Clay stared out the window watching the scenery pass. The sign announcing 'You are now entering Lester County' made him chuckle. Now on his home ground.

Pulling into the hospital drive, the car stopped at the large, red lettered sign saying EMERGENCY. Clay murmured a 'thank you', jumped out, ran to the double sliding doors. They parted as if he was expected. The waiting room was filled with his friends, some of their parents. Hesitating only long enough to scan the room, he spotted Becca slumped in the corner. In a brisk walk he went to her. Stopping in front of her, he took her chin in his hand, raised her head.

Becca's eyes said she was relieved to see him. Sitting down in the empty space next to her, he drew her to his side. She buried her face in his soiled shirt to sob.

***

"Dad." The words broke into Clay's thoughts.

Clay knew which son it was. "Andrew."

Andrew sat down next to Clay, sliding his bare feet into the still waters, creating more ripples.

That's how it goes. Life goes on. Things happen. Ripples get bigger.

"I wanted to talk to you before you left for work."

Clay chuckled. "Not working today, but this is the best time to get me. What's up?"

"Well…" Andrew drew up his chest. Clay looked at his oldest son. "…I guess I want to get married."

"You guess?"

"Well, no. I know I want to get married."

Clay knew the answer to the next question, but asked it anyway. "Who's the lucky girl?"

Andrew blushed. "Haley Hamilton."

Clay spoke under his breath. "Becca's daughter." A slight pang of protectiveness hit his heart. He wanted his son to have what he lost. The love of his life.

Clay looked over the water. "Nice girl."

"I love her, Dad." Andrew blushed as he said the words.

Clay shot his son a sideways glance. "And I am guessing she said yes?"

Awkwardly Andrew force out an answer. "Sort of."

Clay rolled his eyes. "Sort of?"

"I haven't done it formally. But we have talked. We're on the same page." Andrew's word came out fast.

Giving Andrew a little mumble, a brief nod. "It's always good to be on the same page."

Unless the story changes.

"She needs to finish one semester of school, so while she's gone I want to start building our home." Andrew's face lit up.

Clay turned back to his fishing. "The lot on the north shore?"

"Yeah, is it okay?"

"Sure, good piece of property." Clay ran his tongue around his mouth.

She's leaving. I hope she comes back.

Reeling in his line. "Sounds good son."

Andrew's sigh laced with frustration. "Really? I am so mixed up."

Clay looked over. "About what?"

Andrew kicked the water, ran his hands down his thighs. "I love her so much. If I lose her I would die."

Been there. Done that.

Clay swallowed. "Well, son. You have to take a chance if you really love her."

"It's going to work out. Not like you and Bec..." Andrew stopped. "...sorry Dad."

Clay patted Andrew's knee. "It's okay son. There were events that played into our break-up. Things happen."

Clay stood, reeled his line in. "I wouldn't trade one moment with her for none without her." He looked down at Andrew. "Do you understand what I am saying?"

Andrew shrugged.

"She was worth the pain." Clay patted his son's shoulder. "Go for it."

Turning he walked down the dock. His mind filled with the memory of the most painful moment in his life.

262

***

When Tilley told Clay that Becca made it home safe, he went home long enough to shower and change. Grabbing a cold drink, he drove over to her house. He sat in the truck outside her house waiting for her to get up. He was worried for her. Not knowing what actually happened in Gwen's hospital room, Becca's face changed from sorrow to stone. Her pushing him away startled him. Only wanting to comfort her, he gave her the space she demanded.

But he felt he needed to stay close. She would need him. He was here for her. Always.

After four hours, Clay heard the front door open. Becca came out, but behind her she drug a suitcase. Not understanding, he jumped out of the truck. Meeting her at her car, he stopped her.

She was cold and aloof. He wanted to take her in his arms, make her believe everything would be alright.

But her icy, unfeeling words stabbed his heart. "Let me go Clay. It's for the best."

As if hit with a physical object, he let go of her. She shoved him aside, threw her bag across the front seat, got in the car before he could react. Watching the dust from her exit, stunned, he shook his head.

She'll be back.

He assured himself. But she didn't until now. Too many years later. Too little too late.

* * *

Becca called Jilley on the phone. "Hey, the kids are leaving today. Do you want to come over for a last lunch with them?"

"Love to. I'll come around eleven?"

"Good. The truth is I need your moral support. I hate to see them go."

"They *are* coming back?"

"Yes. They both love it here. It's just...the summer was so great. I guess I hate to think of being without them."

"Are you afraid of being alone?"

Becca leaned against the wall. Thinking about what Jilley said. *Was she?*

Forgetting how long she wandered, lost in her thoughts, she heard Jilley's voice.

"Hello?"

Becca chuckled. "Sorry, I was thinking. I don't think so. I like having my own space. I love it here in Aunt Tilley's house. It's just this is the first time the kids and I could be ourselves, enjoy each other. But you're right. They will come back. Haley is planning on being back in a couple of months. She and Andrew are planning on getting married."

Jilley squealed. "No way! Wow! What a turn of events."

"I know du-du-du-du." The Twilight Zone song rolled off her lips.

"Are you okay with it?"

"Oh, yeah. I can't think of a nicer boy. Andrew is the real thing. Just like..." Becca stopped before she finished the sentence.

"...his dad." Jilley finished for her.

"You know me so well."

"Becca, you have got to let go of your guilt for the past. You were young. You made a mistake. A major, life altering mistake. The worst in your life..."

"Okay I get the picture."

"He's still here, honey. You can go for it again."

Becca sat down in the kitchen chair. Leaning her elbow on the table. "I don't know. I hurt him bad. He's still mad."

Jilley laughed. "He's not mad. He's chomping at the bit. It's his male pride, his stupidity

stops him. Plus, are you going to live the rest of your pathetic life without taking the chances you should have taken?"

"Let's cut right to the chase, Jilley." Becca chuckled.

I so missed the honesty of a good friend.

Jilley's laughter echoed over the phone. "Sorry babe, but you need to step out of that comfort zone of yours, get a little bam, bam, bam."

This last statement made Becca break into an embarrassed laugh. She knew her face was getting red from just the thought.

Haley walked into the kitchen. Her face revealed her confusion at her Mom's actions. "Mom?"

Becca waved at her. "Jilley..." She could hardly catch her breath. "Haley just came in. See you at eleven?"

Jilley smirked. "I'll be there."

Becca looked at the phone as she hit the disconnect button. Laying the phone down, she gathered her composure around her, looked up at Haley. "That was Jilley. She's coming over to see you guys off."

Haley sat down across from Becca. "And that is funny?"

"No, Jilley just said something...humorous."

"Good. How about I fix lunch? Show off some of my cooking skills."

Becca smiled. "That would be great. I am thinking of inviting Susie and Franny? And is Andrew coming by?"

"I'll call him. Sounds like fun."

Becca grabbed a tablet and a pen. "What do you need?"

"Let me do it. I'll run into town, get what I need. Be right back."

Becca put the pen down.

Her daughter is going to do this.

"Okay, what can I do?"

266

"Have another cup of coffee, then you can help me cook when I get back."

"Fine." Becca watched as Haley left.

Looking around, she did get up, pour another cup of coffee. Looking out the window, she saw Susie and Franny in their gazebo.

The uneven ground made walking with a full cup of coffee difficult. Spilling it, she held it away from her. Reaching the two women, she sat her cup on the table, shook the liquid from her hand.

"Morin' girls."

Susie chuckled. "How are you this fine morning?"

"Good." Becca pulled out a chair, sat down. "Say, the kids are leaving today. How about a good-bye lunch? Jilley's coming. Haley is cooking."

Franny piped in. "And what is Jonny doing?"

"Being Jonny and not much else." Becca chuckled.

"Is he up?" The slam of the back door answered Franny's question. She was up, on her way toward him.

Susie and Becca watched the two embrace, sit down on the steps of the back deck of Becca's house.

"Do you think it's serious?" Becca asked.

"As serious as Franny gets these days." Susie sighed.

"So you think they both will finish school?"

"I'm sure of it. Franny is in no hurry to settle down. My fear is she will break his heart."

"Not if he doesn't break hers first. You do know he wants to be a starving artist?"

Susie giggled. "She wants to be a legal aid lawyer."

Becca cocked her head. "...they will starve together."

Together they sighed.

***

The kitchen was ablaze with activity. Becca was amazed at how efficiently Haley handled the cooking. What she decided to serve was new, very up-scale as far as Becca could tell. The aroma of the food flooded her senses, making her extremely hungry.

There was also a flare to the arrangement of the dishes. Haley invaded the pantry, found some quaint, antique-looking plates, serving dishes and table cloths.

Making a quick, but proficient centerpiece, the dining room table looked like a bistro from the streets of New York. The mixture of styles seemed to blend together to create a simple flow.

Becca carried the dish Haley handed her, placed it on the table. Then stood back to admire her daughter's work.

Both my kids are artists. Glad they got to expand their creative sides this summer. Also glad I got to see it bloom and blossom.

The knock on the front screen door caused Becca to look up to see Andrew standing there.

He looks just like his father.

"Come on in." She shouted.

The tall, handsome young man lumbered in. "Mrs. Hamilton." He greeted her with a nod.

He looked nervous.

Do I unnerve him?

"Becca, please. Call me Becca." She smiled as he barely cleared the doorway.

Haley came busting out of the kitchen. "Andrew." Just the tone of her voice conveyed her love for him.

He walked over, kissed her on the cheek. "Wow, this looks great."

Is she blushing?

"Thanks, hon."

Jilley's voice preceded her arrival. "Is this where the party is?" Waving a bottle of wine, she burst into the room.

Becca felt laughter consumed her whole body. "Why yes it is." She hugged Jilley.

Jilley offered the wine to Haley. "I hope this goes with your meal."

Haley and Andrew looked at the label together. Andrew whistled as Haley gulped a big breath. "Wow this is a rare vintage." Haley hugged Jilley. "Do you mind if we save it for a special day?"

"Not at all. As long as I am invited to share it."

Haley laughed. "Most certainly."

"Most certainly what?" Jon Jr. entered the dining room from the hall. Freshly showered, his mass of hair looked, at least for the moment, to be under control.

Haley showed the wine to him. "Jilley gave us this bottle of wine."

Jon Jr. raised his eyebrows. "Nice, Jilley." Giving his nod of approval.

Susie and Franny entered from the back way. Franny went to Jon Jr. He gathered her to his side, kissed the top of her head.

Haley set the wine on the buffet table behind her. "Sit everyone. I only have one more dish to bring out."

Andrew spoke to her. "Need help?"

She kissed his cheek. "I'm good. Go sit."

Everyone circled the table. Jilley and Susie flanked Becca at the far end. Franny sat next to Susie with Jon Jr. next.

Andrew sat across from Jon. Jr. leaving the seat next to Jilley for Haley.

Sitting down one last dish, Haley took her seat. "I hope you all enjoy. This is my passion. My heart's work."

As the dishes of inviting food passed from person to person, everyone took some of each. Becca was pleased with their reactions. Looking up at Haley's face, the validation reflected in her eyes.

Taking a mouthful of the salad, Becca finished chewing then said. "Haley this is great. You should open a restaurant."

Haley blushed, took Andrew's hand. "That is kind of our plan." She looked at him, smiled. "To open a place in town..." She looked around the table. "...when we get married."

The excited reaction bounced around the table.

Jon Jr. stood, slapped Andrew on the shoulder.

Jilley grabbed both Haley's and Becca's hands. "What a great idea."

Susie smiled and nodded.

Franny just smiled, looked over at Jon Jr., and winked.

Becca let go of Jilley's hand, stood. Picking up the glass of iced tea, she raised her glass. "To you my darling daughter. Only the best. Andrew. You are a lucky man."

Now Andrew blushed. "I know, Mrs....Becca."

The people around the table all raised their glasses to toast in unison.

Sitting down, Becca saw how much in love the couple was. Her heart burst with pride and joy for them both.

Jilley leaned over, whispering to Becca. "You know if she marries him, she will never leave Lester Lake."

Becca cocked her head. "And this is a bad thing?"

"Nooo. This is a good thing. You will always have her near."

The thought warmed Becca. Together she and Haley would build a life here. If she doubted the fates leading her here, now she knew it was the right thing.

Susie patted Becca back. "You have one settling down."

Becca picked up Susie's hand. "And we have two more the jury is still out on." Picking up Jilley's hand also, Becca shook both of them. "Thanks girls."

Jilley frowned. "For what?"

"For being there after all these years." Becca addressed Jilley. "And..." she turned to Susie. "...for being there the first day I landed. I was such a wreck."

The three women looked down the table at the young people. The new generation of Lester Lake.

***

As soon as Jilley, Susie and Becca finished the clean-up, they walked together outside where Haley and Jon Jr. stood by their car with Franny and Andrew. Seeing the car packed and loaded, Becca felt the tears ready to spring.

Let's get this over with.

Breaking rank from the other two women, she walked to Haley first. Andrew stepped back to let her pass. Hugging her daughter, she whispered. "I love you. And all you have become and want to be. Be safe."

Haley hugged her back. "Will you be okay alone?"

Becca chuckled. "You see those two women on the porch. I am hardly alone."

"Andrew will be here if you need anything."

The young man stepped up, put a reassuring hand on Becca's back. "I'll look out for her, honey."

Caught between the two of them she could actually feel the love.

Slipping away, Becca walked to Jon Jr. "Son." He held Franny's hand. "Take care. Paint lots. I love your work."

Jon Jr. let go of Franny's hand to hug Becca. "Thanks Mom. For believing in me. And the chance to paint here."

Becca held him tight.

My little boy is a man.

She pulled back, looked into the eyes that always carried a hint of mischief. Brushing the

hair away from his face. "I am proud of the man you are becoming."

Jon Jr. smirked. "Becoming?" His killer smile creased his mouth. "I think I am a man."

Becca laughed. "Almost." She winked at Franny.

Haley and Jon Jr. gave their significant others a long good-bye kiss as Becca rejoined her friends on the porch. The three links arms, watched the sporty convertible pull out onto the road.

Andrew waved at them, went to his truck. Franny went to her house.

Jilley squeezed Becca's arm. "You okay?"

All that was left was the dust cloud from the car. "Yeah. I'm good. Thanks for coming."

"You want to go get drunk?" Jilley asked with all seriousness.

Susie and Becca answered together. "No!"

Jilley released her hold. Waving her arms, she went down the stairs. "Okay. Fine. Anytime though." At her car, she paused. "It was fun?"

Susie and Becca separated.

Susie went on down the stairs. "Fun, yeah. Later."

Becca turned to go in the house. Throwing her words over her shoulder. "Another time, maybe."

Jilley yelled after her. "It got Clay there."

Becca turned around shooting Jilley a frown.

Jilley waved. "Just saying."

Becca continued on into the house. She chuckled as she heard the sound of Jilley's car fade from her driveway.

The ringing of the phone jolted her. Hitting the talk button, she wandered down the hall to the studio, stood in the doorway looking at the painting Jon Jr. left.

"Hello?"

"Becca. This is Sparky. I just received your divorce papers."

Jordyn Meryl

CHAPTER FOURTEEN

Becca walked into Sparky's office. She smiled at the small town feel of the space. Decorated with quiet taste, it spoke of a man who honored the people he served.

Sparky walked out to greet her. "Becca." He took her hands into his.

"Sparky." She frowned. "Do I call you that when you are doing your lawyer thing?"

A smile creased his eyes. "You can."

Putting his hand lightly on her back, he motioned toward a room to their left. Becca walked in, sat at the wooden table in his office. Looking around, she saw pictures of his family and friends, sport memorabilia, a large hand crafted desk.

Sparky sat across from her, a file lying to his right. As he opened it, Becca took a deep breath.

This is it. The end to a huge chunk of my life.

276

"Your husband has set some up strong terms for this divorce."

"This does not surprise me. Lay them on me."

Sparky read from the top paper in front of him. "He wants the house, the furnishings, his cars, you can keep yours." He looked up, tilted his head. Becca chuckled.

Sparky continued. "He will pay you alimony for five years or until you marry, whichever comes first. "

That made Becca laugh. Sparky stopped talking, looked up at her. She nodded. "Go on."

"You may come back to the house to pick up any personal items, but any furniture, art work or jewelry will need to be agreed upon by both parties. Since the children are adults, there is no provision for them."

Becca shook her head. "Idiot."

Sparky leaned back in his chair. "Will he take care of them?"

"Probably not. But that is between him and them. He's right, they are adults." She leaned forward. "Is that all?"

"For him. What do you want to counter offer?"

"Nothing. You know my finances. I have more than enough money, a beautiful house on the lake and a place to start a new life. This is the life I should have chosen to begin with."

Sparky smiled. "So you're staying."

"Yes."

"So there is nothing you want from the house?"

"No, when I left I took the things important to me. Pictures of the kids and I. The 'junk jewelry' as Jon likes to call it, given to me by Haley and Jon Jr. He can have all the expensive jewelry he bought for me to impress other people, the designer clothes, the art for the sake to brag, the shallow life he lives. I am good. Where do I sign?"

Sparky smiled and handed her the paper he was reading from and a pen.

Signing her name to this was a relief. For the last several years, she had not felt this good. It was like a heavy chain broke away from her body. She slid the paper back across the table.

"Is this it?"

"If that's how you want it. It is."

Nodding, Becca smiled. "Good." She stood.

Sparky came around the table. "I am glad you're staying." He took her arm, walked her to the door. Before he let her go, he took her shoulders, made her face him. "Are you all right?"

Becca bit her lower lip, nodded. "I am."

He kissed her cheek gave her a big bear hug. "Nice to have you back, Becca. Welcome to your new home, Lester Lake."

She patted his cheek. "Not new. I am finally back home."

Sparky opened the door for her. Stepping outside, the sun gave her an uplifting feeling. As she got in her car, she knew where she needed to go. Heading out of town, she opened the window on her side, let the late summer wind whip her hair.

Free at last! Free at last! I'm free at last!

***

The small town of Spring Hill welcomed her as she pulled up to the art gallery. Stepping out, she felt her steps were lighter. Walking in to the cool building, she removed her sunglasses as her eyes adjusted to the shaded room.

An older man greeted her. "May I help you?"

Becca stuck out her hand. "Hi. I'm Becca Young-Ham..." She stopped, grinned. "...Young. Becca Young. Tilley Young's niece."

The man smiled. "She said you would come one day. I am Arthur Shawnmaker, proprietor of the gallery." He took her outstretched hand in both of his. "She talked of you often."

Becca felt tears forming. "She knew I would come? Tell me about her."

Arthur tucked her hand in his arm, walked toward the Tilley Young room. "She was a visionary. Her art work always came from the heart. I remember the first time she walked in with one of her canvases under her arm."

This man gave her a string connection to the aunt she dearly loved and missed. It felt intimate and real. Becca hugged his arm, leaned her head on his shoulder as she listened, seeing it all in her mind.

"She was so unsure, but her drive to be a good artist overtook her common sense that told her she couldn't do it. Thank god her heart won out. I sold the painting as soon as I advertised it, then commissioned her for more."

They reached the bench in front of the portrait of Jeffery. Becca straightened up. "Do

you know who Jeffery is?"

Arthur patted her hand. "No, she never said, but I had the feeling he was someone special in her life. He was painted with lots of love. You don't know?"

"No idea."

The bell on the front door rang. Becca released her grip as Arthur untangled himself from her.

"I need to greet this person."

"Go on, I am going to sit here for a while."

"Stay as long as you like. I'm glad you finally came in."

As Becca walked around to sit down she kept her eyes on Jeffery. Now she could see how much love Aunt Tilley put into the painting. Sitting surrounded by Tilley's artwork gave her feeling of being grounded. Here she was grounded. Where she belonged. It had been a long time coming, but she was here now.

Home.

She felt a person coming up behind her before they spoke.

"Becca." Clay's voice washed over her like a cool waterfall.

She didn't turn around. Afraid to speak for fear of crying, she looked down at the floor.

Out of the corner of her eyes she watched him straddle the bench, sit down. "Are you okay?"

Nodding, she tried very hard to keep herself together. Clearing her throat. "Yeah."

She turned to look at him. His familiar face forced her to let go. "I just signed my divorce papers."

He took her hand. "I am so sorry. Been there. Done there that."

Cocking her head, she frowned. Recalling him going in the gallery the time she sat across the street. "Why are you here?"

He smiled. "I promised Tilley I would take care of business until you came to claim your inheritance."

"So you waited for me?"

His eyes bore into hers. "Sort of. Tilley always said you would return to the lake. It was in your soul."

That released the flood. Becca reacted with great sobs. Clay took her in his arms, held her shaking body as she cried out her pain. The pain of losing Aunt Tilley. Of wasting too many years married to the wrong man. For leaving Clay. The life she could have had but didn't because she chose the wrong path.

His arms gave her comfort, peace, a sense of wellbeing. She snuggled down into his body. This is what she missed. The feel of being in Clay's arms. In her heart of hearts she knew she still loved him. Always had. Denying it only pushed it away, it did not erase the feelings. As the sobbing subsided, she took the handkerchief Clay offered. Wiping her eyes, she sat up, blew her nose.

Laughing, she tucked the cloth into her hand. "I'll wash it, get it back to you."

Clay nodded. "How about we go get a drink?"

"Sounds wonderful."

He stood, took her hand, pulled her up. She couldn't tell what he was feeling. But for now, she felt better than she had in a long while. More like her real self.

Letting Clay lead, she glanced at the paintings on the wall. Suddenly she jerked back. There was a picture of a bridge.

Crawl River Bridge.

Clay dropped her hand, grabbed her. She staggered back against him. That night came back as if it were yesterday. The reason Becca left Clay.

***

The three car loads of young people were still on a musical high when they crossed Crawl River Bridge at 3:00 am in the morning. Convoy style, they drove the speed limit, as no one was in a hurry to get home on this warm summer night. Clay and Becca rode alone in his truck.

Becca could feel the first airs of fall. Summer would be over soon. Scheduled to drive home Monday, she looked over at Clay, her heart sank.

I need to leave him for a year at least. Then?

She had no answer for herself or him for that manner.

His profile in the lights from the dashboard made him look almost Greek god-like. His skin reflected gold. Without looking over at her, a smile crossed his face. "What are you lookin' at?"

"You." She stretched out her arm, laid her hand on the back of his neck.

"Why?"

Turning to face the front windshield, she sighed. "Just like looking at you....Watch out!"

A car from nowhere crashed into the car in front of them broadside. Clay whipped the steering wheel around so they barely missed the accident. Martin and Gwen were in the first car. Becca watched in horror as their car went airborne, hitting the thick metal railing of the bridge. Flipping up, it twisted a couple of times, then did a nose dive into the river. Clay's truck slid into a pole, causing Becca to jerk backwards. Sparky's car behind them stopped next to Becca's side.

Not moving any more, Clay opened his door. Looking toward the broken bridge rafter, he yelled at her. "Are you all right?"

Becca nodded her head, opened her door. "Yes. Gwen. Martin..." Stepping out, she found her feet were like lead.

Clay yelled back over his shoulder. "Sparky come help. Jilley go for help. Becca stay put."

Everyone obeyed his directions in stunned silence. Sparky jumped out, Jilley slid to the driver's seat. With a squeal of tires she left the scene.

Becca stood plastered up against the truck. Watching Clay disappear over the side of

the embankment, she ran to the edge of the broken bridge.

Below, she saw the car upside down, half submerged into the river. Gwen laid on the river bank, Martin back by the car, his door open. Clay and Sparky slipped and stumbled down the side of the rocky embankment. Both stopped at Martin. Clay motioned for Sparky to stay, as he ran down to Gwen. Kneeling down he placed the side of his head down to her face. Becca saw her arm reach up, grab Clay's.

She couldn't stand there any longer. Sliding down the mud, she scampered to get to her friend. Almost falling into Clay, he stopped her descent with his hands. Losing her footing, she ended down on her knees, skidded to Gwen's side. Gwen's face was a bloody mess. A shard of glass embedded itself in her chest. Becca looked back at the car. Gwen had been thrown through the windshield.

In the distance, Becca could hear sirens. As they grew louder, she took Gwen's hand. "Hang on. Help is coming." Tears flowed freely down Becca's face.

Clay said nothing. The muscles in his jaw tensed, his eyes full of tears streaking down his mud cover face. He wiped them with his shirt sleeve.

Clay handed Becca Gwen's other hand. "Stay with her."

Becca nodded.

Clay rose, walked around her over to Sparky and Martin. Sparky stood up, his hands in his back pockets. Becca couldn't hear the words, but their faces told it all. Martin was dead.

Gwen moaned. "Martin?"

Becca turned back to her. "He's fine, Gwen. Clay and Sparky are with him.

The other car landed in the trees. The two boys inside were crawling out of the windows with a shell-shocked look.

Bright colored lights reflected on the water. The sirens deafening. Becca didn't look up, she just held Gwen's hand and prayed.

Don't let her die. Please.

A group of people came down the hill. Becca could feel and hear them behind her. They talked gibberish. Clay's voice sounded in her ear. "Let go baby." His hands pried hers from Gwen's.

"No!" She screamed, as Clay lifted her up, swung her around. Half carrying, half dragging, somehow he got her up the hill. At

the pavement he picked her up in his arms, finished carrying her to Sparky's car. Jilley stood beside it.

Clay put her in the backseat, Jilley crawled in behind her. They hugged each other, sobbed.

Becca heard Clay's voice tell Sparky. "Take them to the hospital. Follow the ambulance. I need to stay here and talk to the police. I'll be along soon."

Becca felt his hand pet her hair. Then the door slammed.

***

Strange sounds disturbed Becca's sleep. Beeps, bells and flashing lights. Jerking up, she

still had ahold of Gwen's hand. Gwen's eyes searched the room.

"Martin?"

Becca went to her side. "Gwen. He..."

A peaceful look came over Gwen's face. "He didn't make it did he?"

The sobs deep in Becca's chest rose to catch in her throat, blocking her voice. She wanted to answer her friend with the truth. Gwen deserved the truth.

"No." She finally pushed out.

Gwen's hand relaxed in Becca's. Becca grabbed it back, squeezing it. "Stay with me Gwen. Don't leave."

Gwen's weak voice put chills over Becca. "I want to leave. I see Martin. He's waiting for me." Her eyes closed, the beeps
286

changed to a steady tone. Nurses and doctors filled the room, pushing her aside. Walking backwards she felt stunned. At the door a woman pushed her out, closed the door in her face. Becca stood on tip-toes to watch through the small wired window. She felt a person behind her. The staff inside the room stopped working and covered Gwen's head with a sheet. It was then that Becca accepted that she was dead. Falling back against the body behind her, she felt the familiar touch of Clay.

Sobs wracked her body as he wrapped his arms tightly around her. The ungodly pain in her stomach made her double over. He held tight, pulling her into him. When her legs buckled, he lifted her up into his arms, carried her to a small empty waiting room, and sat down to hold her as she cried.

Her sorrow stopped as suddenly as it started. She straightened up, untangled Clay arms from her, stood. Looking out the door, she saw Gwen's parents being led away by the priest. She felt Clay next to her. She was suffocating. Him, the room, the building. She moved toward the door.

Clay grabbed her arm to stop her. "Where are you going?"

Becca hesitated, then looked up at him. "Home."

"I'll drive you."

"No...I need to walk."

"Bec it's two miles. I'll take you."

"No." Her sharp words, jerking her arm free, shocked him. She saw the pain in his eyes, but her pain overshadowed his. She needed air. To breathe. Turning, she walked fast toward the exit doors. The closer they came, the faster her pace. She heard him call her name when she reached the doors. She paused for a second, then hit the handle bars with all the pent up anger in her. Running, she dodged cars and people. Then she was on the dirt road leading to Aunt Tilley's. Her lungs hurt as they gasped for new air, but she kept running. Faster. The faster she could run the faster she would be out of this nightmare.

Bursting through the door, she heard Aunt Tilley say. "She's here, Clay. She's okay. Give her some space... I will."

Becca didn't stop. Her destination, her room. Once inside, she slammed the door, fell on

the bed as great wracking sobs shook her body.

***

When Becca finally woke up, she had no idea of time. The sun was shining so it must be day. Looking up at the ceiling, she had no more tears to cry. Then she made a fatal decision. Unbearable pain could be denied if she hardened her heart. With all her effort, she left the bed, walked to the bathroom. Looking in the mirror, she was shocked at her appearance. Her skin the color of gray, her eyes dark circles. Pushing back the mop of hair, she turned to go in to the shower. Every time the pain wanted to surface, she pushed it down.

288

Back in her room, she dressed in jeans and a tee shirt.
Throwing her clothes in a suitcase, she left the room.

Going down the hall, she ran into Aunt Tilley. "Becca. I thought I heard you."

Becca pushed by.

"Where are you going? Oh Becca, don't run away."

Becca stopped, but didn't turn around. "I'm not running away. I need to get back home." She started walking again. She couldn't face her, couldn't deal with the look of pain and betrayal she knew would see in her eyes. . "Thanks for everything, Aunt Tilley. I'll call later."

Marching on out to her car, she heard the crunch of gravel under boots.

Please don't let it be Clay.

"Becca." She slumped as she heard his voice.

He came to her side. "What's going on?"

Becca threw her case across the front seat. It hit the passenger-side door with a thud. She couldn't look at him either. He touched her arm. She jerked it back. "Look, I need to get back to school..."

"What about us?"

The words felt like a knife plunging into her heart. Taking a deep breath. "There is no us. Never will be. I was foolish to think I could have a life in this dirt water town." She knew she hurt him, but in her defense, she wanted him to give-up on her. And dangling a future in front of him would be cruel.

Opening the door, she pushed him aside. Never looking at him, she started the car, drove forward. Bouncing over the rough ground, she finally reached the dirt road. Gunning the motor she pressed down on the gas pedal. She made the mistake of looking into her rear view mirror. Clay stood in the middle of the road.

Her tears continued as she drove away from Aunt Tilley's, subsiding halfway home. Stopping for gas, her mind took the course of least pain. She had felt the pain long enough, now go to non-feeling.

The house she called home loomed in front of her. But this time it did not welcome her as it usually did. Pulling into the garage, she removed her bag from the car. The house was silent as she entered. Going to the stairs, lifting the bag, throwing it over her shoulders, she walked

silently to her room. Dropping her load in the middle of the floor, she collapsed on her bed.

When she did open her eyes the room shared the darkness with the night. Her clock said three. Guessing it wasn't afternoon, she concluded it must be morning. The weight of sorrow became too much to bear. Twenty-two and her world just crashed. The only way she could deal, she thought, was to focus on not thinking or caring. Moving in a fog of denial, she decided to go back to school early.

290

***

Clay guided her to the chair at the outdoor patio across the street from the gallery.

A waiter appeared. "Can I get the lady something to drink?"

Clay still towered over her. "Water, please."

Becca raised her hand. "Wait. Also a bloody mary with Absolute Vodka. Make it a double with a beer chaser."

Clay raised his eyebrow. The waiter looked at him for the okay. Clay nodded. "Give the lady what she wants."

As the waiter left, Clay sat down across from Becca. He slumped in his chair, cocked his head. "You okay?"

Becca looked at the face she had loved for a lifetime. "Yeah. It just all came crashing back. I refused to think about it, so I didn't. The painting of the bridge. I didn't see it before when I came here."

"I just released it to the gallery. Tilley painted it right after you left. All the pain and grief she felt for the two kids who died. They were her best friend's children. You leaving. It ripped her heart out."

Becca bowed her head.

Clay continued. "So she painted. I went to see her one day, saw it. She asked me to take it, keep it until it was time to show it. I asked her when that would be. In Tilley fashion she said I would know. When you came back, I knew what she meant."

Becca stared at her hands. It seemed everyone knew her better than she knew herself. The silence hung between them.

After a while, Becca looked at Clay. "Thank you."

His knee dropping smile creased his face. "For what?"

"For being my friend."

"Always, Becca. Always."

The waiter sat a tall glass of a red mixture with olives, lime and pickle down in front of Becca. Followed by a frosted glass of beer. Becca removed the trimmings, took a long drink.

"Anything for you sir?" The waiter addressed Clay.

"A cold beer, thank you."

Becca raised her finger. "Bring me another one." Draining the glass, she picked up the beer.

***

Again Becca woke up with a killer headache and faint memory of getting to bed.

This has got to stop! At least I am not in jail.

Swinging her legs over the side of the bed, she held her pounding head in her hands. Still in her clothes.

A shower!

Stumbling to the bathroom, she took off her clothes, threw them in the hamper, and stepped into the running water. As the mist cleared her head, she remembered what happened last night. The painting of the bridge, the painful memory of Gwen and the accident, Clay across from her while she drank several bloody marys.

He must have got her home. She recollected nothing. Only a feeling of freedom, of releasing a hurt carried too long.

After finishing her shower, and getting dressed, she took her first cup of coffee out to the dock. Sitting yoga style, she recalculated her life. Her marriage was over. With a flick of the pen she ended the farce. She faced up to the pain that had crippled her decisions years ago. And the big one. She acknowledged, at least to herself, that she loved Clay Lester. He always was the missing part of her life.

But things had happened. She had two kids she adored, Clay had his six sons. She laughed to herself.

A soft voice sounded behind her. "Care for company?"

Becca looked over her shoulder to see Susie approaching the dock. "Come join me."

Susie sat down next to her. "So what are you doing out here?"

"Gathering my thoughts." Becca placed her hands, palms up on her knees.

"Is this a good thing?"

Closing her eyes, Becca spoke with conviction. "Yes. Yes it is. I am now a free woman."

"Oh, wow. Are you okay?"

Becca rocked back. "I am. And..." She stretched her arms above her head. "...I faced the fact I love Clay Lester."

Susie clapped her hands. "What did he say?"

Lowering her arms Becca chuckled. "I haven't told him."

"Why not?"

"I think I got too drunk. Unless..." Becca frowned, tilted her head. "...no I don't think I told him. Because if I did..." Becca laughed.

"If you did what?"

"I don't think I would have woken up alone." Becca grinned.

The two women giggled.

Susie spoke through her laughing. "So what are you going to do?"

Becca leaned back. "Seduce him. I did it once. I can do it again."

CHAPTER FIFTEEN

Becca shut the laptop lid. The kids had been gone for a week.
Both Haley and Jon Jr. just touched base with her. They kept in
touch by email and Skype. Haley remained focused and on track.
Finishing her last class at the university, she now concentrated on
the cooking internship from the Cordon Blue. Jon Jr. told her
Kevin Lester came to visit as they were at colleges only a few
miles from each other. Oh, yes he also met the black sheep,
Thomas.

While she missed them, she enjoyed the quiet freedom from
other people. Mid-morning, today was a crisp fall day, full of
autumn colors of brunt orange, sunset gold, blazing reds.
Standing, she stretched, picked up her coffee cup, headed for the
kitchen. Passing the studio, she stopped, then entered. The

desire to paint hit her strong. Setting the cup down, she started gathering up supplies.

The outdoors called to her. *"Go find a place of serene beauty. Today is a day not to miss."*

Wearing jeans, a light sweater, tennis shoes, she grabbed a painting smock as her last item. Lugging her treasures to the car, she picked up her bag on the way. Shutting the door with her hands full, she placed her load in the back seat of the car. Before she started the car, she picked up a hair tie to bunch up her mop of hair.

The idea of an adventure made her giggle. Her plan was to just drive until something hit her fancy. Heading to the north side of the lake, she looked in awe at the amazing colors bursting on the picturesque landscape.

Alone on the road, she drove at a snail's pace. She knew the lake was on her left. Rounding a bend, she saw a decorative wooden sign reading 'DRAGONFLY COVE.'

Sounds inviting.

Easing the car onto the single lane, dirt side-road, she bounced as she drove over ruts and potholes. All roads led to the lake, so she figured she would eventually find herself at the water's edge. A small hill stood before her. As she crested it, she took in a breath. Before her was a beautiful log house. Not a cabin, a grand house with large windows showcasing a view of the lake to die for. Stunned by the beauty of the view, she was taken aback when it hit her where she had landed.

This is Clay's house! This is where he brought me when we made plans for our life together. Shit! I need to get out of here.

Glancing up at the house she saw him standing on the deck. Leaning with both arms on the railing, he looked straight at her. His jaw set in a straight line.

Okay, girl make this good.

Throwing the car into park, she shut it off, unfastened her seat belt. Opening her door, taking a deep breath, she slid out of the car. Feeling the gravel under her feet, she threw her shoulders back, brushed at her clothes. Why? She did not know, a nervous thing.

Rounding the front of the car, she kept her sights on Clay. He just stood there looking at her. Shading her eyes with her hand, she yelled up at him. "Hi. I was just looking for a place to paint. Took this road."

Lowering her hand she turned in a circle. "Wow, this is quite a place."

"Do you want to see inside?"

She turned back to face him.

Not really. It will drive home just how much I gave up.

"Sure." Going to the deck stairs, he met her halfway. "So this where you live?" She could see the depthless blue of his eyes.

Clay cocked his head. "Yeah, I live here."

Since he stood two steps up from her, her eyes traveled up his body. Worn black cowboy boots, what would be called 'working boots'. His faded blue jeans hugged his rock hard thighs. The belt buckle hung at his waist just above... Passing on up to the powder blue plaid shirt fitting a rib cage firm and buffed. The blue accented his eyes to a knee-weakening intensity. He gave her a wry smile. Leaning on the handrail, his body blocked her way.

Becca stopped. Close enough to smell the freshness of a shower on his skin, she started rambling again. "So it is such a pretty day, I thought, go paint. So here I am..." He moved aside so she could pass. Brushing against him on the narrow steps, she kept moving and talking. "...this is a gorgeous place."

Reaching the top, she looked out over the deck at the breathtaking view of the lake.

I should paint this.

She felt Clay beside her. Unable to decide what to do with her hands, she stuffed them in her jeans pocket.

"Come on in." He gently placed his hand on her back, guiding her to the sliding doors. Opening them with ease, she stepped into a man cave. The décor was rustic, big oversized chairs, a large looming stone fireplace. A mass of windows on the back opened up to another spectacular view of the lake. Leaving him, she wandered through the room. Touching the furniture as she passed, she felt she had entered a dream of what might have

298

been. Going to the windows, she glanced at the wall to the left.
All different types of artwork collaged together of dragonflies.

Looking closer she found one a rough, handmade piece.
Under it a plate read 'Africa'. "You travel a lot, Clay?"

His voice sounded from across the room. "Yeah. When I can."

"Africa? You went there?"

The smile sounded in his tone. "Yeah, a safari. Quite an
adventure."

"Did you kill anything?"

"No, didn't go to kill. Just to see."

"Why did you name this Dragonfly Cove?"

"Mainly because it has the largest dragonfly population on the
lake."

Becca twirled around. "Really?"

He shrugged, nodded.

"So you built your house?" She walked back over to the
windows.

"Yes. At first I built just a small cabin. A place to come, get
away from everything, to fish. Then when the boys and I moved
here, I added on."

Still with her back to him. "Moved here? Isn't this where you
and your wife lived?"

"Oh, hell no. Veronica didn't want any part of the lake life. We lived in a house over in Country Club estates. She wanted it when we divorced, I didn't."

"So she lives over there and never lived here?"

"Yeah." For some odd reason the answer made her happy.

"I would have lived here with you." Becca spoke low, mostly to herself.

"What did you say?"

Becca turned around. "Nothing. This is just a grand house. You build it all?"

"Mostly. It was a work of love for me."

Becca raised an eyebrow.

"It was a home for me and my boys."

Becca nodded. Putting her hands behind her back, she strolled to the kitchen area. A modern-day kitchen with an old-fashioned charm.

Clay's voice vibrated on her back. "I am just fixing some lunch. Join me."

"Okay. You cook?"

Clay chuckled. "Raising five boys, you either learn how to cook or you starve."

Becca caught the mistake in numbers. "Five. You forgot one."

"No..." He walked around her to the counter. "...five. Thomas stayed with his mom." He motioned to the table. Becca sat down

300

at the small table in the breakfast nook. Again the floor to ceiling window captured another awesome view of the nature outside.

"So...are you at odds with your son?"

Clay set a plate in front of her. "Not as long as I keep bailing him out of his messes."

"Is he in trouble?"

Clay sat across from her. "Nothing serious, like drugs or anything. Just makes bad choices with women, gambling, the fast life he chooses to live."

"I'm sorry." Becca looked seriously at him. "Must be hard."

Clay smiled at her. "It's okay. Five out of six ain't bad." He chuckled.

Picking up the BLT sandwich, Becca took a bite, swallowed. "Oh... This is good."

"Thank you my lady." He mockingly bowed his head. "So, your kids get back to school?"

Becca nodded, her mouth full of food.

Clay nodded. "I guess there is to be a wedding between our families."

Becca nodded, finished her chewing. "Yes. Your Andrew. My Haley. Who would have thought?"

"Strange turn of events." Clay looked out the window.

Becca felt awkward.

You need to get over this, girl.

Clay rose, took her empty plate. Without speaking, he took them to the sink. Becca folded her napkin, placed it on the table.

Following him, she stood just behind him as he rinsed the dishes. "Look. Clay. We need to clear the air."

He jerked around, his eyes shooting fire. ""You walked out on me."

"Not you. My friend died." Becca wanted to touch him, but she was afraid of his reaction.

"So did mine. So did all of ours. What gave you the right to cut and run?" He stepped toward her.

She started to step back, then decided to stand strong. "I didn't say I did it right."

"Good. I'm glad we have that established." Clay ran his hand through his hair. "Why didn't you come back?"

Becca held his glare. It was time to own her actions. "I was scared."

"Of what? Me?" Clay's look changed to confusion.

Becca felt her snarky side rise. "Don't flatter yourself. I was not afraid of you."

"Of what then?"

Becca placed her hands on his chest. "Of facing the truth. Having the courage to accept it."

"And what pray tell is the truth, Becca?" His bitterness still lingered. His eyes shot sparks. Never had he been hotter.

"That I loved you. And if I loved you anymore and lost you, I wouldn't be able to live. Gwen died so she could be with Martin, because living without Martin would be no life for her."

There I said it.

Without words, he grabbed her, crushing his mouth to hers. Her hip flowed into his as their bodies aligned to each other. Returning his passion and anger, she kissed him with all the pent-up emotions she had denied for so long.

Clay backed her up against the wall. His hands moved over her ribs to remove her sweater. His mouth moved down to her breasts. She relaxed, allowed her body to feel what she kept from it all those years. Her hands pulled open his shirt. Each sound of the snaps giving way pushed her buttons of desire.

He cupped her butt, lifting her up. She wrapped her legs around his waist. Carrying her, she encircled her arms around his neck, buried her face in the sweet smell of him, kissing and tasting his skin.

When he stopped moving, she felt herself flying away from him as he tossed her onto a bed. Towering over her, she smiled at the hunk of a man. He started to undo his belt buckle. She sat up, taking his hands. Together they released his manhood. The slow, sexy, smile she remembered from him returned.

Lying back, she brought him with her. As he kissed her, his hands removed her jeans. His mouth traveled down her, licking and sucking her into a dizzy swirl of passion. Her fingers raked though his hair as she moaned. Twisting with the pain of wanting him, she seized the moment.

The feel of him haunted her dreams. Bringing to the surface the empty void in her life, she accepted him. The first climax sent shock waves through her over-aroused, too long denied body. The cap of the second one captured her soul.

Clawing at his back to release the pressure, the third and final one sent her over the edge. He peaked with her and together they capped the cliff of crazed desire.

Holding him tight to her, afraid he would vanish if she let go, she clung to him like a life line. His breathing slowed as he rose to look at her.

Releasing her death grip, she allowed him room to breathe. He brushed her hair from her eyes.

"My gawd, Becca. I have so missed you."

The tears busted out. "Clay, I am so sorry." Blubbering she stroked his face. "I know it was the mistake of my life. I knew it years ago. I am so sorry..."

He stopped her words with a kiss. "Shhh. It's going to be alright."

"Is it?"

"Yes. Becca. This time you are not going to run."

"This time?"

Clay moved off of her. Took her in his arms. "Do you love me?"

Becca sobbed. "Yes. Yes. I always have. Always will."

"And I have always loved you. So this time there is no reason we shouldn't be together. Right?"

"You still want me?"

"Yes, darlin'. I still want you." She could feel his body quiver as he chuckled.

The relief she felt being back in his arms, his life, his heart overwhelmed her. "Oh Clay. I love you so."

For several minutes they clung to each other. Finally Clay moved, untangling them. Getting off the bed, he picked up her jeans, gave them to her. Becca slide off the bed, slipped into them. Watching Clay get dressed made her smile.

"You are still gorgeously hot." Becca stepped over to caress his waist.

Clay kissed her upturned lips. "You my darlin' have not changed. You still have a body that gives me a hard on."

She smacked his chest. "How romantic is that!"

His laugh warmth her. "It's the truth. Since you came back I have taken many a cold shower."

The crude words were the best she ever heard. "So I still got it?"

Clay swung her around. "More than ever."

The kiss they shared now was not only passion, but a coming back to a safe place.

Home.

Walking out of the bedroom arm in arm, he swooped down, picking up her shirt. Taking it from him, she left his embrace long enough to pull it on.

He helped her pull it down. "So were you really out to find a place to paint?"

Becca chuckled. "Yes. Truthfully, I did not know you lived here. But I guess the fates guided me." She walked to the center of the room. "This is a beautiful house." Regret covered her. "I would have loved to live here with you. Raise our kids. Build a life."

Clay came behind her, circled her waist, drew her into him. Speaking against her hair. "It's the past Becca. Let's just move on from here."

Becca nodded. "Okay. Let's start all over."

"To our new beginning, Luv."

***

Walking her to her car, Becca showed him her painting supplies. "See I really was looking for a place to paint."

Clay opened her door, gathering her in his arms. Pinning her against the car, he let his lips drag the pleasure of her taste into his mouth.

She'll remember this kiss.

306

Pulling back he kissed the tip of her nose. "When can I see you again?"

"Anytime. Just come on over."

Am I really swooning?

"Tomorrow after work."

"I'll cook dinner?"

"You cook? I figured you had a cook to do it for you."

"I did. I fired her. I fired all of my old life when I came back to Lester Lake."

"Roughin' it, huh?"

She went up on her tiptoes, kissed his cheek. "No. Just makin' it real."

Clay patted her butt as she climbed in the car. "Honey, I'm as real as you can get." Shutting her door, he stroked her cheek.

Becca laughed. "I can vouch for that."

It was hard to let her go, Clay stood back, watching as she turned the car around to drive away. To finally have the woman he loved in his life was like the end of a dream and the start of reality. The memory of the last time he saw her taillights disappear surfaced.

No! This time is different.

He ran his fingers through his hair.

Make this time different.

Clay walked back into the house. He went to the sink, began washing the dishes. His mind recapped what just happened. His physical body felt a great relief from his sexual tension. His mind tried to wrap around the possibilities.

Could Becca and I still have a life together?

The back door slammed, bringing him back. Looking at the plate in his hand he realized he was still washing the same one. He turned, saw Stephen walking into the house.

"Hey Pops. I just passed Becca on the road." Grabbing an apple from the bowl on the counter, he took a big bite. "Was she here?"

Clay kept his back to his son. "Yeah. She was on a painting expedition."

Stephen laughed. "Yeah, I bet. Dad getting a little afternoon delight?" Stephen walked on into the great room. Plopped down on the couch, flipped on the TV.

Clay grabbed a dish cloth, wiping his hands as he stared absent mindedly at the screen.

If he only knew!

***

The drive back to her house was the best ever for Becca. Her body still tingled from the love-making. She smiled all the way home. Pulling into her driveway, she bounced out of the car, up the steps.

Once in the privacy of her own house, she let out a yell. "I still got it." Her back hit the hall wall with a thud. "I so needed that."

Swinging her hips she strolled on into the bathroom, singing as she undressed. "I am one hot mama. Got me a cowboy lover. He is the best, in the west. One hot mama."

The sting of the water hitting her bare skin only heightened her desires. She let them surface, spinning around to fill her spirit.

Tomorrow I will get another dose of Clay Lester. And every day for the rest of my life.

Becca shook her fist at the ceiling.

Don't fuck this up for me this time.

A shot of cold water hit her back. She jumped, slipped, landed on her ass. With the shower crashing over her she leaned against the wet wall.

Point taken.

***

Waking the next morning, Becca's cloud of happiness surrounded her, letting her know it was real at last. Her body ached for Clay. She allowed her mind to wander to the fact that tonight he would be here in her bed with her.

Snuggling down, she stretched her arms above her head.

This truly is the first day of the rest of my life.

The ringing of her cell phone interrupted her thoughts. Looking at the caller id, she saw it was Jilley.

"Hey girl!" Becca answered the phone.

The surprise in Jilley's voice was obvious. "Becca? Why so chipper?"

"It's a good day."

"It's only eight in the morning. How do you know it's a good day, yet?"

"Trust me, it will be."

"If you say so. Can you meet for lunch?"

Becca crunched up her nose. "The Club?"

"No. Let's get a greasy, fattening, delicious hamburger at Brick's."

Becca sat up, swinging her legs over the side of the bed. "Now that sounds good. Fries?"

"But of course."

Becca stretched as she stood. "Good I have some errands to do. Say around noon?"

"Make it one. The crowd will be gone."

Walking over to the window, Becca smiled at the serene scene of the morning dew hovering over the lake. "Okay, but I can't get drunk this time. I have plans for the evening."

"Doing what?" Jilley's voice snapped to attention.

"Tell you later." Becca turned from the window.

"Will I like these plans?"

Becca smiled to herself. "You will love them." Her phone clicked. Pulling back she checked the incoming call.

Clay.

"Jilley. I have a call coming in. See you at one."

Jilley wasn't going to be put off easily. "Who is...?"

Becca switched lines. "Clay." His name rolled off her tongue in an easy, tasty, good way.

"Just calling to see if what happened yesterday is real or just a dream." His rich voice reminded her of his touch.

Holding the phone with both hands. "It's real."

"How are you today?"

"In love with you."

His low, rough voice sent a chill do her stomach. "Good, because I am still in love with you."

"Where are you?"

"Driving to work. What are you doing?"

"Just getting up. Jilley called. Woke me up." Standing, she walked to the window.

"Do you know I have never woken up in the morning with you?"

The thought thrilled her. "Then we need to change that."

"Oh, we will darlin'. Tonight."

Becca felt the peak of desire hit her core. "Count on it."

"Later, babe."

"Back at you."

Disconnecting the call, she walked to the closet.

This is a blue jean day. I have lots to do.

***

After stopping at all the places on her list, Becca walked into a nearly empty bar at

Brick's. Jilley was waiting in a booth at the back. With a kick in her step, Becca smiled at David on her way to the table.

Jilley's wore a frown as she watched Becca. "Why are you so happy? If I didn't know better I would swear you got laid..." Her face changed to total surprise. "...You did!" Grabbing Becca's arm she drug her into the booth. "Tell me!"

Becca was laughing so hard she cried.

Jilley ranted on. "Oh, please tell me it's Clay, not Jon. It is Clay isn't it?"

"Are those the only two choices I have?"

Jilley grabbed both of Becca's hands. "Just tell me it is Clay?" Jilley shook her hands.

"What about my Dad?" David appeared at the table.

Becca knew she was blushing and shook her head.

Jilley let go of Becca, leaned back. "Nothing. Just catching up on old times. You want?" She addressed David.

"Your order?" He gave her a questioning look.

Jilley now blushed. "Yeah, okay. Two burgers with everything. Fries on the side."

312

"How do you want the burgers cooked?"

Jilley frowned at him. "Medium."

"Cheese on the fries?"

Jilley waved her hand. "Sure."

An amusing gleam in his eyes. "And to drink?"

"Water! Are you writing a book?"

David cocked his head, looked at Jilley. "Just taking your order, ma'am."

Jilley narrowed her eyes. "Fine. Now you have it." She stared at the boy.

David winked at Becca. "I'm good, ladies." He strolled away.

Jilley and Becca's eyes followed him until he disappeared into the kitchen.

"Now." Jilley swung her look to Becca.

Becca's rolled her eyes. "Okay. You deserve this. Yes. Clay."

"When? How?" Jilley's jubilant shriek bounced around the room.

Taking Jilley's hand, Becca leaned forward, spoke in a lower voice. "Yesterday. I just happened to wander onto his property and..."

"Bada Bing Bada Boom." Jilley made semi-cruel gestures.

Becca laugh. "Something like that."

"And..."

"And we are going to give it a try. He's coming over tonight."
Becca slapped her hands on the table. "Oh, Jilley. I feel again like
I did when I was twenty-two. All giddy and fuzzy."

"As well you should." Jilley smiled. "I am so happy for you."

Becca bit her lower lip. "I just hope nothing screws it up this
time."

David appeared silently again, putting the two heaping plates
of food in front of each of them. "Enjoy ladies."

Becca nodded. "Thanks David."

He nodded, smiled. "You're welcome."

After he left, Jilley took a big bite of her burger. Chewing, she
chuckled. Once her mouth cleared, she picked up her water. "To
you and Clay. It's been a long time coming."

Becca raised her glass, clinked Jilley's "Hear, hear."

***

Becca fussed the rest of the afternoon over the meal for Clay.
Listening to a local radio station playing a mixture of soft rock
pop. She bounced around the kitchen. She had never been this
excited to put on one of the many dinner parties Jon insisted they
present for the for the masses of 'friends'.

Friends! A bit of an overstatement.

There were colleagues, important clients, strangers. Ne're a
friend in the bunch of them. Not like Susie and Jilley. She smiled
as she remember the "girl's nite out". Drunk, she poured her
heart out to them. They held her in their confidence.

314

Now those are friends.

As the meat marinated and the salad crisped, Becca went outside to the dock to arrange the new outdoor furniture. A picture in a magazine inspired her. Setting candles and flowers around, she smiled and hummed as she worked.

The evening would be cooler now that fall was coming. She had purchased a fire pit, just in case. Sitting down for a minute, she surveyed her work. Her mind wandered to what she hoped would happen.

Leaning back, she closed her eyes. The images of Clay as they made love came sweeping over her, arousing her. Just two more hours she would be in his arm.

CHAPTER SIXTEEN

"Mae, I'm done for the day." Clay shouted to his secretary as he came out of his office. Dropping a pile of signed papers on her desk, he smiled raised his eyebrows.

Mae looked up at the big clock on the wall. "But Boss, it's only three."

Clay shifted to one leg. "Is there a problem?"

"No, just...what do you have to do?"

Clay leaned both hands on her desk, smiled at the woman who had beendear to him for years. "I, my lady, have a date." He cocked his head.

"Who? Haven't you dated every free, and not so free, woman in Lester County? Are you branching out? You know what happened the last time you did?" She leaned her chin in her hands.

"Very funny. No. I have finally found the real thing."

316

A look of sadness mixed with worry crossed Mae's face. "Oh, Clay. You know the only one for you is Becca..."

He winked at her.

"...Becca, it's Becca?" She stood, came around the desk, hugged him. "Go. Go!"

Clay hugged her back, laughing. Letting go, he headed for the door.

Mae yelled after him. "Go buy flowers. And wine. And chocolate..." Her suggestions followed him out the door.

Strolling to his truck, he threw his keys into the air, whistled a catchy tune. Once inside he leaned back before starting the engine.

Mae's ideas were good.

Taking his cell phone from his side clip, he speed dialed Becca's number. Her voice slipped over him like a refreshing rain.

"Clay?" There was a slight edge to her tone.

"Hey darlin'. Just calling to say I will be there in about an hour."

He could hear the sigh of relief. "I'm here."

For two decades he waited to hear those words. "Love you, Becca."

"Love you too, Clay."

Disconnecting, he swung into the parking lot of the only florist in town. Going in, he heard the bell ring over his head.

The middle-aged woman at the counter looked up. "Clay. What brings you in? Someone die?"

Am I that pathetic?

"No one died, Peg." He walked over to the cooler filled with all kinds of flowers. "I need some roses."

"What color?"

Clay stopped.

Did she have a favorite color?

He looked at all the colors. "I have no idea."

"Well..." Peg slid the glass door on the cooler back. "...since its fall, the orange is always a good choice."

Clay looked at the orange ones. While they were beautiful, they didn't quite say what he wanted. "What about red?"

"Typical. Says true love." Peg almost yawned.

"Okay. A dozen?"

Peg gathered up the deepest red roses in her case. Going to her work counter. "What kind of a vase."

Clay fished the cash out of his wallet. "No vase." He looked over at Peg.

Peg wrapped the roses in a tissue. "When do you want them delivered?"

"No delivery. I'll take them with me."

Peg raised an eyebrow. "Who are these for Clay?"

Small town people! Need to know everything.

"A very special lady." He laid some cash on the counter, took the bundle from Peg.

Peg frowned. "Mae? It's not her birthday yet. It's in January."

Clay took a deep breath. "Not Mae."

"So who?"

"Have a good day Peg." He left the shop.

A liquor store was just across the street. Tucking the roses under his arm, he jogged over. Entering, he realized he had no idea what kind of wine Becca liked.

Was she a sophisticated expensive wine person or a...?

"Hey Joe." Clay addressed the man in the store. "Has Becca Young, er Hamilton, ever been in here to buy wine?"

"Becca? Sure."

"So what's her favorite?"

Joe walked over to a shelf, picked up a sparkling white wine. "This. She always buys this."

"Great. Give me two bottles."

Holding the roses under his arm, he paid, taking the bag from Joe.

"Thanks." Clay could see the knowing smirk on Joe's face. "Please don't say anything. Not yet. Please?"

Joe winked. "You got it."

Swinging his truck onto the road to his house, he hit the bumps at a hefty speed. A cloud of dust swirled up as he stepped from the truck. Leaving the flowers and wine on the seat, at a half run, he took the deck steps two at a time.

Making a bee line for the shower, he quickly undressed. Giving himself a quick once over, he stepped out, wrapped a towel around his waist, walked to his bedroom. Picking out fresh clothes and a good pair of boots, he dressed hurriedly. Fastening his belt, he bumped into Stephen in the hall.

"Whoa, Dad. Where are you off to?"

Clay skipped around his son. "Out."

"What about dinner?"

Clay chuckled as he side-skipped through the house. "You're a big boy. Figure it out."

Stephen yelled after him. "Where are you going?"

Clay didn't answer. He jumped down the steps, trotted to his truck. Becca's house was just a few minutes from his.

Slowing down, he pulled into her driveway. When he stepped out of the truck, he could smell grilling meat. Smoke snaked around the corner of the house. Gathering up his treasures of wine and flowers, he followed the smell. Once at the back of the house, he saw Becca standing at the grill, her back to him. Stepping softly, he came up behind her. Dressed in a long flowing dusty blue sun dress, her feet bare.

320

When he reached her, she was still unaware of his presence. Putting the arm holding the wine bottle around her waist, he drew her into him. She giggled, leaning against him. As he kissed her neck, he brought the flowers around.

"To the love of my life."

She took the roses, turned in his arms, kissing him with a luscious eagerness rousing a slow burn of anticipation, forcing it to curl through him.

He moaned as he devoured her. Her body formed to his. Savage desire made him draw a harsh, ragged breath. His body hardened at the thought of spending the night with her. The little purr sounding in her throat enticed him to draw the kiss out.

So into the kiss, both escaped into a timeless stage.

Finally Becca pulled back, speaking against his lips. "The steaks are going to burn."

Clay groaned. "All right."

"We have all night. " Becca kissed him lightly, turned back to the grill.

Clay took the fork from her. "I'll do this." He handed her the bag with the wine. "Here, put this on ice."

Becca pulled out the bottle. "My favorite." She narrowed her eyes at him. "How did you know?"

Clay gave her a wry smile. "I have my ways."

She slipped into his arms, snuggled against his chest. "You certainly do have your ways."

He kissed the top of her head. "We'll work on that later." Patting her butt. "Now let a man do his thing."

Giggling, she stepped back. "Okay. I have things to do in the house."

Clay was in deep concentration when a voice startled him.

"Clay?"

Jerking around Clay laughed. "Robby."

"What are you doing here?" Robby strolled toward Clay with his hands in his pocket.

Clay gave Robby a good-humored grin. "Having dinner with Becca."

"Are you two...you know...together?" Robby lowered his voice.

Clay leaned in, whispered. "Yes. We are."

The smile breaking across Robby's face was priceless. "Seriously?"

Clay flipped the steaks. "Seriously. Hey can you find me a cold beer?"

"Right here." Becca walked up on them. She handed both men a cold bottle.

Robby's look of amazement still on his face. She patted his arm. "I saw you walk across."

She slid her arm around Clay's waist. "How are we doing?"

He smiled back at her. "We are just about done."

322

Becca started back for the house. "I'll get the rest of the stuff."

"Need help?" Clay offered.

"Nope. I'm good." She flung over her shoulder.

Clay waited until Becca went in the house before he finished his answer. "Close your mouth, Robby."

Robby gulped. "I'll be damned."

Clay laughed. "Aren't you glad?" He turned the fire down on the grill.

"Oh, hell yes. Wait until I tell Susie."

"You know what Robby, tell the whole world. This time nothing will come between us."

They both turned as they heard the screen door slam. Becca came toward them with a tray.

Robby and Clay looked at each other.

"I need to run." Robby scooted away.

As Becca got closer, Clay met her, took the tray from her. Walking together to the table, he sat it down. Looking around the table, he saw how much effort Becca put into making this dinner special. It was as important to her as it was to him.

"Looks good." Clay pulled her to him.

Becca laid her head on his shoulder. "Clay Lester. I have not been this happy in many years. And it is because of you."

"No, honey. It's because of you. You faced your demons, stood strong."

Becca pinched his ribs. "You are my demon. And my salvation at the same time."

Clay stiffened. "Let's eat. I want to get you to bed early, darlin'."

***

That night Becca came to Clay fully. He wrapped her in his love, rekindling the youthful fire. Carefully, he led her to her bedroom. Standing facing each other, the moonlight illuminated the room sending a ray of moonbeams to shine on them. Her eyes encouraged him to accept the goal to bring her to the uttermost crest, then over.

Sliding his fingers under the straps on her dress, he moved them to the front to the single tie holding back the bloom of her breasts. Freeing them, he introduced them to his hot waiting mouth. The dress fell to the floor, leaving Becca standing naked and inviting in front of him.

As she started to unsnap his shirt, he stopped her. "This night is for you."

Her body quivered under his touch as he lowered his mouth downward. Kissing and licking his way, he remembered the places to touch her. They were burned into his mind from the first time they made love. Awake, he thought of them together reliving the passion, the outright animal lust encompassing them. Asleep, his dreams were always Becca, no matter how many woman he bedded.

324

With the sweet taste of her in his mouth, he laid her down. Running his hands over her silky skin, his mouth went to the V of her thighs. They tensed as he let his tongue search and probe. Goosebumps rose on her skin as she arched with her first orgasm. She shuddered under him and he delved deeper.

Her scream echoed in the quiet as he brought her up again, letting her peak to the more powerful second summit. She squirmed and twisted under him. His face dripped sweat on her crotch. Sizzling, it danced on her hot skin.

Moving up on her, he spoke in a low voice. "Say my name, Becca."

Her eyes were closed, she opened them, drawing in his soul. Like a waterfall over a cliff, she whispered. "Clay."

"Remember that. You are back where you belong."

A smile creased her eyes. "I know." Her voice faltered as he entered her.

Driving his steel into her, she arched up to meet his demand. Her tunnel tightened around him like a vice, drawing him deep inside. The sensations collapsed around him as every cell in his body erupted with sweet indulgence.

Her passion matched his as together they escalated up the mountain of rapture. Climbing and clawing, the crown came in an explosion of exhilaration.

Tumbling over the last raw edge, she shuddered as she called his name. "Clay!"

Shaking with release, he buried his head in her breasts. "Becca."

Feeling more content than he could ever remember, he rolled from her, gathered her to him. Their bodies merged together, mixed with sweat, the dampness cooled the hotness of their skins. Holding her close, reveling in the feel of her as he cradled her body, the long time coming of this moment slipped into his spirit.

Finally, he had his Becca back. In his arms, in his life. This time he would shield her, protect her. She would never want to run from him again. He thought about why she left. In reality he couldn't blame her. They were young. Probably the worst thing ever to happen to her. She made a bad choice. How he hated her for all those years.

Hate her? Get real guy. I always loved her, I just hated what she did.

His anger was gone. The minute he kissed her, felt her kissing him back, his love for her

came barreling back.

She stirred. He kissed the top of her head.

"Clay." She rose to look at him. "Stay here tonight?"

"I was planning on it darlin'."

326

She leaned her arm on his chest. "Good. I want to wake up with you next to me."

"And you will. For the rest of your life. If that's what you want?"

"I want. I can do this for the rest of my life. Grow old with me Clay."

He chuckled. "We have a long ways to old. But know I will be there with you."

***

The quiet of the morning allowed Clay to reflect on all that happened. Becca snuggled into his body. His arm rested around her. Having her next to him was a wish he tried so hard not to indulge in. Never did he think he would get this chance. Her steady breathing the only sound breaking the calm of the moment, even the creatures of the lake were silent. A sure sign winter was approaching. His mind wandered to making love in front of a fire, walks on the leaf crusted paths, holidays, then to welcome spring again.

Becca stirred, turned her face to him, opened her eyes, smiled. "Mornin' cowboy."

The word aroused Clay. He was her cowboy. He was whatever she wanted. "Mornin' darlin'. Care to take a ride on my horse?"

She giggled, turning in his arms. Running her hand down to his manhood, she cupped it. "I see he's taut, ready to go."

Clay let a robust laugh come up from his gut. He was hard before his brain even thought of it. "He is. And I am." His hands traveled over her side, over the soft curves to her thighs. She moaned as his fingers probed the sweet spot. He felt her wetness, worked his magic. Her body quivered as he let his lips follow the same trail as his hands.

Clay never forgot how to please a woman. The fact he loved this woman, made nourishing her sexual hunger his pleasure. Becca was starving for the touch of a lover. And he would be the feast she craved.

Her mature body trembled with anticipation. The shy young girl was replaced by a grown woman who let her desires play out. His body just ached. The pain always there, but when he first saw her, it spiked, he never got any relief. Until now. Of all the women he had, none aroused him like his Becca. None left him as satisfied. The only true release came in the soft, hot clasp of her body.

"Oh, Clay! Tell me what a fool I was to leave you." Becca spoke in a low raspy voice.

Licking her belly, Clay chuckled. "You were a fool to leave me." He spoke against her skin. He toyed with her, slowly rocking his hips against hers. She squirmed as she grabbed his butt, bringing him to her.

328

He entered her slow, little by little. Watching her face, he gauged her climax. As his came, she crashed with him. Deeper he went as she rose off the bed to take in more of him. Sweat formed in the valley of her breasts. He licked it off, she moaned, then erupted into

screams. The third orgasm climaxed both of them.

Wet from sweat and passion, he slid off of her. Holding her in his arms, she took small quick breaths. The rays of the morning sun shot sunbeams across the room. If he had his way, he would stay in bed with her all day.

Her words came slow. "I wish we could stay here all day."

He laughed. "I was just thinking the same thing."

"Can we?"

"Not today, darlin'. I have a ton of work to do. And what would the town think if we didn't surface for several days?"

Becca giggled. "Who cares?" She turned up her face to take in his lips. "They have to get their own man."

"So now I am your man?"

"Yes. Yes you are." She kissed him again.

"Then that makes you my woman." He looked at her with a serious face.

Becca spoke, with regret in her voice. "I always was. Just too stupid to acknowledge it."

Locking his eyes on hers. "Acknowledge it now."

Her brow knitted in confusion. "Sure. How?"

Flashing a wicked smile. "Go out with me Saturday night."

Becca rose up. Joy exploded over her face. "I would love to."

"Then it's a date."

Clay slipped out of bed. Taking her hand he drew her to him. "Come take a shower with me."

Becca scrambled off the bed.

Walking into the bathroom, both naked, Becca laughed. "I've never walked around naked."

Clay frowned at her. "Never?"

She shrugged. "No. I had my own bathroom."

"Oh, poor little rich girl." He mocked her voice.

Becca put her hands on her hips. Her standing there naked, giving him her best disapproving look, was too funny. And too inviting. He grabbed her, molded his body to hers. It felt so good to him. No other woman felt this way.

Becca wrapped her arms around his neck. "We are like rabbits. Screwing all the time."

Clay kissed her. "We have many years to make up for. Besides, you were always the only girl I wanted to make love to."

Becca pushed him back. "The only girl...Just how many girls have you been with since me?" He caught a slight edge to her question.

Clay hedged. "What do you want me to say?"

"Just answer the question."

"Okay. There was a period where I fucked every girl that would let me." He held her

tight, afraid to let her go for fear she would hit him.

She squirmed against his embrace. "And that period ended...when?"

Tightening his hold, he looked her straight in the face. "When I got married. I was faithful to my wife."

Stopping her struggle, her eyes snapped in challenge. "Since your divorce?"

"Hey, I'm no monk."

Continuing to study him. "So you been catting around until I jumped in your bed?"

Giving her a sexy half-smile. "Is that a question?"

"Answer." She snarled at him.

"No." Clay shook his head. "No, I really haven't been with anyone since the divorce. A couple of one night stands..." Letting the sadness of his life without her seep in.

Becca softened her look. "Oh, Clay. I am so sorry." She stopped moving.

"For what?" He brought her close.

Regret showed on her face. "For screwing up both our lives."

Lowering his head until their foreheads touched, he whispered. "You know what. It is what it is. We are together now. That's all that counts."

Becca pulled him into the shower. The hot water beat down on both of them. Clay backed her up against wall. Going down on his knees he took her core into his mouth. The sweet taste of her and the water gave him a hard shaft. Coming up, he lifted her, placed her on him. She wrapped her legs high on his back. Slipping down to the floor, he took her with the same intensity as always. She pleasured him as she always did.

***

Standing in her doorway watching Clay leave, Becca felt a warm tingly feeling slip over. Wrapping her robe tighter around her body, she hummed as she went down the hallway back to her bedroom. In the closet she searched for clothes. Finding a pair of jeans, she flipped through the shirts hanging neatly on the rod, picking a pastel blue. Looking at the top shelf, a picture on a box caught her eyes. Jumping on her tip-toes she grabbed for the box. Not able to get it to budge, she picked up a hanger, tried to hook the lid. Giving it a jerk, it and two other boxes fell to the floor. One spilling shoes on the floor, while the other spilled something else. Letters, packs of them tied with a faded ribbon.

Picking them up, she looked at the clean handwriting.

To: Miss Tilley Young

In the corner, a return address:

PFC Jeffery Blaine

Jeffery!

Being as gentle as she could with the excitement building, she took the first envelope, carefully removed the paper inside.

My dearest Tilley,

Whoever said war is hell was right. Viet Nam...

Oh no. He was in the Viet Nam war.

Becca sat down cross legged, began reading the letters from Jeffery.

***

Hours later, she heard her front door open.

"Becca!" Clay yelled.

"In the bedroom!" She heard his heavy boots echo closer as he walked down the hall.

From the doorway he shouted again. "Becca?"

"I'm in the closest. I found Jeffery!"

Clay appeared in the doorway. "What? Did Tilley keep him in the closest?"

Becca took his hand, drug him down to her. He straddled her with his legs, leaning his chin on her shoulder.

"Aunt Tilley had a high school sweetheart. He was drafted to go to the Viet Nam war. There almost three years. He must have written to her every day. Delightful letters of love and their plans for the future."

"Wow. I never knew." Clay took one of the letters from her. As he read she nestled back against him. His soothing voice made the words come alive. Becca could see Aunt Tilley as a young girl waiting for her man to come home from the war.

Handing Clay the next letter, Becca looked at the last envelope, it was different from the rest. Yellow, it looked official. Miss Tilley Young typed on the front. A stamp of the US Army in the corner. Clay just had finished his letter, when Becca sat up, gasped. "Clay."

"What darl…" He took the strange envelope from her. Opening it, his words cut though her heart. "We regret to inform you…"

He died.

After hours of reading of their love for each other, Becca felt the pain for Aunt Tilley. She lost the love of her life. And she never spoke of it. Tears flooded Becca's eyes.

Clay hugged her, spoke against her cheek. "It's okay, Becca."

Burying her face in his shirt, she blubbered. "Oh, Clay. They were so in love. How tragic."

Clay allowed her the tears. He rocked her gently for several minutes. When she was done, she wiped her eyes on his sleeve.

Speaking against his chest. "Clay?"

His chin rested on the top of her head. "Yes darlin'?"

"We are not going to waste any more time on the past."

"Works for me."

This made her laugh. Pushing against him, he fell backwards. Climbing astride him, she looked down at the face she loved the way Aunt Tilley loved Jeffery. Working at his buttons, she slipped her hand in to run her fingers over his chest.

His eyes sparkled with mischief. Stroking her backside, he smiled as she massaged his chest. She saw him in a different light. He was the love given to her for a second time. She

would not screw this up. With her hands on his chest she felt his heart wildly beating.

Leaning down in one movement she covered his mouth with her own. Seducing him with hot, deep glides of her tongue, she claimed him. Moaning, he tried to move, but her thighs on his ribs held him tightly.

"This time it will be me pleasing you." She felt him tremble under her. Spurring her on, she moved back to undo his jeans. His manhood sprang lose. Her hand closed around him, circling, stroking. Watching the pleasure on his face as her fingers toyed with his member, she felt a bolt of fire lance through her.

His pleas only heightened her desire. Lowering herself slowly, she accepted his fullness. The robe opened giving freedom to her body. An orgasm quickly rose in her.

Clay's hands kneaded her breasts, her nipples drawn into tight, small points. His thumb and forefingers working her concentration into a frenzy.

Shudders wracked her body as she shook from the exertion of his release. When he cried out her name, Becca threw her head back and laughed. The mixture of joy and delight caught her in her soul. A warm sweet emotion went through her. She'd forgotten passion could feel like this.

Exhausted, she removed herself from him, rolled to his side. Lying together, each took deep breaths.

Clay finally broke the silence. "Damn woman!"

Becca chuckled. "You're welcome."

***

Walking into Brick's Bar on a Saturday night is like a human trying to part the Red Sea. But Clay walking in with Becca was a close second. A hush fell over the crowd. Most everyone knew their tragic love story. Clay held Becca's hand as led her through the crowd. Jilley and Sparky, Robby and Susie were meeting them. Quiet filled the small bar as they snaked their way to the table.

Then a single handclap echoed over the room. Soon a round of applause filled the air. Slaps on the back, hugs greeted them. The Romeo and Juliet of Lester County were together at last. Clay looked back at Becca. She smiled at him, squeezed his hand.

Jilley jumped up and down when they finally reached the group. "Becca. It's like royalty have arrived."

Becca leaned into to whisper to Jilley. "Was it that publicly known?"

"Afraid so, darlin'. The Crawl River Bridge tragedy and the broken heart of the county's favorite son could have been a country music song."

Clay wrapped his arms around Becca. "Dance with me darlin'."

Placing her hand in his, she let him wind their way to the dance floor. Drawing her into his arms, he two-stepped her to the music. Her body followed his as if they had been doing this for years. Burying her face in his shoulder, she inhaled the raw smell of him. A mixture of musk, sawdust and a man after a shower, she knew tonight she would once again be in his arms.

Glancing around at the other dancers, she knew she was in good company. Clay's world, now hers.

"What has you in such deep thought?" His words broke through her thoughts.

"Just thinking how good it feels to be here with you. Thank you for giving me another chance."

"There never was a question about giving you another chance, as you called it."

"Then what was it?"

"It was loving you for all these years and finally..." He pulled back to look at her. "...finally having you back."

Tipping her head up to look into the depth of his midnight blue eyes. "I am back. I promise I will never leave again."

"I'll hold you to that." His look was stern, challenging.

"Honey..."she wiggled against his lower body. "...hold me however you want, whenever you want."

A throaty laugh vibrated on her neck.

I am totally in love with this man.

Finishing their dance, they returned to the table. Sitting with old friends, they all laughed as they did years ago.

David came up, swung a chair around, sat on it backwards. "So Pops. Gotcha a hot date there?" He winked at Becca.

Clay put his hand on David's shoulder. "Yes, son. Your ole' man finally found a girl, no let me correct that, a woman, to rock my bones."

David shook his head. "TMI. Dad!"

Becca laughed at Clay's son's discomfort.

"Sorry, son. You asked." Clay took hold of Becca's hand, kissed the back of it.

David smiled. "Glad to see you two together." He stood, replacing the chair to the next table. "Becca. You look stunning tonight."

Becca nodded. "Thank you, David." Locking eyes they both understood, they only wanted what was best for Clay.

The rest of the night Clay rubbed her leg under the table, sending hot spikes up her body. She returned the favor by toying with him.

By the time the evening ended it was early morning. Walking together to his truck, Clay backed her up against the side. "You have teased me all night, woman. Are you ready for some good lovin'?"

Becca twisted against him. "The question is, are you?"

CHAPTER SEVENTEEN

Waiting for Haley to arrive, Becca busied herself making a light lunch. The fall semester had ended for both of her kids. Jon Jr. was coming later to spend the holidays.

The sound of tires on gravel alerted her of her daughter's arrival. Grabbing a dish towel, she ran to the front door. Out the screen, onto the porch, the two met. Hugging, they both laughed.

Becca saw Haley's little car filled to the top. "So you are here for good?"

Haley's face beamed. "Yes. I am."

"Come on in. I fixed some lunch. We can unpack afterward."

"No hurry. Andrew is coming over later. He can help."

Becca chuckled to herself.

Andrew is coming. Of course

340

As the two women sat down at the kitchen table, Becca looked across at her daughter.

Haley started chatting. "So I finished my entire studies…"

Becca stopped her fork in midair. "Is there a graduation?"

Haley gave a careless shrug. "…there is, but I don't want to go back for it…"

Becca tipped her head back. "Why?"

"It would be too awkward. You, Dad, Andrew." Haley shook her head.

Asking softly, Becca leaned forward. "Did you tell your Dad about Andrew?"

"Yeah. He is not pleased I am marrying some 'hick from the sticks' as he calls him," Haley said with a breeziness, dismissing the statement.

Becca reached out to Haley. "I'm sorry."

Haley took her mom's hand. "It's okay. Dad is moving on with "His life".

"And what is that? Is he…" Becca searched for the right words.

"Seeing someone?" Haley cut in. "No. At least not a woman. He is running with the big boys. Being his idea of important." Haley cocked her head. "What about you, Mom? You're divorced now. What about…"

"Clay?"

"Yes, Clay."

"Well..." Becca looked down at the table, then raised her eyes. "We are 'seeing' each other."

Haley broke out into a big smile. "That's great!"

Becca searched her daughter's face. "Really?"

"Yes, mom. You are allowed to be happy, move on." Haley gave her an approving grin.

Becca nodded. "I have moved on."

And on and on and on.

Becca just smiled back, took a bite of her salad.

***

Two weeks later, Jon Jr. rolled into Lester Lake. He drove a new car with a big speed boat behind it. Becca stood on the back deck watching him lower it into the water. Kevin and several other young men helped, as did Robby.

Men and their toys.

Haley stood behind her. "I see Dad came through with his checkbook."

"Should I feel guilty that my son is a con man to his own father?"

"Not at all. It's between him and Dad." Haley walked over to a chair. The winter had been mild this year. Today was a clear, sunny day with temps in the high 40s. Taking a seat, wrapping her sweater around her, she looked over the lake.

Becca sat next to her daughter. "So what did he offer you?"

342

Haley smiled, turning to face Becca. "You know him so well. A new car, a house, my own restaurant."

"If...?"

"If I didn't marry Andrew." Haley's fighting spirit flared slightly.

A sense of pride swelled in Becca's chest. Her daughter made the right choice. The one Becca had been too chicken to make. "Hard choice?"

Haley shook her head. "Not at all. I love Andrew. We will make a good life here." She smiled at Becca. "Isn't that what's important, Mom?"

Becca knew any answer she gave would be a trap. Her hesitation alerted Haley.

"Why did you leave, Clay, Mom? You truly love him. I've seen you together. He adores you."

Becca looked down at her hands. "It's a long story."

"I have time."

Becca nodded. It was time to tell Haley the truth.

***

Since her kids had arrived, Becca and Clay's time together was slim. But tonight was starting to play out as a night for them to be alone.

Haley and Andrew were going over to a neighboring town to look at a café. They planned on spending the night.

With Becca willing to put down some money, no strings attached, and Clay willing to invest also, Haley was looking to start her business. The kids were deep in plans for a wedding and finishing their house, so it was exciting times.

Jon Jr. and Kevin were going for a guy's night out in another town.

Clay's voice on the phone drove a warm yearning up Becca's body. "So I will sneak over after dark..."

"Sneak? We aren't children." Becca snickered.

"Sometimes I feel like it. However, catching a quick moment in the back of the truck brought back good memories." His voice carried a hint of naughtiness.

Becca clutched her phone with both hands. The giddy feeling of making love on the sly like they had when they were young did feel exciting, just a little sinful.

Purring into the phone. "Tonight we can be together in my bed."

"Lady, you just made me an offer I can't refuse. Later darlin'."

"Later."

***

The soft crush of gravel told Becca Clay was rolling in. At the dining table, she logged-off her laptop, shut the lid. All day she waited for him. What to be wearing to greet him went from coy country girl to naked. Totally naked seemed somewhat slutty, so

344

she settled for nothing under a long fluffy robe. She didn't want any clothes in his way.

Let him use his imagination as to what is underneath.

Waiting for him enter, she took in a gasp as he pushed open the unlocked door. The scene was set. A blazing fireplace gave the room a toasty inviting feel. There was wine in the ice bucket, simple finger food on the coffee table.

In the soft glow of the room, he looked good. His normal tight jeans, a rustic blue shirt, his boots, shinning black with scroll deigns. Becca did not move. As his eyes found her, his killer smile crossed his face. In two easy strides he came to her. She raised her face, opening her mouth, eager for the taste and feel of his lips. Slowly, lazily, never breaking eye contact, he lowered his lips. Accepting the warm demand of his kiss, a luscious anticipation with a slow burn of delight curled through her. An unexpected measure of wildness in his kiss brought her to her feet.

As she stood her robe fell open. His hands moved inside, caressing her burning skin.

"No hello, how are you?" She giggled against his lips.

"Hello, how are you. My gawd you feel good." He drew her naked body to him. "I see you are ready for me."

"And you sir, have on too many clothes." Becca pulled at the front of his shirt and in one motion bared his chest. Pushing it off, she next tackled his belt buckle. She had learned how to work it, so it took little effort to free his hardened shaft.

Becca looked down at him. "No underwear?"

Clay let his jeans fall to the floor, picked her up as he stepped out of them. "You weren't the only one planning ahead."

As he carried her to the rug in front of the fireplace, she licked his neck. "Are you going to leave your boots on cowboy?"

Laying her down on the rug, he chuckled. "For the first time I am."

Becca threw back her head to laugh. "The first time? Will I be able to walk tomorrow?"

His mouth touched her neck, placing soft, wet kisses. "Not if I can help it."

Becca stretched out her body as his lips traveled down, leaving a trail of hot spikes where they touched. The fire cast a lustrous glow across his chest as he rose above her. She came primed and ready. Her body knew to allow the waves of pleasure to peak, it greeted him

with an open tunnel ready to be entered.

His eyes bore into hers as he penetrated her. The climax took them both immediately, completely. Their cravings knew how to coincide with each other. Feeling each other's trembles, knowing each other's highest points of no return, both shuddered with pleasure as they capped together.

346

Becca waited for Clay to catch his breath as she took small gulps of air. Their heat was hotter than the fire they laid in front of naked.

Coming down, Clay rolled to his side. Tracing along her side with his fingers. "Gawd, I missed you."

His words reflected her own lack of his loving. Running her hand down his cheek, she touched his lips. "I have missed you so much."

"In time darlin'. The kids will move out and we will always be together."

"Stay the night?"

He grinned. "Yes, this night I can. I encouraged Andrew to have a night to himself." He rolled on his back, laid his arm over his eyes. "I know, selfish."

Becca looked down his unclothed body, admiring every inch. When she got to the boots, she giggled.

He looks so sexy all sweaty, naked with his boots still on.

Hearing her laugh, he looked over at her. "What's so funny?"

Shaking her head. "Nothing. I just feel so good."

Sitting up, he frowned then smiled. "How about some wine?"

"Yes, we have all night." As he stood, she couldn't help but laugh. The sight of him was the best.

***

"Rock it like you mean it"

The song, true to its word, rocked Becca right out of her sound sleep. Her hand searched the night stand for her cell phone. Feeling the familiar object in her hand, without looking she pressed the talk button.

Holding it to her ear. "This better be damn important."

Clay's phone rang behind her. She felt the covers move across her as he rose up to answer it.

This doesn't feel good.

As Clay answered his, Becca listened to the calm voice. "There's been an accident. Your daughter, Haley, is alive but in serious condition at Lester Memorial Hospital...

The panic in Clay's voice made her turn around. "Ben. Andrew? On my way."

Becca clicked the off button. Her eyes locked with Clay.

Brace yourself they said. We're in for a ride.

Without speaking, they both left the bed, went to gather the clothing chucked around the room. They dressed without speaking. Pulling and jerking, Becca had no idea what she was putting on. Pants, a shirt, shoes.

Where are my damn shoes!

They finished together and Clay took her hand. If he hadn't been leading her, she doubted she could even find the door. Her mind went blank. Things seemed to move in slow motion even though they were running. The warmth of his hand kept her grounded. Outside at the truck they parted, opened the doors, hit the seat with a thud at the same time.

Becca clasped her hands together. Her prayer more like begging.

Please let her be okay.

Her mind went back to Martin and Gwen.

And Andrew. Oh, God, please both of them.

The truck barreled down the dirt road, fish tailing as they hit the paved street, turning left. Becca saw the lights of the city. Trying to get her bearings, she just realized it was still dark.

What time is it?

The dashboard said 3:00 in a bright white light. Daring to look over at Clay, she saw his jaw muscles tense, the vein in his neck bulging. Without speaking or turning his head, he reached out, took her hand, squeezed it. Great sobs threatened to explode.

No! Not now! I must stay in control. Haley needs me.

Forcing them down, she took a deep breath. Focusing on the scenery, she realized the hospital was just a couple of blocks away. The early hours found the streets deserted. Clay had to be speeding. The buildings flew by. He whizzed through a red light, took the last turn at a dangerous angle. One block, straight ahead. The emergency room sign jumped up in front of them.

Thank God.

The truck suddenly came to a standstill. Becca stopped her head from hitting the dashboard by bracing her arms in front of her. Yanking the doors open, they jumped out. As they crossed paths in front of the truck, Clay again took her hand, guiding her to the doors. The noise startled her as they slid back.

Ben Cooper came toward them, but he spoke to Clay. "They are both in surgery. Critical, but still alive."

Becca felt her knees buckle. Clay grabbed her, pulling her into his body. His solidity and strength let her grab for him. Burying her face in his chest, she pulled him close.

Ben steadied her with a hand on her arm. "Are you okay Becca?"

Turning her head to look at him, she nodded.

Clay's deep voice vibrated on her head. "Ben, Becca is the girl's mother."

Through tear-filled eyes she nodded once.

Clay spoke against her cheek. "Ben's who called me."

Again she nodded once.

Ben pointed behind them. "The waiting room is right there." He put his hands on their backs, gave them a slight shove.

Breaking away from Clay, she walked to the small, dimly-lit room. Stopping short she looked around. A double chair, four single chairs, a couple of tables, a lamp, magazines, a Bible- all in muted beige tones. She felt the movement behind her.

Clay's voice. "Thanks Ben for everything."

350

The slapping of a back. "No problem, Clay. I'll keep close, give you the updates as they come."

Another slap. "Good."

Hands on her back guided her to the double chair. She allowed it, afraid she might collapse. Again the surreal slow motion. Fighting the nausea climbing up her throat, a pair of hands pushed her down as she plopped on the seat. A heavy weight crushed her shoulders, her heart pounded, knees shook.

Clay sat down next to her, draing her into his arms. "Hang tight baby. They are going to make it. Trust me."

The tears exploded in a gush of pain and fear. Collapsing against him, she drew in his strength. Words wouldn't form, so she just nodded her head. The vibration and musical ring from her phone made her draw away. Checking the caller ID she saw it was Jon Jr.

"Jonny." She knew her voice betrayed her, but she didn't know how to conceal it.

"Mom? What's wrong? I got a call from the police. They said Haley been in an accident. Is she alright? Where are you?"

"I'm at the hospital. Yes, she been in an accident..." she turned and looked at Clay, lowered her head. "She's in surgery..."

What else should she say?

Jon Jr. gasped. "On my way."

Becca's thoughts leaped feverishly. "Jon, call your dad."

No argument from him. "Okay...I will."

The phone went dead. Becca stared at it, turned to Clay. "Should you call people?"

Clay's lips went into a tight line. He reached in his pocket for his phone. With one hand, he speed dialed a number. Becca could hear it ring and with every unanswered one, Clay frowned a little more. Then they heard a muffled voice.

"Yeah?"

"David."

The voice raised in pitch, his attention caught. "Dad? What's wrong? What time is it?"

"David, listen. Andrew has been in an accident. We're at the hospital. Find your brothers. Call your mother..."

"Okay, Dad. Is he alright?"

"We don't know." The pain in his voice echoed down.

"We? Who is we?"

"Becca and I. Her daughter was with him." Clay looked over at Becca.

"Haley? Is she okay?"

He rubbed his eyes. "We don't know that either. Just get here."

"On my way." The phone went dead.

Becca rubbed his cheek. "Seems like we both are chicken to talk to our exes."

352

Clay grabbed her hand kissed the palm. "I just cannot deal with her drama right now."

Their eyes caught. "I know."

Clay pulled Becca back to him. Resting his chin on the top of her head, she felt his light kiss, then heard his sigh. She nestled into his body.

***

Within fifteen minutes, the ER doors started sliding back and forth. The first to arrive was Jon Jr.. Becca jumped up from the chair, rushed to him, hugging him as if she let him go he would disappear.

"Mom? How is she?" Her son always did ask the right questions.

"We don't know." At the word we, Jon look around her.

"Clay." His attention went back to Becca. "Andrew?"

Becca nodded.

"Oh, wow." He looked at Clay. "Sorry."

The door, then footsteps as two of Clay's sons arrived. Matt and Kevin stopped in the hallway, just short of the waiting room. Becca turned to Clay, but he stood on his feet, heading out the door. Once they saw their father, they both approached him with a million questions. Clay herded them into the small room. Becca moved Jon Jr. to two chairs on the far wall, pulled him to sit down.

They watched as Clay tried to explain what he knew. But for every answer they shot out five more questions.

Finally, Clay got them to sit down. "It's a waiting game, sons. Just keep positive thoughts."

He turned, running his hand through his hair. Becca saw the agitation in his face. She was about to get up, go to him, but the door opened again. Two more sons, David and Stephen, entered. Stephen's eyes were already red from crying. She sat back down, took Jon Jr.'s hand, patted it.

Clay embraced his youngest son, drew David in with them. Matt and Kevin sat very still, but Becca could tell they were fighting tears. Kevin wiped his eyes, Matt patted his knee. The five men sat together as Clay quietly tried to explain again.

Just as he got things quiet, the door opened, in walked Veronica and Thomas. Becca watched Clay's face as he rose slowly, moving hesitantly to the door. Thomas, pushed back by his mother, slipped over to his brothers.

Veronica's high pitched voice rang out. "What the fuck happened here?"

Clay took hold of her arms. "Calm down. Andrew and Haley were in a car crash."

"Haley!" Veronica pushed him away, jerked her head towards Becca. "Your daughter?" The words were said with a mean accent on daughter.

354

Becca knew this is not the time or place... "Yes." She raised her chin up, looked Veronica

straight in the eye.

"Figures." The one word spit out like a toxin.

Clay dropped his hands to his side. "Go sit with your sons. You'll know as soon as we do what's going on."

Clay walked out to the hall. Becca watched him pace, running his hands through his hair. Very uncomfortable in the small space with Veronica, she turned to look at Jon Jr., giving him a weak smile.

"Did you get a hold of your father?"

"Yes, he is going to the airport. I think Dr. Stan is giving him a ride here in his plane. Or maybe he's coming too. I...I don't know. He will be here soon, I'm sure."

Becca's attention was drawn away by Ben walking down the hall. Veronica retreated into the small restroom just off the waiting room. Letting go of Jon Jr.'s hand, she slipped out the door, hustled to him.

She heard the edge of hysteria in her voice. "Ben?"

He stopped when he reached her. "Becca."

Becca stuttered her question. "Can... you tell me... what happened?"

She felt Clay's hands on her shoulders. Ben's eyes looked up. Clay must have given him a quiet signal to tell her.

"As near as we can tell they were broadside on the Crawl River Bridge."

I can't breathe.

Becca's world swayed.

Crawl River Bridge. Where Martin and Gwen died.

Wondering why she wasn't in a pile on the floor, she realized Clay kept her upright. "Clay."

"I know baby." Over her head she heard his voice. "What happened?"

Ben continued, glancing at her, it felt like he was waiting for her to collapse. "A car broadsided them. A bunch of drunk teenagers."

"And how are they?" The hairs on the back of her neck rose.

Ben shook his head. "Not a scratch."

Clay spoke to her. "It's not going to turn out the same, Becca." His arms wrapped around her, keeping her tight to him.

Ben was confused. "What's the same?"

Clay spoke to Ben. "Something that happened long ago."

No words could be said that would make this all right until her daughter and his son were safe.

"That's all I know, folks. Sorry."

"Thanks, Ben. This is enough for now." Clay spoke over her head.

Ben glanced at the wordless woman, concern crossed his face, but he only hesitated for a moment, looked up at Clay, then turned away.

Clay half lifted her, carried her to the wall. Blocking her in with his body, his voice low but firm. "It's not going to turn out the same. Listen to me! This is not the past repeating itself."

Becca bit off the urge to scream. "Oh, Clay. How do you know?"

His voice cold, steady as stone. "Because God wouldn't do this to us again. Now get a grip."

Becca had to smile. A deep cleansing breath escaped through her lips. "Okay. A grip."

Grabbing the front of his shirt, she buried her face in his chest. The smell of Clay, along with the strength he carried, made her believe him.

He spoke tenderly to her, touching her cheek with his breath. "It will be all right this time, Becca. I promise."

Nodding she fought the tears, bucked up so she could speak. Leaning back against the wall she touched his face with her hand. "I am so glad you are with me for this."

"Together we will get through this. Hang on."

God I love this man.

The sound of the door opening and voices they both recognized made them turn. Sparky, Jilley, Susie and Robby came in together. The somber looks on their faces were replaced with relief when they spotted Clay and Becca.

Susie and Jilley broke away from the men, rushed to Becca. Clay stepped back as the three women embraced, all three crying.

When Becca surfaced the three men stood there looking helpless. She quickly went to Sparky and Robby, hugging them. "Thanks for coming."

Robby held her a little longer. "Sure Bec. We are so sorry."

Pulling back he turned to Clay. "So what do we know?"

Becca went to Clay, tucked in under his arm. Clay spoke, his voice cracking. "A car hit them as they were crossing Crawl River Bridge.

A gasp escape the other's lips. The irony did not escape the group. Jilley took Becca's hand. "Bec, don't think that."

Becca squeezed her hand. "I'm trying not to." Releasing a heavy sigh, she hugged Clay to her. He returned the hug, kissed the top of her head.

"Are all your boys here?" Robby addressed Clay.

"Yeah. And Becca's son also."

Robby rubbed his hands together. "So how about we..." He pointed his thumb between him and Sparky. "...take them to eat?"

Clay nodded. "Good idea." He looked down at her. "Becca? Is that good?"

Becca moved away from Clay. "Yes." She took each of the women's arms and they walked together to the waiting room. Kevin was sitting with Jon Jr. All the boys looked up as the adults walked in together.

Robby addressed the room. "Boys, how about some breakfast?"

Stephen, Kevin and David stood up. Jon Jr. looked at his mom. Becca smiled, nodding her head. "Go. We won't know anything for a while." Matt stood up with Jon Jr.

Thomas came around the corner. "Did I hear breakfast?"

The men herded the boys out of the room, Becca could still hear their chatter as the doors opened, then silence as it closed.

Sitting down, Jilley and Susie sat down on each side of Becca. Clay stood, looked around. "Where's Veronica?"

"Veronica is here?" Jilley's voice rose in surprise.

The bathroom door opened and out she walked. "Yes, the bitch of Lester County is here. Isn't that the title you gave me?" Her glare settled on Jilley.

Jilley stiffened. "If the title fits…"

Veronica started for the woman. Clay grabbed her, stopping her attack. He backed her to the chair farthest away, pushed her down. "Stop it! Your son is in trouble. It doesn't matter what they called you. You can debate the issue at another time, another place." He spoke through clenched teeth.

Veronica glared at him, then slumped back in the chair. "Fine." Pointing a finger at Jilley, she sat. "This isn't over."

Jilley started to get up, but Becca and Susie grabbed her. Accepting their direction she glared back. "Bring it on bitch."

Clay threw up his hands. "I'm getting coffee. You four try not to kill yourselves."

Stomping out of the room, Becca watched him leave, then turned her gaze on Veronica. Beneath the bitter, hard eyes she saw the pain of a mother. Drawing her lips into a line, Becca gave her a small smile. Veronica didn't return the look. She just turned her head to look out the window.

***

Her body stiff, Becca moved in Clay's arms. Someone must have shut the door. She could see the hustle and bustle of the hospital, but didn't hear the sounds. Looking around, she saw various bodies sprawled over the room. Some on chairs, some on the floor. The window reflected the morning colors of dawn. Her movement stirred a reaction in Clay. She stretched her legs out. He moaned, put one arm over his head.

"Morning." His voice was raspy.

Becca decided to sit on up. Her aching body complained but she pushed it. Clay rubbed her back as he shifted to a sitting position.

The opening of the door jerked them both to their feet. A man in a green scrub suit addressed the couple. As he spoke, the people in the room stirred, quietly and somberly they sat up.

"Andrew is out of surgery. He did good. He's in the ICU. His parents may see him." His face took a sobering look. "Haley is still in surgery."

Becca gasped. Clay's hands steadied her.

The doctor continued. "She received more injuries, however everything is going well. You should be seeing her surgeon soon." The doctor shrugged his shoulders. "That's all I have for now folks." He just stood there in the silence.

Veronica jerked up, almost knocking Thomas to the floor. Becca turned, nodded to Clay. He moved around her, walked toward the door. Veronica reached it first, jerked it opened, hitting the doctor. Clay held out his arms in an apologetic gesture. The doctor nodded, let him pass first.

Jilley came up behind Becca. "I heard."

Becca leaned back, soaking in the comfort of her friend's arms.

***

Clay saw his son through the window as the nurse led them to the ICU room. His face swollen and bruised, tubes seemed to be everywhere. As he rounded the corner of the door, the sounds of machines beeping and humming sent a spike in his chest.

Andrew's eyes were closed. Veronica went to the other side of
the bed than Clay. She pushed back her son's hair, staring at the
mangled mess in front of her. He noticed the hard shell she
always displayed crumble. If he knew anything about her, he
knew she loved her sons more than anything. Standing back, he
let her have her time. Talking in a low voice, he couldn't hear her
words, but the tone was one of comfort. Her eyes looked up at
him. In them he saw her anguish and fear.

"He's going to be okay, Roni. He's strong."

She nodded, allowed her tears to flow down her cheeks.
Finally she looked around the room. Finding a chair she went
over, sat down. "I'm staying," she announced as if someone
would dare challenge her.

Clay didn't respond. He chuckled quietly. Taking his son's
hand, he squeezed it. Slowly Andrew rolled his head to Clay's side
of the bed, forced them open. Trying to speak through dry lips,
Clay heard the soft word. "Haley?"

Clay leaned close to Andrew's ear. "She's doing fine. She
needs you strong. Fight hard son. Fight hard."

Andrew's head nodded slightly, his eyes closed. His breathing
shallow, but steady. Clay held his hand for a moment then laid it
down. Since Veronica took the only spot to sit, he walked out to
the hallway to find a chair he could bring in, when he noticed a
gurney being wheeled into the room next door. Looking at the
person on it, he saw the blond hair of Becca's daughter. A man in

green scrubs followed the gurney, then veered off towards the ER. Clay caught up to him, walking quietly beside. The man looked suspiciously at Clay.

"I'm Andrew's father. The boy in the accident." Clay explained.

The man nodded.

"I know you can't tell me anything about her condition but I need to be there when you tell her mother."

The man extended his hand. "Doctor Brown."

Clay shook it. "Clay Lester." The doctor's eyebrow shot up. Clay was accustomed to that.

If you live or work in Lester County when someone says their last name is Lester, a connection is made. Clay smiled, nodded.

The waiting room door stood open, people were spilling out. Quiet blanketed them as Clay and the doctor walked into the room. Clay searched for Becca, found her by the window. Without speaking, he walked to her, took her hand. She straightened, frowned at him, let him guide her to the doctor. Standing behind her, he braced her by holding the top of her arms.

Watching the doctor over the top of her head, he listened.

"She came through the surgery well, considering her injuries."

Jon Jr. slipped to his mother's side, talking her hand.

"She was hurt worse as she took the brunt of the impact. They hit her side of the car. She is in the ICU. You can see her now."

Becca nodded, squeezed Jon Jr.'s hand, pulling him with her. Clay followed. The three of them walked in silence to the room. Becca and Jon Jr. went in together. Clay waited at the doorway. His heart hurt for her. Hurting from his own pain, he was willing to carry both. Going to the hallway he looked between the two rooms.

This is going to be okay. Rough, but okay.

***

At midnight Clay walked down the hospital hall to get a cup of coffee. Everyone had left but him, Becca and Veronica. Rubbing the back of his neck, he turned when he heard soft footsteps. Becca followed him. Her face was drawn with fatigue and worry. Stopping, he waited until she caught up to him. Holding out his arm she moved into his body.

"How's it going baby?" He swung her around, guiding her toward the beverage room door.

"Best it can. How's Andrew?" Her voice betrayed her weariness.

Clay tried to sound upbeat. "Holding his own. Haley?"

"Improving every moment. Every hour is a step toward her healing." Exhaustion tipped the edge of her tone.

In the room, he went to the coffee pot, she went to the fridge, took out a bottle of cold water.

Becca looked around. "Veronica still here?"

Rubbing his forehead, he frowned. "Yeah. She hasn't left his bedside."

Becca walked over to Clay, rubbed his arm. "She's a mother in pain. Give her a break."

He smiled, drew her into his side. "I know." Kissing her, she was the one thing keeping him grounded. This time together they would fight pass this crisis. "Is Jon here yet?"

"On his way from the airport. Should arrive at any moment." Becca sighed, hugged him.

"Are you okay with this?"

She shrugged. "Have to be. He has every right to be here. She's his daughter too."

Together they walked back to the ICU rooms. Parting, they each went in to be with their

children. Clay heard the bitterness in Becca's voice behind him. Looking over at her, he watched her back stiffen.

"Jon."

CHAPTER EIGHTEEN

"And just what the hell happened here, Becca?" Jon's ever subtle voice slipped through clenched teeth.

Becca spoke low but without the intimidation Jon expected. "Our daughter was in a car accident."

"I suppose she was with that kid."

"Andrew, yes they were together." Becca turned to the other man in the room. "Stan. Thanks for getting him here." They met at the foot of Haley's bed, Stan gave her a peck on her cheek.

"You're looking good, Becca. Considering."

"Thanks. Did you look at the chart?"

Stan nodded. "Yes. She's doing good for the injuries she suffered. She's a fighter."

Becca patted his hand. "She has a lot to fight for."

"The boy?"

"Yes. They are very much in love. They both will fight."

366

Stan patted her hand back. "Good. That's better than any medicine."

"Excuse me!" Jon's voice echoed behind her.

She rolled her eyes at Stan, turned around. "Yes, Jon."

"What were they doing? Was he drinking?"

Becca took a stance. "They were out together. No they weren't drinking, as far as I know. They were crossing the bridge, a car hit them." She leaned close to Jon's face. "Shit happens Jon. Deal with it. Our daughter needs us together to support her."

Becca could see her words took him back. He frowned, then his face softened. "Yes, of course." The real Jon was back. Calm and in control. Show no emotions.

Whatever.

Becca walked to the window, leaned her forehead against the cool glass. A past incident crossed her mind. Why? She didn't know. It just played out in its own way.

***

"Becca. Where's my gold cuff links?" Jon called from the bedroom. Looking in the mirror, Becca fluffed her hair, frowned at the tone he always took as 'Jon-the-superior-businessman'. Giving herself a final look, she smoothed down the expensive, but plain, Christian Dior, white dress. Her make-up and hair were perfect, according to Jon's specifications.

367

Leaving the bathroom, she walked over to the dressing table, opened the jewelry box. Taking out the objects Jon asked for, but god forbid he look for, she walked over, dropped them in his hand. Wearing a black tux, he did look very handsome. Looks was not Jon's problem. His problem was that he wanted to be seen as above everyone else. And he wanted people to know that his wife and kids were as well. Always on display, Becca learned the fine art of pleasing Jon.

Quite simple. Flash around like you were the Queen bitch, everyone accepted you as such.

Becca picked up the diamond earrings, the ones she had instructions to wear tonight. They were purchased for the occasion by Jon. Not a gift of love or even appreciation. They were for show. Jon's show.

Standing back, Becca again made a check list of her appearance. Nodding, she completed the task. Jon came up behind her, looked at her reflection in the mirror over her shoulder.

"We look good together."

Becca sighed, turned to get her jacket. John laid his coat over his arm, motioned for her to pass by him. Gathering up the long dress, she went out into the hallway.

The nanny met her, nodded. "You look very lovely Miss Becca."

"Thank you, Rita. We will be late. These things have a habit of lasting forever. And Jon likes to the first to arrive, the last to leave." Becca winked.

Rita had been hired per Jon's request that they have a nanny. Becca didn't want a nanny, but knew it was useless to argue. So she appeared as if she thought he had a great idea, insisted she do her part to hire 'just the right one'. After interviewing several women, Rita came to her door. A kind, pleasant woman, Becca felt she could relate to her.

So they made a pact. Rita would nanny when Mr. Jon was here. Becca took care of the kids when he wasn't. For this they paid Rita a considerable amount of money. Win/win for all.

Jon passed the two women opened the front door. "Come on we'll be late."

Becca hugged Rita, whispered. "Thank you."

Walking ahead of Jon, Becca waited until he opened the car door for her. Sitting down in the soft, leather seats of his Lexus, she took hold of the seat belt as he shut the door.

Once inside, on their way, the instructions started. "The Morrows are the couple to watch. He just started at the firm. I guess they are from the Midwest somewhere. She teaches school or something."

"And they are on point, why?"

Jon always failed to hear the sarcasm in her voice. "He thinks he is going to go places, so get acquainted with her, find out their plans. You know what to do."

Yes, she did. Her duty, to give Jon the info she got from the wives. She never did know what he did with it, but if she gave him something, he left her alone. Not once had she found out anything of great importance, but he acted satisfied with her report, so whatever.

Pulling up to a rich, old house that once housed the family of a wealthy perfume manufacturer, it now was the place to hold large parties for the very wealthy. Built as a duplicate of a castle in England, Becca loved the house for its charm and history. When she was first married to Jon, they had come to a party at the house. So intrigued, Becca came back one day for a tour. Taking notes, she became well-versed in the grand times and important events of the mansion.

It proved to be an asset when the conversation lagged. She could whip out some quaint fact of the place to get her through the dry spot.

Jon stopped the car. A valet opened Becca's door, offering his hand. Standing up, she watched his eyes travel over her. Embarrassed when he noticed her watching him, he let go of her hand, shut the door.

Jon offered his arm and they entered the foyer with all eyes on them. Mission accomplished. She presented herself well as Jon's wife.

Escorting her to the bar, Jon ordered a white wine for her, a brandy neat for him. Handing her a glass, Jon scoped the room.

Becca leaned over, whispered. "Which ones are the Morrows?"

"The couple in the corner with the Baileys."

After taking a sip of her wine, she nodded to Jon, walked toward the group of people.

"Marvin, Betty. So good to see you again."

The older couple introduced her to the middle age man and woman next to them. "Becca, this is Claude and Sissy Morrow."

Becca took hold of first the woman's hand, then the man's. "So nice to meet you. I am Becca Hamilton.

"Jon's wife." Claude let the surprise in his voice surface. A tall, gangly, handsome man, dressed in an ill-fitting tux, he looked nervous, out of his element.

Becca nodded. "Yes, that is me."

Sissy was an attractive woman, lacking style in her pink, beaded gown. Her medium length, dishwater blonde hair lay flat, plastered to her head. Becca always like to put the newbies at ease. She knew Jon didn't.

Her attention focused on them. "So where are you from?"

"Iowa." Sissy spoke up. Claude stood silent, observing Becca.

"Never been there. Tell me why you came here."

For the next two hours, Becca listened about life in the heartland from Sissy. Every once in a while she would glance over at Claude. It must have made him nervous. After the first half hour he excused himself to mingle.

Becca would catch sight of Jon now and then, working the room. His favorite pasttime. Once, he came over to meet Sissy. Chatted for a half a second, then kissed Becca's cheek, moved on.

Sissy spoke to Becca as Jon left. "My, you have a very good-looking husband."

Becca titled her head. "Yes. And he is all mine." Taking a big swallow of her wine, draining the glass, she grabbed another from one of the trays passing by.

One of the wives, Dolly, of another partner came up to Becca. "Becca, I've been looking for you. Lunch tomorrow at the club?"

Becca loved doing this. "Sure." She turned to Sissy. "Would you like to join us?"

Taken totally by surprise, a look of happiness crossed Sissy's face. "Yes, I would love to.

What time?"

Becca shrugged. "Oneish. Right Dolly? Oh have you met Sissy, the newest member of the team?"

Dolly tried to hide her displeasure. "No, we haven't met."

Dolly was the trophy wife of one of the older men in the company.

Her plastic surgeon's bill alone probably bought the doctor a new BMW.

Inside, Becca chuckled. To her it was a game. The conquest to keep the other people in her life at arm's length, but make them feel they really mattered.

Becca smiled the phony smile she practiced. "Good. We will have a grand old time."

Sissy was pleased beyond belief, Dolly flustered to the point her neck turned red.

Game point and match!

Becca crept away from the two women. Looking for the ladies room, it took her several minutes to get there as many people stopped her to say something. Once inside, she met a couple of other partners' wives, Sally and Cleo.

"Becca, how nice to see you. You look stunning in that dress. Who is the designer?"

Standing in front of the double mirrors, Becca fussed with her hair. "Dior."

"But of course." Sally said, visually impressed. "You have such remarkable taste."

"Actually, Jon picked it out. Had it shipped over." Jon did pick out most of the outfits he wanted her to wear. He kept up on those things. If nothing else, Jon was a business man in every aspect of his life. He paid attention to what styles to wear, what

cars spoke of prestige, where to be seen and who to be seen with. Becca was glad. She could really give a rat's ass about all these minor details.

Cleo and Sally left the room; Becca stood alone looking at herself in the mirror. She never felt like she was a phony. It was her way of getting though life. It worked was all that mattered.

Taking a deep breath, she checked the time on her expensive diamond watch. Three more hours, then she could crawl into her bed. Sleep, always a good escape.

Straightening up, she walked back into the party. Going to the bar, she ordered a raspberry martini. Jon always got her a white wine. To him it was a proper drink for a lady. Becca needed something a little stronger to get through the night. Snaking her way through the crowd, she went out onto the balcony, a large stone replicate of a massive English terrace, overlooking a flower garden the size of a football field. She set her glass on the edge of the rock railing.

The night was still warm, but refreshing. Gathering her jacket around her bare shoulders, she hugged herself. Thoughts of 'what the fuck are you doing' always wanted to sneak into her mind on occasions like this. She shoved them aside.

I am doing what I need to do to stay sane in an insane world!

"Becca." The voice of one of the young assistants broke up her argument with herself. "What are you doing out here all alone?"

"Marc." She addressed him without turning around. Marc, one of the brightest spots in the evening. Always charming, he would someday achieve the highest levels of his chosen profession. "Looking at the full moon. You know the creatures of the night come out when there is a full moon."

Marc came, stood next to her, leaned on the stone railing. "And what creatures are those?"

Becca looked over at him with a sly wink. "The good ones. The bad ones like the least amount of light possible."

Marc chuckled. "So... You look gorgeous as always."

"And you clean up nicely."

The playful banter stayed just that, harmless. Tethered on the edge of flirting, they never crossed the line. Both had too much to protect. Becca, her sheltered life. Marc, his ambitions.

Picking up her glass, she drained the last of the martini.

"Can I get you another?" Mark motioned towards the glass.

Becca shook her head. "No. That hit the spot."

"What are you two doing out here?" Jon's voice echoed behind them.

Marc stood up gave Becca a wink. "Hitting on your wife."

Jon walked over, stood on the other side of Becca. He gave Marc a playful grin. "Any luck?"

"Sorry to say, no. She is totally yours." Marc saluted Jon. "You are a lucky man, Jon Hamilton."

Jon did not reply. Becca laughed quietly to herself.

Marc turned to leave. "Later guys."

Leaning on the stone, Jon looked out over the garden. "So how's it going?"

Becca shrugged. "Fine. The Morrows are just Midwesterners in a different environment. You?"

"Heard some rumors about a takeover. Will need to follow up."

Jon took Becca's glass from her. "Have you had many of these?"

"Just the one."

"Good. Let me get you another wine."

"Thank you dear." Becca sauntered by Jon, reentered the party.

***

"Daddy?" Haley's weak voice alerted Becca.

Turning sharply, she rushed to the bed.

Haley's eyes were barely open. "Mom?"

"Yes, dear." Becca leaned close, as she could barely hear Haley's words.

"Andrew?"

"He's in the next room. He's doing good." Becca felt her daughter's relief. Taking the

young girl's hand she stroked it carefully around all the tubes. "How are you feeling?"

"Like I was run over by a truck."

"You kind of were. What do you remember?"

"Lights. Then a crash. Then nothing."

"Are you in pain?"

Haley shook her head. "No. Not right now." Haley turned her head back to look at her dad. "Daddy? How did you get here?"

"Dr. Stan flew me here. How are you princess?"

Haley smiled weakly. "I've been better. Thanks for coming." She dismissed Jon, turned back to Becca. "Go check on Andrew. Tell him I love him. Please?"

"Of course." Becca gave Jon a 'don't you dare start' look. Jon nodded.

Walking over to the next room, Becca stood in the doorway for a moment. Clay and Veronica stood on each side of their son's bed.

Andrew's eyes were open, he was trying hard to escape the fog to speak. "Haley?"

Becca stepped up. "She's awake." Standing at the foot of Andrew's bed, she smiled. "She wants you to know she loves you."

Veronica and Clay turned in her direction. Andrew gave her a weak smile. "Thank you. Tell her I love her too."

"Will do." Becca glanced at Clay. He winked at her.

It is going to be okay. This time.

***

The kids healed quickly. Transferred out of ICU after a few days, their rooms were on the same floor, next to each other. The hospital staff knew of the two lovers who survived the crash. They went out of their way to accommodate them.

Becca walked down the long hallway to Haley's room. It was early morning so the rush hadn't started yet. The day nurses nodded as she passed by. Entering her room, Becca was surprised to see the doctor already there.

"Dr. Brown?" She looked from the man to her daughter. "Is everything okay?"

The doctor had kind eyes, a quiet, assuring bedside manner. "Yes. Things are real good." He turned to Haley. "Ready to go home?"

Haley's face glowed. "Yes!" She scooted up on her bed.

"Fine. You'll need help. I am assigning a physical therapist to come work with you."

Haley couldn't contain her enthusiasm. "I have mom. I live with her." Plopping her head back she smiled at the doctor. "I will do whatever you want."

Dr. Brown patted her hand. "I know you will. You have been an ideal patient. If it wasn't for your spunk and determination, you would not have healed so fast."

Writing on the clipboard in his hand, he turned to walk away.

Haley's voice, full of hope. "Andrew?"

378

Stopping in front of Becca, with his back to Haley, he smiled. "He's going home too.

Just limit the visits. You both need to heal."

They exchanged smiles. Becca touched his arm. "Thank you so much. You saved her life. I am forever grateful."

She could tell the words pleased him. "It was my pleasure. Take good care of them. They have a long future in front of them."

Nodding, Becca stepped aside to let him pass. Winking at her daughter, she walked to the bedside. "So it's home to heal."

Haley took her mother's hand. "And I can't think of a better place to be than in Aunt Tilley's house by the lake."

"What is this? You're going where?" Jon's voice sounded behind Becca.

Haley looked around. "Home, Daddy. I get to go home."

"Great. I'll call Stan, have him send his plane..." Both women looked at him, stopping his words.

"Sorry, dad. But I'm staying here. With Mom."

"No way. At home I can get you the best of care..."

"Dad. I am staying here. This is my home now. Not your house."

His eyes flared at Becca. "This is absurd. I can provide for her better than you."

Becca moved from the bedside. Passing Jon, she patted his arm. "Maybe. But this is where she wants to be. It's her choice." Turning back to look at Haley, Becca winked. "I'm going to get some coffee. Want some?"

Haley smiled. "Sure."

Jon spoke to Becca. "I'll have a cup."

"Fine. The drink room is two doors down." With that she left.

Once outside of the room, out of sight of Jon, she leaned against the wall. She didn't like being rude, but Jon seemed to bring it out in her. Turning her head to the side, she saw Clay walking her way.

Once he reached her, he leaned his hand on the wall. "You okay?"

Becca nodded her head. "I will be. Jon's in with Haley. I needed to get out of there before I bitch slapped him."

Clay looked down at the floor, chuckled. "Your restraint never ceases to amaze me."

She slapped his chest. "Stop it." The laughter came out anyway.

He looked up at her, leaned in to gave her a sweet kiss. "Hang tough babe. How is Haley?"

"She gets to go home. I think Andrew too."

Clay's face lit up. "Good. I can't wait to get him out of here. Let me check with him. You good here?"

"I'm fine. Going to get some coffee. Later."

Jordyn Meryl

CHAPTER NINETEEN

The pain shot up Haley's leg as she swung it over the side of the bed. It didn't alarm her. Every day it became less. Physical therapy worked wonders. Being young, she accepted the 'No pain. No gain' philosophy. Anyway, the pain reminded her she survived. So had Andrew. Together they counted their blessings, cut their losses.

It had been three months since the accident. At first she gritted her teeth to buck up. Now she could move better, walk stronger. Her mom had been a blessing. Her dad a pain in the ass, but then he backed off. Sitting on the side of the bed, she thought back to when he finally went home.

***

Jon stayed at the small bed and breakfast in Somerset. The owner, Nell, tried hard to please him, but never succeeded. This did not surprise Haley, her dad had never been an easy person to please.

"Hello princess." Her dad bent down, kissed her head.

Haley sat on the back porch waiting for his daily visit. Out of the hospital for a little over a week, she really wanted him to go home. Tired of explaining why she wanted to be here in this 'one horse town' as he called it.

"Mornin' Daddy." She watched him drop down in the chair next to her.

Heaving a big sigh, his next words were always the same. "Watching the grass grow?"

Haley chuckled to herself. "Something like that."

"Honey…" He turned to her. "…I should get back home. Work and all you know."

Haley hoped she hid her joy, trying real hard to sound sincere. "I understand."

His eyes bore into hers. "I can still make arrangements for you to come home with me."

Forcing her tone to stay calm. "I am home."

"So you really think you're going to be happy here?"

"I do."

"I have my doubts…"

"Excuse me Dad. But you seem to have several doubts about a lot of things, your marriage for one."

The look on his face told her she hit the spot. Biting her lower lip, she looked away. Her intention wasn't to hurt him, just get him off her case. "Please. Accept what I want to do. If it doesn't work out you can do the 'I told you so' thing. But for now, please just let me be."

For the first time she saw her dad's eyes glisten. "Touché." *He reached out, took her hand.* "I guess I screwed up."

"No, you didn't. You changed directions. I hope you're happy. Really. We-Mom, Jonny, you and I-need to move on."

Jon nodded. "If you ever need anything..."

"I do. I need you to walk me down the aisle."

The pause spoke volumes, but Haley held on for the answer she wanted.

Jon frowned. "Okay. I will. But I am..."

She put her finger on his lips. "Quit while you're ahead, Dad."

For a split second father and daughter shared a moment, broken by the sound of the screen door opening.

Becca stepped out. "Jon. Thought I heard you. How's it going?"

Haley spoke to her mom, but kept her eyes on her dad. "We're good. Dad's getting ready to go back home."

"Really? So soon?" *The sarcasm dripped from Becca.*

Jon patted Haley's hand, stood. "Yeah, I need to get back to things. I can see she's in good hands." *Bending down he hugged her.*

384

Kissing his cheek, she whispered. "Thanks daddy."

"I do love you."

"I know."

Following his exit, she smiled slightly as he passed by Becca. He stopped, took her hand. "Take good care of our girl. Please let me know if she or you need anything."

Haley saw her mother narrow her eyes. "Sure, Jon. Thanks."

As he started to enter the house, Haley shouted at him. "See you at my wedding?"

He stopped, then nodded. "Agreed. Let me know where and when."

Becca stepped aside as the door slammed shut behind him. Slipping over to his vacant chair, she plopped down. "He has agreed to your marriage?"

Haley grinned. "Not exactly. He only agreed to give me away. Is that okay?"

Becca leaned back in the chair. "Of course, honey. He's your father." Becca put her hand to her chin. "Should be an interesting day."

***

Jon Jr. leaned on the front of his car at the airport's private hangers waiting for his dad to arrive. A bright sunny day with a chill in the air. He flipped up the collar on his black leather jacket, adjusted his sunglasses.

Jon's rental car came across the pavement to the small private jet waiting for him.

Jon Jr. walked over to greet his dad as he got out. "Hey Dad."

Taking the bag out of the back seat, Jon turned around. "Son. Nice of you to come to see the ole' man off."

Jon Jr. slapped Jon on the back. "Not a problem, Dad." As they walked toward the plane, Dr. Stan stepped out on the small stairs. "Dr. Stan." Jon Jr. waved.

"Junior. Are you going with us?"

"Not this time."

Jon handed his bag to the attendant. "Can if you want." His pleading touched Jon Jr.'s heart.

Shaking his head. "I'll be home sometime. Did you see Haley today?"

Jon faced Jon Jr. "Yes." Heavy sigh. "She asked me to give her away at her wedding."

"Wow. You going to?"

Jon nodded. "Yes. I owe her that much. I owe you too. I don't want to lose you two."

Jon Jr. hugged his dad. "You're not. We just grew up. Don't sweat it. It will all work out in the end."

Breaking apart, the two men smiled. Jon spoke first. "I guess everything is working out. Just seeing Haley so hurt... I realized life is precious."

"Make a good life for yourself, Dad. We all are moving on."

386

"So you're sticking with this art thing?"

"With a business major on the side. I am still my ole' man's son. I feel good about all of this."

Jon nodded. "Good luck son."

"See you later, Dad."

Jon Jr. watched his dad climb the stairs. For the past three weeks he spent more time with Jon, than he had in his lifetime. Sometimes change works for the good. At first, seeing his parents break up, he worried what would happen to his family. But things did work out. His Mom rekindled an old love, his sister fell in love with a great guy, he now pursued his dream of being an artist. And his dad? He would find his niche. Life goes on.

Standing alone as he watched the plane lift off, he smiled. Life does go on, if you're lucky. They were lucky this time.

Checking his watch while he walked back to his car, Jon Jr. wanted to get to his mom's house. He had an art project going that he wanted to finish. The light would fade soon, he should hurry.

***

Andrew pulled into Haley's driveway. The doctor had finally given him the okay to drive. Being away from her so long tortured his soul. They made as many plans as they could on the phone. Jonny, Kevin and even his dad took turns taking him over to her house. Although he figured Clay's reasons were more personal, like Becca. Chuckling, he thought about his dad trying to figure out how to see her with both Andrew and Haley at the houses 24/7. The ole' man possessed some spunk now that Becca solidly occupied his life.

Good for him.

Watching them at the hospital, Andrew could tell how much in love they were, how good it was for them.

Kudos to both of them.

Andrew's brothers stepped up to finish his house. They allowed him to sit on the side to supervise, but he did no work. His pride in them skyrocketed. Even Thomas came to help. A crisis such as this either brings a family together or destroys it. His took the high road.

Stepping out lightly, he leaned on the cane to steady himself. Looking up, he saw Haley

standing on the porch.

Smiling, he raised his free hand. "Let me come to you."

Her smile radiated. "Okay."

Slow, but moving, his stiff body painfully climbed the stairs. Reaching the top, he held out his arm to Haley. She slipped into his arm, curling into his body.

"You did good cowboy." She murmured against his chest.

He laughed. "If I was a real cowboy, the bull won't have crippled me, little darlin'."

Breaking apart the two hobbled into the house.

388

Becca came out of the kitchen. "Hey you two. Haley here's a letter from your dad."

Taking the white business envelope, Haley frowned.

Her dad sending a letter. This looked serious.

Ripping it open, she pulled out a short typed letter with a check folded inside. She looked first at the letter, handed it to Andrew. He read the computer written words:

Haley honey,

This is for you and Andrew. I know I was a total jerk at first, but almost losing you made me realize, it would break my heart. Hopes this helps, more if you need it. Just tell me.

Love,

Dad

He heard Haley gasp, then showed the check to him.

No way! It's for one hundred thousand dollars!

Her eyes misted, looking at Andrew as he observed the check.

His voice cracked. "Seriously?"

Taking both of them from him, she handed them to Becca. Hugging him, she laughed. "How about that Mom?"

Becca's voice carried her surprise. "I'll be damned."

Jonny came out of the studio. "What's going on?" He looked over Becca's shoulder. "No way! The old man came through."

Andrew, both stunned and pleased, hugged Haley. "Take what you need for the wedding. The rest goes toward your café."

Things sure were looking up.

***

The dress Haley found in a magazine was *the* one. Ordering it from New York, she paced as she waited for UPS to deliver it. She had tracked it online, and it was arriving today. Hearing the rumble of a big truck coming, she raced to the front door.

"Mom, it's here."

The big brown truck stopped in the driveway. The young man getting out was a friend of Andrew's. "Hey Haley. I have a package for you."

Haley was now on the porch. "Yes, I have been expecting it."

The screen door slammed behind her, Becca walked up to the steps as the delivery boy handed the package up. It was big and heavy. Both Haley and Becca grabbed for it.

"Sign here and it's all yours." The delivery boy pushed a machine under Haley's face. Balancing the package with her knee, she signed. "Thanks, Joe."

"So what is so special?"

"My wedding dress."

"I'm glad I was the one to deliver it to a special lady." He jumped down the steps. "Later."

Both women answered. "Later, Joe."

Carrying the box together, they maneuvered down the hall, into Haley's room. Tearing it open, Haley gasped. The sparkling white gown lay in front of her. Lifting it carefully, she admired the beadwork, the silkiness of the fabric.

"Mom!" Haley squealed. "It's gorgeous."

Becca stood to her side. Looking over at her, Haley saw the wetness form in her mother's eyes. Becca nodded.

"Help me get it on."

Together they unpacked the gown, worked to put it on Haley.

It was perfect. The scooped neckline accented her breasts, hugging her ribs to flow into a soft scalloped skirt followed by mild train.

Haley swirled around. "Oh, Mom…"

Becca crossed her arms. "You look lovely. It is the perfect dress."

Haley cocked her head. "This is really going to happen, isn't it?"

Becca adjusted the dress. "Yes, honey. Why wouldn't it?"

"You know, when the car hit us, I had my doubts." Trying to cover her fear with humor, she grinned.

Stopping what she was doing, Becca took Haley by the shoulders. "I can't imagine."

"You don't have time to think. I just remember bright lights. Seeing Andrew, bleeding. Pain, so much pain…"

Her mother didn't speak. Just looked at Haley, sadness on her face.

"It's been a rough winter, Mom. But come June, I will be married. Our bodies healed, our love grown stronger."

Nodding, Becca still didn't speak.

Haley locked eyes with her. "What about you, Mom? Is Clay a part of your future?"

Becca smiled. "Yes. He is. He always will be."

"So you regret..."

"Time wasted. That's all. No more regrets." Becca hugged her. "None for you either, sweetheart."

* * *

Andrew turned around to look at the back of his tux, traditional black, it flattered his

body. His Dad and David were with him to get fitted also. Clay walked out of the dressing room, followed by David.

Strutting in front of the mirror, Clay held out the jacket. "Not bad for an old man."

"Yeah, Dad. You still got it." David slapped him on the back.

"If this isn't a good-looking group of men." Haley's voice made Andrew turn around. Seeing her walk toward him, made his heart jump. All the physical signs of the accident were gone. She walked strong, straight, and beautiful. She never ceased to take his breath away.

Moving up to him, she straightened his jacket, adjusted his waist band. "Looks good." She looked around Andrew to Clay and David. "You boys clean up nice."

Andrew watched Becca come up behind an unsuspecting Clay. Putting her arms around his waist, his surprise turned to pleasure as he looked at her, turned to take her in his arms, kissing her cheek. Andrew had never seen his Dad so happy.

"So we did good?" Andrew addressed Haley.

Haley pulled his shoulders down as she kissed him. "You always do good, honey. Just needed to check up on the tuxes."

The memory of the crash came back as he realized this moment almost hadn't happened.

He tried to get to Haley, but he couldn't move. Being lifted on the gurney, he fought the darkness closing over him. She just lay there. Her skin pale. Opening her eyes once, she looked at him, then they closed again. People were shouting, a fog settled around him. Finally it took over. The next thing he remembered was seeing his dad's face. Trying so hard to talk, he asked about her. Becca answered him. Saying the comforting words. 'She's okay.' Taking a deep breath he settled into the cocoon draping over him.

Coming back to the present, he gathered her to him. "So are we good?"

"We're good." Haley turned to the others. "Lunch?"

Clay and David agreed, Becca just laughed. "Go get changed, cowboy."

Clay kissed Becca quickly. "Yes, ma'am."

***

Having lunch at Brick's, the five of them kidded, laughed. Andrew and Haley wanted to check on the flowers. The lunch crowd started, so David went to work.

Clay and Becca lingered over their drinks.

"So we are going to be related by marriage." Clay ran his thumb over her hand.

Tingling her, Becca looked at his face. "I couldn't be happier. You?"

"I so admire their spunk. The accident and all, they survived a lot."

Becca looked down at the table. "I do too. They are both strong people."

"So are we, Becca. When this is over, it will be you and me."

His words warmed her soul. "I am so looking forward to it."

Clay got serious. "No reservations? No doubts?"

Becca shook her head. "Not this time."

Clay took her hand. "Then how about we get out of here, spend some time together."

They stood together. "What do you have in mind?"

"I still have a blanket in the back of the truck." He raised one eyebrow.

Becca moved into him. "So what are we waiting for?"

He kissed the side of her neck. "Damn if I know."

***

Clay took her to the spot on Tilley's property they had to as youngsters. Driving with the same anticipation he felt back then. Hidden in the trees, he stopped the truck under the same weeping willow. Both climbed into the truck bed, he spread the quilt out.

She came to him as she had years ago. Willing, hot, desirable. Laying her down, he slowly undressed her. Each touch saw her peaking for him. His mouth moved over her, tasting the sweetness of her skin, sweeping down to the center of her core. Spurred by the frantic need straining within him, stroke after sensuous stroke he felt her shudder beneath him. Fully aroused, desire pushed him to satisfy her completely, hitting the highest point of her passion.

Becca clawed at his bare back, begging him to take her.

"In time. Relax." He spoke softly, feeling her body plea for swift gratification.

She twisted to fit him best. Rising up, he entered her slowly, thrusting, then pulling out.

When she hit her highest point, he took her, plunging in, appreciating the grip of her tunnel milking his manhood. His body quivered with the strain.

Tumbling over the last edge of pleasure together, he rolled to his side as he eased out. Wrapping her in his arms, he held her tight until her body stopped shaking.

The fresh smell of her hair comforted his mind as his body regained control. "Becca…"

She didn't answer.

He continued on. "Do you know what you do to me?"

"If it's the same as what you do to me, then yes."

He chuckled. "We always were good together."

"That's a fact."

"Here's another fact. You are never getting away from me again."

"Don't want to."

He drew back to look at her. "I'll come after you this time."

Becca rose up on her elbow. "Why didn't you come after me?"

Clay shrugged. "I was young, hurt, mad, proud. Take your pick. Would it have made a difference?"

Becca looked him straight in the eyes. "Probably not. I was so closed off, I would have hurt you worse."

"Well, there you have it." He pulled her into his chest.

CHAPTER TWENTY

The wedding day

Becca opened her eyes to the gray that comes just before dawn. This was her daughter's wedding day. No reason to try to go back to sleep. The plans were done, now it is game on.

Stretching, she rolled out of bed. The sunrise over the lake was the most beautiful she ever seen, a sunny, perfect, early summer day. Just what she ordered.

Going to the hallway, she looked in on both her kids. Haley stirred slightly, but remained asleep. Jon Jr.'s deep snore told her his sleep was solid.

The morning carried a slight chill, so she grabbed her robe and slippers from the bathroom. In the kitchen, she started the coffee, laid out the makings for a big breakfast. Turning on the oven, she figured this would probably the only full meal any of them would eat today.

The wedding was to be held on the dock at their house. A simple affair with friends and family. Jon Sr. arrived yesterday, true to his word he would give his daughter away.

Sipping her first cup of rich coffee, she thought back to last night, the rehearsal dinner.

***

Veronica insisted the rehearsal dinner be held at "The Club". Andrew and Haley agreed just to keep her happy. Veronica was not happy with any of this. Voicing her opinion many times, she felt her son should not settle. Becca secretly felt it was because Haley was her daughter.

When word got back that Clay and Becca were together, the ripples coming from his ex-wife spread far and wide. The only thing was, no one listened to her. She rained terror over the county to an unresponsive audience. So they appeased her, allowed her the one night.

Jon Jr., Haley and Becca arrived together. Andrew stood outside, pacing while he waited for them.

"It's a zoo in there." He stated as Haley walked up to him.

Kissing him, she patted his chest. "It will be alright. Just a few hours, this part will be done."

Haley had a way of calming Andrew. His face showed his relief-she was with him now. Taking his arm, she raised her chin, walked in.

Jon Jr. offered Becca his arm, laughing. "Show time."

398

A large poster announced the dinner for Lester and Hamilton. Following the young man who presented himself to the group, they entered a small, private room off the main dining room where a long table stood decorated with white, black and sea green, Haley's colors. Veronica stood at the head of the table directing the waiters and the people who entered.

"Andrew." Her shrill voice cut like nails on a chalk board. "It's about time. Haley..."

Veronica's eyes went down the simple black dress. "...you look...nice."

Becca saw her daughter hide the smile that threatened to explode.

"Here, you and Andrew sit here." Pointing to the two chairs next to her. "Haley, you are on this side, with your family. Andrew, you're over here with me, your dad, and your brothers."

Rather than take issue, everyone followed her orders. Becca went, stood by the chair to Haley's right. Jon Jr. next to her, then darted off to greet their father.

Jon Sr. came up to the girls, going to Haley first. "Honey, you look beautiful."

"Thanks Daddy."

Turning to Becca. "Becca, you look..." He frowned. "...very different. Where did you get that dress?"

Becca's dress, a long, navy blue dress of satin with a cross over neckline accentuating her breasts. "This old thing! Why online. Don't remember the designer. I just liked it."

Their eyes locked. Jon blinked first. "It suits you."

Becca took a deep breath.

Let it go.

"Jon, I would like for you to meet Andrew's mother, Veronica." *Looking toward Veronica, she saw Clay slip in.*

Oh, thank god.

"And Clay, his father."

Jon walked around the table, fussing over Veronica. "My, you look stunning. A woman of class I can tell."

Becca blinked.

Is she blushing?

Gushing, Veronica took on a sugary sweet tone. "So you're the elusive husband."

Ex-husband.

Seems Veronica has a little trouble remembering to include the ex.

Becca frowned, looked at Clay. A wry smile played around his lips. He winked at her. She relaxed her shoulders.

None of this is important. What is important is Haley and Andrew.

Becca glanced over at her daughter. Holding Andrew's arm, she stood staring at the scene before her.

Veronica's annoying voice carried on. "I can see where Jon Jr. gets his good looks."

Becca cut in. "This is Clay Lester, Andrew's father." She accented the 'Lester", hoping Jon got it.

Tearing himself away from Veronica, he shook hands with Clay. "Glad to meet you. You have a delightful wife."

Clay chuckled. "Ex-wife."

The surprised raised Jon's eyebrows. He turned back to Veronica. "Why would anyone leave such a delightful woman?"

Clay grimaced. "I could ask you the same."

At the remark, Veronica's gave him a dark look. Jon Sr. didn't even get it. Of course, he had no idea Becca and Clay were together. Not something Becca wrote home about.

The rest of the Lester boys entered the room, taking the focus off the conversation. Everyone searched for their chairs. Place cards told the ranking of the guests. Becca, Jon Sr., Jon Jr. and Franny, and Haley's bride's maid on Haley's side. Clay, Veronica, David, Thomas, Matt, Kevin and Stephen on Andrew's side.

As the waiters served the first course, Clay rubbed his foot along Becca's leg under the table. Looking at him, she half-hid her smile.

Thank god this is just one night...

***

"Mom?" Haley's sleepy voice sounded behind Becca, bring her back to this day.

Becca turned, still smiling at her memories of the evening before. "Hi, honey. Sleep well?"

Haley walked over, gave her mother a quick hug, poured a cup of coffee. Sitting down, she pushed a mop of hair out of her face. "Somewhat. I'm nervous, but not so much..." She took a sip, then looked up at her mom. "I am just excited to get married. Does it make sense?"

Not to me. I didn't have any feelings when I married your dad.

Instead, Becca smiled. "Kind of."

"What time are they coming to set up?" Haley looked at the kitchen clock.

"Around ten."

"It's seven now." Haley sat back. "I've got time to enjoy this good coffee."

"And breakfast. I need just a minute to get it ready."

Becca expected an argument, but instead Haley smiled. "Sounds good. This will be my last breakfast as a single lady."

Becca laughed as she put a quiche in the oven. "It's not like your last meal."

Hearing her daughter's chuckle. "No. but it will be nice to share it you. Just the two of us."

***

At nine thirty, Jon Jr. made his appearance. Dressing in jeans, he grabbed some coffee and toast, darted out of the door at the sound of a truck pulling into the yard. Becca watched him from the window.

Kevin and Matt drove down by the dock. Jumping out of the truck, the three, joined by five more young men, started following Jon Jr. orders. It was his job to set up the ceremony spot. Pleased to do it, he took it very seriously. Another truck arrived with the tents and tables.

The wedding stood to begin at one. Everything had been orchestrated to arrive at the proper time. Haley planned out every detail. Her mother was to be just the 'mother-of-the bride'. People in the community were more than willing to help.

After her shower, fixing her hair and face, Becca wrapped up in her robe, went to her

closest to lay out her dress.

This dress would make Jon Sr. proud, a designer dress.

A tea-length dress, in soft pale green, Haley picked it out. Slipping it over her head, she loved the feeling of the silk. It did flatter Becca. She was anxious for Clay to see it.

Their time had been so limited, but after tonight, she would be devoted only to being with him. And...her body trembled...he would be staying the night. Jon Jr. was going out with his friends, staying at David's with Kevin.

Haley and Andrew were spending their first night at the house he built, then off for a few weeks to a sunny beach. Jon Sr. would be going back to whatever was his life. Veronica could retreat back into her cave.

Be nice!

Just one more day.

"Mom!" Haley shouted from her bedroom.

"Coming."

Walking in, she saw her daughter ready for her dress. Her hair done, her make-up perfect. Franny came over to help. The two girls stood in the middle of the room.

"How am I?"

"Good...no, you look so beautiful, darling. Let me get the veil, we will put your gorgeous dress on."

Jon Jr. ran into her in the hall. Dressed in a black tux, looking so like her handsome son.

Grabbing his arms, she stopped him. "How is it going out there?"

"Great, everything's done." He looked around her, out the window. "Andrew and David are here. So is Clay."

"Go out get everyone in place. Where's your dad?"

"Right here." Jon Sr.'s voice sounded from the kitchen.

Becca let go of a sigh of relief.

The plan is coming together.

Jon Sr. rounded the corner.

404

Becca held up her hand. "Stay there. We are just about ready." She bolted back to Haley's room.

"Did I hear Dad is here? And Andrew?"

Becca nodded. "Yes. And Yes. Everyone's here."

Together Franny and Becca helped Haley step in to her grown. Zipping up the back, it fit as if it were made for her.

Walking around to face her daughter, Becca felt her pride swell up. "You are the most beautiful bride."

Haley leaned over, kissed her cheek. "Thank you, Mom. For everything. I love you."

Becca could feel the tears rising in her eyes.

No, this is not my time!

Turning quickly, she stepped out into the hall. "Jon, she's ready."

Standing back, she waited as he passed. Watching the two come together, her lack of feelings at her wedding nagged at her.

"Mom?" Jon Jr. tapped her shoulder. "I need to get you to our seats."

Becca nodded, took her son's arm.

Walking down the white aisle runner, they passed friends near and dear. Escorting her to the front row on the bride's side, they left the first chair empty, sitting in the next two. Becca glanced over at the groom's side. Clay sat on the outside. He winked at her, smiling his approval. Veronica leaned forward, glared at Becca.

Becca winked back at Clay, gave Veronica a phony smile, turned to look at the front.

Bitch!

Taking a breath, she looked at the wedding site. Jon Jr. had done a magnificent job. In white and sea-green, everything was perfect from the lanterns to the massive amount of white roses. Music played in the back ground.

Becca patted Jon Jr.'s arm. "You did good."

Jon Jr. smiled. "Thanks Mom. I just wanted it to be perfect for her. She's been through so much. She deserved the best. And she is marrying him."

The music stopped then swelled. A song Haley and Andrew picked out, while not traditional it spoke of their love for each other.

Watching Andrew's face, Becca knew when to stand to turn toward the bride. Lovely in her dress, Jon Sr. also handsome, the two glided down the aisle.

Becca was afraid of breaking into great racking sobs of joy. Her chest heaved as she fought with all her might to stay in control. Nothing in her life touched her with so much power and overwhelming love.

She knew she wasn't losing a daughter. They would not only live close to each other, but they shared a bond that would only grow stronger. Plus, she could not have asked for a better son-in-law. No, this was a good thing. As they walked by, she looked over at Clay. He watched her, giving her one nod. She resisted the urge to fly into his arms. The safe arms of the man she always loved. Instead she just nodded back, knowing he understood.

Turning to face the front, after Jon Sr. handed Haley to Andrew, he came to the seat next to her. The preacher nodded, everyone sat down.

Becca listened to the words of the ceremony. Truth be known, she had not paid attention to her own. Hearing the vows and promises, she understood marriage was a sacred thing. She had done herself and Jon an injustice not to take it seriously.

"I now pronounce you husband and wife. You may kiss the bride."

A shout rose up as Andrew took Haley in his arms, kissing her. Facing the crowd, they walked calmly down the aisle, shaking hands, accepting kisses on the cheek. After the couple and attendants, Jon Sr. presented Becca his arm. She smiled as she accepted it.

Walking over to where the reception had been set up, each took a chair. The people

Haley hired were exceptional. All local businesses, they put on a class act.

For two hours, Becca played the dutiful mother of the bride. As more drinks were toasted, people started gathering in groups abandoning the seating chart.

Becca left Jon to go over to Jilley, Sparky, Robby and Susie. "Whew. Glad that's done."

Jilley patted Becca's hand. "Nice job, friend."

Becca shook her head. "I didn't do much. Haley planned most of it."

Jilley looked over Becca's shoulder. "Say, Jon and Veronica are quite chummy."

Becca jerked around. True. Jon was all charm and Veronica was all but falling over him. "Yeah they hit it off last night at dinner."

"Oh my gawd! You don't think..."

The thought made Becca burst out laughing. "That would be weird." Feeling a hand on her shoulder, she heard the voice she needed to hear all day.

Clay!

"What's weird?"

Becca took hold of his hand. "What if...Jon and Veronica..."

Clay laughed a hardy laugh. "Your ex and my ex? No way...no wait." He held up his hands. "I can see this."

Everyone joined in the joke. Clay pulled a chair out, sat next to Becca, putting his arm on the back of her chair, stroking her neck.

As the night settled over the party, Haley and Andrew announced they were getting ready to leave. One last dance. Clay took Becca on to the dance floor. She snuggled down in his arms. Looking over his shoulder she saw Jon dancing with Veronica.

Rubbing her forehead on his shoulder, he whispered. "What?"

"Nothing. I am just glad to be in your arms again." She pulled back to look at him. "You will spend the night?"

He cocked his head. "Yes, every night if you want."

Laying the side of her face on his chest. "I want."

Finally the couple got ready to leave. Kissing Becca, Haley whispered. "It was grand Mom."

Becca nodded. "It was."

Everyone gathered on the dock as the happy couple left in Andrew's decorated speed boat. As the crowd dispersed, Becca bid each good-bye.

Standing on the dock alone, still watching the lights on the boat disappear around the bend, she crossed her arms, holding in the urge to cry.

Gentle arms surrounded her from behind. Clay spoke against her cheek. "They will be good together."

Becca nodded. "Yes, they will."

Looking around, she saw everyone had left. The cleanup crew had everything loaded. Her yard looked as if nothing had even been there.

A drop of rain hit her face. Looking up she saw low clouds crossing the sky. She welcomed the fine mist touching her skin.

"Becca." Clay's voice was low, serious. She turned to look at him. "What is it?"

"Dance with me." He opened his arms to welcome her in.

"It's raining." She laughed, holding her hands palms up.

Drawing her into him he whispered. "Then we'll dance between the raindrops."

Their bodies formed together, swaying to their own music.

Clay pulled back, looked at her. "I saw some serious thinking on your face today. Why such deep thoughts?"

Shaking her head she looked into the compassion of her love, lover, friend. "I just realize how wrong it was to not marry for love. Not only for me, but also Jon."

The corner of Clay's eyes wrinkled as he smiled. "I was thinking the same thing." He stopped moving, stood back.

Becca stood still, the rain came down drenching both of them.

"So…" he dug in his pocket, producing a small ring box. Going down on one knee he raised the opened box to her. "…marry me?"

410

Mesmerized by the beauty of the ring, she reached out to touch it. "Oh, Clay…" She looked at him. "Yes. I want nothing more than to be your wife."

He took the ring out of the box, an elegant vintage ring of white gold, antique scroll work, diamonds surrounded a large emerald cut diamond. Placing it on her finger, he held her hand.

"Where did you get this? It looks like an heirloom."

"It is…" The rain came down harder. Both ignored it. "…it was my grandmother's. My grandfather had it made for her. She gave it to me to give to you twenty years ago."

"And you kept it?"

"Always. No one else has ever worn it besides you now."

Water dripped from his hair. Becca wiped it from his skin. Standing, he took her face in his hands, kissed her with all the love he carried for so many years.

Becca jumped up into his arms. Wrapping her arms around his neck, she buried her face in the nook of his neck.

EPILOGUE

Becca leaned her hip against the kitchen counter, deep in thought, as she looked at the lake on the unseasonably warm, early spring mid-morning. The sun shone brightly, not a cloud in the sky. Finishing the last sip of her coffee, she set the cup in the sink. Hearing the rustle of material behind her, she smiled to herself.

Jilley's voice echoed softly in the empty room. "You okay, hon?"

Feeling Jilley's arms wrap around her shoulders, Becca leaned her head on her dear friend's forearm. "I am."

"Second thoughts?"

Becca chuckled. "Not this time."

Jilley rested her head against Becca's. "So what are you in such deep thought about?"

Becca let out a deep sigh. "Gwen."

412

Together they had visited their friend's grave.

***

Gwen had been laid to rest in the small cemetery Becca remembered from her youth. The trees had stood for centuries guarding the residents. Jilley led Becca to a grave under one of the mighty oaks.

Becca dropped to her knees in front of the tombstone that read "Gwen Josephine Strong. Dear daughter and friend."

Running her fingers over the chiseled lettering, she allowed the tears she had so desperately buried to flow. The flowers in her hands crushed against her chest. Hugging them as if they were life itself, she felt Jilley's embrace and leaned into the comfort of those arms.

Her body shook with sobs. "Gwen! I am so sorry you died. That your life was taken from you too young. Too soon."

Wiping her eyes with the back of her hand, she continued. "And I am sorry I ran away. I made the worst choice of my life because I was afraid. But I should have taken a lesson from you. I should have trusted my love."

The pain crested as Becca sobbed deeper. Finally, it gripped her stomach, forcing her to bend over. Bending the flowers in her arms, she heard the stems break. Jilley's arms tightened, her body swayed with Becca.

The release was like a lock opened, releasing her soul. As her crying subsided, to her surprise, she felt Gwen's forgiveness and her love. Becca touched the word "Friend". "That was nice that they put that there."

Jilley released her strong hold, sat down on the ground. "Her folks asked us if it was okay. I was so pleased."

Becca bit her lower lip. "I didn't know her middle name was Josephine?"

Jilley laugh. "No one did."

Becca looked over at Jilley through her tears. "Her best kept secret?"

"Wouldn't you?"

The laughter that forced its way out surprised Becca, but there it was and it felt good. Together the two women laughed. Becca finally felt free and at peace with her past.

Jilley stood, pulled Becca up. Becca looked at her mangled bouquet. She laid them tenderly at the foot of the tombstone. "Sorry Gwen."

Arm in arm the women turned to walk away. Becca glanced at the next marker, "Martin Moore." She stopped. "They laid them together?"

"Yes, their parents knew that was the way it should be."

Becca patted the top of the cold marble. "I know you are with her, Martin. Thank you."

***

"The car is here." Susie's voice cut the moment.

Becca laughed as together they turned to look at the third person in their party. "A car? I really expected a pick-up." She pressed her hands down the dress she had picked to be married in. A light taupe, flowing silk, it felt light and free.

Jilley and Susie wore spring colors. Jilley in fresh yellow, Susie in lush lavender. The flowers a bounty of rich spring colors.

Becca took a deep breath. "Showtime girls. Let's roll."

The car was a white limo. The driver, Clay's son David. As the three women stepped down the steps, David gave a low whistle.

Jilley patted his cheek before she got into the car. "You always were my favorite."

Susie followed. Just as Becca started to get in, David stopped her. "You are so beautiful. I am so happy for my Dad today."

Becca caressed his face. "Thank you, David. For everything. I couldn't be happier either."

The ride to the one and only church in town only took fifteen minutes. Jon Jr. stood on the curb waiting for them. As the limo came to a stop, he reached down and opened the back door. Presenting his hand, Becca took it in hers. As she stepped out she admired her handsome son. In the traditional black tux, she chuckled as she looked down and saw the shiny black and silver cowboy boots.

Kicking out her foot, she showed her white, wedding, cowgirl boots. "We are so 'country' now."

Jon Jr. offered her his arm. "Well, ma'am. I reckon it's a good thing."

She hugged his arm. "I love you."

He nodded, escorted her inside the church.

Standing at the beginning of their walk, Jon Jr. leaned down to whisper. "I love you too, Mom."

The tears started. She did and didn't want them. She had learned that tears cleanse the spirit. But she really didn't want to be a blubbering idiot as she walked down the aisle.

Oh, what the hell. It is what it is.

Looking to the front of the church, she saw Clay standing with Robby and Sparky. His eyes looked just at her. Keeping her sights on him, she floated to her long awaited and final destination.

As he took her hand from Jon Jr., her son kissed her tear-streaked cheek. Clay took one finger to wipe them away. Kissing her wet cheek, he whispered. "Are you all right?"

Becca nodded. Words were caught in her throat.

I hope I can talk when the time comes.

The preacher started the ceremony. She gripped Clay's hand. He was her rock, her foundation. And he was going to be her husband. The love of her life, to grow old with.

416

Feeling a blur settling over her, she snapped her mind back. She wanted to remember every moment. As they came to the vows, she felt her love for him rise in her chest.

Listening to the words, she smiled. This time she paid attention. When she said 'I do' it came out strong, looking Clay dead in the eyes.

His words creased his lips with a smile. She knew he meant every one.

When they kissed, she rose up on her tip-toes, gathering him to her. The rest of the people vanished. That was until the yelling and clapping made them pull apart.

Clay took her hand, together they ran from the altar. Bursting through the large, wooden double doors of the church, Becca laughed as before her stood Clay's truck. All decked out with streamers and flowers.

As they skipped down the steps, he opened the door for her. "Your carriage awaits, pretty lady." He cocked his head. "You like?"

Becca jumped up into the seat. "Now this is my idea of a ride."

Other Books

By

Jordyn Meryl

<u>Italian Dream Series</u>

When Dream Change-Book 1

When Dream Collide-Book 2

When Dream Die-Books 3

The Trouble With Angels

Home Before Dark

The Space Between-A Paranormal Romantic Suspense

Coming Soon

Katie's Wind

The House of the Crescent Moon

Please support me by:

Leaving a review at-

Amazon

Goodreads

My Facebook page

Telling your friends and family

An author is judged

by the feedback Of their readers.

Thank you,

jm

Proof

Made in the USA
Charleston, SC
26 May 2015